Witness To My Last Judgement
A Modern Version of the Traditional Near-Death Experiences

Marie-Emily Sendrea

Witness to my Last Judgement
A Modern Version of the Traditional Near-Death Experiences
Copyright © 2022 by Marie-Emily Sendrea

All rights reserved. No part of this publication may be reproduced, distributed, or transmitted in any form or by any means, including photocopying, recording, or other electronic or mechanical methods, without the prior written permission of the publisher or author, except in the case of brief quotations embodied in critical reviews and certain other noncommercial uses permitted by copyright law.

Although every precaution has been taken to verify the accuracy of the information contained herein, the author and publisher assume no responsibility for any errors or omissions. No liability is assumed for damages that may result from the use of information contained within.

The front cover: Marie-Emily Sendrea's painting entitled: "PASSION TRAPPED IN STONES'; oil on canvas, 31.5x39.0 inch (80x100 cm).

Library of Congress Control Number:	2022916561
ISBN-13: Paperback:	978-1-64749-798-9
ePub:	978-1-64749-799-6

Printed in the United States of America

GoToPublish LLC
1-888-337-1724
www.gotopublish.com
info@gotopublish.com

CONTENTS

Acknowledgements v
Overview vii
Preface ix

Instead Of An Introduction

Chapter 1   Fame Versus Love 1

PART ONE
Post-Church Service Routine

Chapter 2   Sunday Routine After Church Service 15
Chapter 3   Departing From The Real World 29
Chapter 4   Figment Versus Fact 33
Chapter 5   The Boundary Of The Unknown 55
Chapter 6   Roaming Into Nothingness 63
Chapter 7   Inside The Starting Place 69
Chapter 8   Undergone Into Nihility 77
Chapter 9   Swift Jump For Catching Life 85
Chapter 10   Bits Of Earthly Life 89
Chapter 11   Bringing Back My Childhood Memories 93

PART TWO
Reminiscence Of My Childhood Memories

Chapter 12   'I' The Child Versus 'I' The Adult 97
Chapter 13   America – The Starting Line............................ 105
Chapter 14   'I' The High-School Girl Versus 'I' The Adult..... 111

PART THREE
Marching Onward To The Goal

Chapter 15   Marching Onward To The Goal........................ 123
Chapter 16   Acquainted With The Elite's Tall Order 133
Chapter 17   The Bitter Flavor Of Honey 145
Chapter 18   'I' The Incriminator Versus 'I' The Perfidious .. 153
Chapter 19   Advancing Towards The Judgement 157
Chapter 20   Who Was Melanie Dupont? 163
Chapter 21   Buoyed By False Hope.......................................191
Chapter 22   The Two 'I's Converge 195
Chapter 23   At Home With A Born-Again Wife 207
Chapter 24   Open Letter To The Reader 211
Chapter 25   Epilogue 213

Mission Statement 215

ACKNOWLEDGEMENTS

I humbly and gratefully dedicate this book to my Creator, who blesses me so generously and makes me, even from my early childhood, open widely my eyes and mind, in order to observe, catch and comprehend the mysteries that compose and surround our earthly life. My Lord helps me see His signature all around me.

Thanks to my husband Dorel for his so-needed care and encouragement, especially in the time when my household chores could not get my attention. Special heartfelt thanks to my beloved Robert who always answers promptly when I cry for help. Thanks also to my entire family for their great outburst of love and uplifting support. I cannot also forget my dear friends who not only express their admiration for my artwork and written stories, but they also encourage me to keep up working, while letting the world acquainted with my stories narrated on paper and canvas.

OVERVIEW

This novel is a modern version of the traditional near-death journey. In transporting its reader from a realm of actual and logical existence to an out-of-the-ordinary realm, this novel accesses an alternative plane of thought and event, finding new narrative intensity in operating within the mind of a single character.

The metamorphic change to which Dee-Anna Turner, the novel's main character, was subjected during her out-of-the-ordinary journey helps the reader grasp the significance of the reality. This reality is namely that our wealth and good reputation gained on Earth mean nothing in God's eyes. Dee-Anna's greed and verve for jumping into the elite's indulgence stress upon this veracity, confirmed also by Solomon in Ecclesiastes: "Vanity of vanities, all is vanity."

First, the reader relates to Dee-Anna's quick wit and cynical attitude as she silently attacks her pastor in her mind, telling him to give up his extravagant standards of living if he wants to set an example for his parishioners. Dee-Anna's mannerisms and remarkable beauty captivate readers right from the beginning, but quickly do they realize that her actions are indeed the bullet that is piercing her very soul. The novel is intended to make readers look at the bullet kept secretly in their own clenched fists. The bullet could be a number of things: bad actions against others done under the fear of poverty; forcing our own destiny; longing for extravagance while attending church as a social function; praying out of routine, but not as a soul need; or justifying and whitewashing all our sins. The list goes on. Unfortunately, only few recognize that God brings unusual encounters and ordinary people into our lives to ring the bell near our ears. Dee-Anna's unusual experience is an example of God's hands at work.

Almost the entire content of the novel makes readers march along with Dee-Anna inside a bizarre realm, and like her, they also ask over and over: "What is this? What world is this, and in what period of time?" It is right at the end when both get their answer.

Even if this novel depicts events occurring in an ordinary life, its uniqueness is drawn from the extraordinary experience Dee-Anna has while forced to witness her own life. Terrified and alone, during her ordeal, Dee-Anna is forced to be a judge of her own pharisaic actions, pacing slowly along with the live-image of herself while moving from one episode of her life to another — starting with her innocent childhood until her corrupt adulthood.

This novel does not necessarily break new ground but rather breaks up old ground, which nobody has been teaching for a long time: Hell! Yes, the ancient teaching of Hell has been pushed to the sidelines and people are forgetting that it is a real place. The novel does not describe the inside of the real Hell, but the horrific place where Dee-Anna is a visitor for one night reminds the reader about such a real place. In Hell, people, whose earthly deeds are nothing but rotten fruits, will spend eternity. Our Christian label does not redeem us and salvation is not locked up forever, as many think. Although redemption is a gift of God and by no means the good work of an individual, this does not mean that we can take the liberty to live morally and sexually unrestrained. If Christians call themselves the 'children of God', their conduct of life should prove exactly that.

Witness to My Last Judgement is not a science-fiction adventure and its purpose is not to scare the reader. It was purposely written for all of us — we the inhabitants of this world, poor and rich, young and old — showing us that we all will die one day and experience the 'unknown'; its shape, location, colors, fragrance, and dimensions nobody knows.

PREFACE

The story of Dee-Anna Turner, the main character of this novel is a wake-up call for all human beings, in general, and also in particular for those who think that their daring actions make them invincible.

The first two chapters portray Dee-Anna's manoeuvres at work, while starting with chapter 3 to the end of the novel the reader sees her Maker's divine hands at work. She is instantly deprived of all earthly possessions, including her beloved ones and thrown into another time and location — like a puppet in a dollhouse. During her near-death journey, Dee-Anna re-sees her own live-image, automatically becoming a participant of her own life — stretched from her innocent childhood to her corrupt adulthood. As a witness, she endures the painful guilt of her manipulative actions and also her soul's auto-destruction, caused by her hypocritical style of living.

Proceeding smoothly, while moving from one chapter to another, the reader travels along with Dee-Anna, both witnessing her tribulation as well as her metamorphosis, in the end. Each chapter details different aspects of that weird place, where Dee-Anna, a formal witness, involuntarily witnesses the unfolding of her own life. Fortunately for her, that hell-like place is somewhere she stays for only a very short time and thankfully did not have to remain there forever. Unfortunately, many human beings will enter Hell and stay there for eternity. This novel helps readers to catch the mirrored reflections of their soul's deeds and turn involuntarily towards their own life, balancing their deeds, and rummaging inside their soul for wrongly masked sins. I know this because I, too, did the same thing while listening to a twenty-minute poetry recital — a symbolic enactment of The Last Judgement.

The content of the novel could make the reader notice a slight correlation with Diana, Princess of Wales. This comes into the mix due to a dream I had of her. Years before her tragic death, at the time when she was in full glory, I dreamt that the Princess was wandering amongst the marble tombstones in a cemetery across a huge chalet made of ornamental red bricks. The cemetery was similar to the ones I had seen in Paris, France during the time I had lived there. Mystified by her silhouette, weaving graciously through the narrow alleyways between the tombs, I wondered why she looked so frightened and alone when I knew that the entire planet venerated her. Impressed and puzzled by her automobile accident that had occurred years later, mixed feelings invaded my soul. Still having the poetry recital freshly in my mind and being perturbed by thoughts linked to human beings' destiny in general and the Princess' tragic destiny in particular, I decided to put these three thoughts together and write a book about human destiny. It took me a long time to structure my thoughts and collect data, changing the story's format many times.

I want to point out that the hypocritical character of Dee-Anna has nothing to do with the Princess' attributes. I liked Princess Diana very much and always admired her exquisite delicacy. Her death made me extremely upset. What I intend to communicate with the content of this novel is in fact my perception that social status does not matter; rich or poor, we all one day must answer God for our earthly deeds. Dee-Anna, the novel's character, meets both attributes; she is poor in the first part of her life and then becomes rich in the latter. In both categories to which she belongs, she manifests good and bad deeds. Our social status is not an excuse for our actions. God knows that we are made out of clay, but His Holy Spirit, set in us, can help us find the holy ground in our lives. Dee-Anna's metamorphic change proved exactly that.

Through the use of the novel's narrative tension, I intend to apply my principle that states: a refined mixture of real experiences with imaginative inputs teaches a person the definition of earthly life.

INSTEAD OF AN INTRODUCTION

CHAPTER 1

FAME VERSUS LOVE

"Charity suffereth long, and is kind; charity envieth not; charity vaunteth not itself, is not puffed up, doth not behave itself unseemly, seeketh not her own, is not easily provoked, thinking no evil... Charity never faileth..."

(Recited by Mr. Tony Blair, England's Prime Minister, from I Corinthians 13:4,5,8 at the funeral of Diana, Princess of Wales, on Saturday, September 6th, 1997)

I was trying to look interested in Dr. McCarthy' sermon. He has served our church well for a long time. What the congregation liked the most about this handsome, tall man was the fact that, he nurtured the members' souls with modern flair. He had the voice of an actor-strong and dynamic. Sermons flowed from his body like lava, blessing the audience one-minute, burning the next. Dr. McCarthy liked to use jokes about his wife in his sermons, and the congregation loved this subtle exchange, but Mrs. McCarthy visibly puckered her lips, pretending to be upset. I always admired Mrs. McCarthy's intelligence and her clever way of dealing with delicate situations, particularly when women of our congregation were involved. She was recognized as a distinct person. Her blond hair, always in style, enhanced her large blue eyes, and her recent eyelid surgery added even more expressiveness to her oval face.

Mrs. McCarthy was small and delicate, the opposite of her husband, who was strong and impressive. This big man loved his tiny wife very much, always surrendering to her wisdom. Every time he tried to impose a controversial idea on the church, his wife's gentle smile made him pause, lift his left hand, and scratch the opposite side of his head as a sign of submission. Therefore, the congregation recognized that Dr. McCarthy and his wife had a model marriage, even though there were people who disputed that.

The church was one of the most modern in Michigan. It had been built immediately after World War II. A few years before, a small group of wealthy people from our church had decided to renovate it, and it had been a great idea, considering the deterioration its structure had suffered from years of weather changes. The shape of the roof had been completely transformed in such a way that both the old building and the new addition could be covered by one roof. All the windows and doors had been updated, replacing the gloomy ones, which prevented light from penetrating the building. The result was astonishing. And impressed by the beauty of our church's building, more people joined our congregation, doubling its number. The church's members could serve the Lord in comfort now, on adequate pews upholstered with fine red velvet and an air-conditioned sanctuary brightened by stylish chandeliers. Some of the members of the church complained about the narrow spaces among benches, but it was all right with the majority, since we were not praying on our knees anymore.

From my seat at the back, I had a panoramic view of the sanctuary and the congregation. I liked to sit there, because I could admire the even white pillars. In my mind I compared them with the naked backs and shoulders of some stylish ladies occupying the Lord's house. That Sunday, I contemplated the sanctuary even longer than usual, shifting my gaze from one corner of it to another. "What a job!" I said to myself, thinking of the decorators' refined work. Out of the blue, my thoughts considered the time when the first Christians had tried in desperation to find refuge inside the catacombs. Pale faces and poorly dressed bodies, grouped shoulder to shoulder against the catacomb's filthy walls, singing to the Lord, paraded in my mind. I looked around, staring at the congregation. "Wow! What progress we Christians have made!" I thought. The comfortable benches were full of quiet people, staring at Dr. McCarthy's gestures, while my mind cried out: "Poor souls! They try hard to copy the deep love the first Christians showed to the Savior, forcing their faces be captivated by this man's fiery sermon. I'll bet their minds are somewhere else. I know it, because I'm guilty of the same sin every Sunday."

I stole a glimpse of my husband, Paul, sitting close to me. I wanted to know if his face looked different from the rest of the audience's. "No, it doesn't," I thought. "Well, we're human."

"Get rid of your worldly desires, brothers and sisters," thundered Dr. McCarthy's voice. My entire body shook, as though taken by surprise. "Don't accumulate earthly wealth!" He yelled. "Replace it with the hope of the Divine Reward instead, brothers and sisters."

"Don't you want to set an example, Billy?" An inner voice revolted. "Be the first one to do it though...and we will perhaps follow you," continued the same voice. I moved my eyes around, staring at some faces in the audience, my mind asking: "You don't like the preacher's idea, huh?"

"But, do you like it?" The inner voice asked me this time. "I'm not Mother Teresa," I threw at the voice, scratching my costly leather purse with my long nails.

"Princess Diana didn't take her wealth with her, " uttered Dr. McCarthy, "While Mother Teresa didn't have anything to take with her. They both died, but their lives on this earth were at the opposite poles; one very rich and famous and the other very poor and famous. But when their earthly time stopped, they both exited the world on the same path... dear brothers and sisters, 'let not lay up for yourselves treasures upon earth, where moth and rust doth corrupt, and where thieves break through and steal'..." thundered the preacher's voice, citing from the Bible.

"Slogans... all slogans," I told myself, moving my eyes around. "I don't think I would have ever been able to do what Mother Teresa did with her life, especially after being mired in such dire poverty, first in the communist Russia a baby and then as a newcomer here in the United States. This doesn't suit me. No! Thank you, Brother Bill!"

"Death can strike at any time for each of us… for me and for you… and for you my young friend," our preacher thundered again, pointing his finger in our direction. "Nobody has a choice. Death never asks you if you want to die or not. Diana wasn't asked. By the contrary, the beautiful, rich girl wanted to re-marry, not to die. As poor as she was, Mother Teresa, too, wanted to hold on life. She wasn't asked about her choice either. Do you think you'll have a choice? Do you think that you'll be asked?"

Murmurs arose from the audience.

"Think about, young lady, having your life cut short unexpectedly," continued the preacher, pointing in my direction. "Just think about that!"

"I hope he's not referring to me," I thought, following his finger with my eyes.

"Poor Diana had plans for the future," Dr. McCarthy went on. "Perhaps, you, too, have plans, my dear lady… and you young man. Who is going to profit from the struggles you have had in your life? A struggle to survive? or overcome an illness, or… who knows? Maybe… to overcome the world. Napoleon had been famous for such a struggle. Hitler also had this dream." I moved in my seat. The mention of Diana and Mother Teresa's death, and also the preacher's well-drafted sermon linked to those events, made me feel uncomfortable during that Sunday morning service. Dr. McCarthy attempted to point out other examples suitable to be compared to the deaths of the two famous women, trying in the same time to make a parallel among the two deaths and also pointing to God's expectations. I embodied myself in each of those examples. Princess Diana's example attracted me the most; elegant and wealthy enough to catch people's admiration, and in the same time capable of comforting people in hospitals and camps. Thinking of her death: "Well… I prefer the part where the roads were paved with countless flowers while the procession slowly moved towards the cemetery where her grave awaited her corpse."

"Lay up for yourselves treasures in heaven, where neither moth nor rust corrupts, and where thieves do not break through nor steal…" Our preacher's strong voice made me focus on the sermon again. "For where your treasure is there will your heart be also," he once more quoted from the Bible.

"Lay down an example first, Preacher, and then your flock will follow," I thought, full of mutiny.

"Therefore take no thought, saying: What shall we eat? Or, what shall we drink? Or, wherewithal shall we be clothed… For your heavenly Father knoweth that ye have need of all these things," Dr. McCarthy cited from Matthew, in the Bible.

I gazed at the preacher's hands, as they laid the Book carefully on the pulpit. "Was Mother Teresa ever concerned with those daily necessities?" He asked the congregation. "The way she lived her life proved otherwise. But she was very concerned about the needy people's lives. She never accumulated wealth in her barns, or checking accounts, but she always put food and medicine in those people's hands."

The preacher paused for a few moments, staring at his flock. A deep silence covered the assembly. I stared at Paul's face. He was quiet, too.

"God make all of us be changed," thundered the preacher. "Amen," I was involuntarily saying, joining the congregation.

Not far away from Mrs. McCarthy, I noticed the new musicians, hired recently by our deacons. "A good thing!" some had said. "We don't need this kind of music in our church," others had replied. The musicians had played jazz music before, and that was all right with the majority in our church, as long as they played religious songs in the church. "In fact this is the new trend adopted by many modern churches," our youngest deacon had replied when dissatisfaction wove among the church's deacons during a recent meeting. "Don't you notice how our young people show their enthusiasm with their thunderous applause when they're listening to the group's performance," the youth minister had asked the deacons at the same meeting. His cleverness had helped him handle the matter and he hadn't met with any objections when he subtly silenced the complainers with his concluding words: "Dear brothers, let's get away with those old, tiresome songs. It's time for a big change. Let's do it, so we'll be like the other modern churches in the world. Let's unite and teach our old members the new songs. Let's hail Jesus with vibrant songs and not tire Him with the old boring hymns. Let's shake the sky with our music! Amen!"

"Amen," I pondered, my eyes on Dr. McCarthy again, trying once more to concentrate on his sermon.

"Wake up brothers!" The preacher yelled. I stared at the huge hands attempting to describe the scope of the love we should have for our fellow human beings. I turned up my nose, thinking: "For some I might have feelings, but not for everybody, dear preacher!"

Without warning, a feeling of revolt washed over me. I suddenly found myself fighting within my own soul: "I'm at the apogee of my life, I have no time to love," I rebelled. And again: "I barely have time for myself… I slaved all my life in order to move up in society. Yes, you thorny life, I fought you and I conquered you."

"Don't be sure of your earthly life," Dr. McCarthy shouted. His voice swatted my thoughts away again. "Conquer the eternal life instead, brothers and sisters… and you young man, and you young sister, and you… and you," the preacher called, his voice wavering, his eyes bulging.

"The sermon is almost over," I whispered in my husband's ear, showing no interest in Dr. McCarthy's request.

"Is it, really?" Paul asked, looking at his gold watch. I smiled, moving my lips closer to my husband's ear.

"It's a habit of our preacher to inflate his voice at the end of the sermon," I whispered again, giggling softly.

The musicians closed the church service that Sunday morning with "Amazing Grace," in a very dynamic rhythm that reminded me of the old "rhythm and blues" music. People applauded, as did Paul and I, while we were standing up, trying to get out of the narrow space between our pew and the one in front of us.

"Hi Dee!" a voice took me by surprise. I instinctively turned my head, as a hand tapped me on the shoulder.

"Oh! Hi Sue! How are you?" I greeted back.

"Don't leave! I want to talk with you," Sue whispered, taking me by the arm and dragging me aside. "But, let me first introduce my future sister-in-law… Pam come her, dear!" she addressed the tiny, timid girl standing in front of us.

"Hi, Pam! I'm Dee-Anne Turner." I introduced myself, shaking hands with the girl. "Nice to meet you! Are you from Michigan, too?"

"No," the girl answered; she was too shy to talk more, or look me in the eye.

Sue gently pushed me toward the corner of the auditorium, while I was looking in despair at Paul, pushed by the crowd toward the main entrance.

"What a piece of luck!" I thought, looking at the heavy woman in front of me, ardent to 'share her big secret' with me.

"Here, boys," I said, waving my arm to get Michel and Daniel, my two sons' attention. They were about to enter the auditorium, elbowing around people, while they tried to find one of us. Politeness kept me in the corner where Sue had dragged me, listening to the endless description of her wedding plans.

"When did you say John proposed?" I asked Sue, watching my kids, who for the second time missed the spot where I was standing with my friend. "Here, boys!" I called again, waving my hand in my children's direction.

"Oh, Dee, I just told you… He finally proposed on Friday… Oh, dear! Listen to this!" she said. I felt lost, petrified at the thought of having that boring woman detailing the proposal. I listened, anyway. "You know how long I have waited for this," she started. "Oh, dear! I was afraid he would get cold feet and never propose. But I took no chance with him! It is true I pushed a little, but it worked. So, Friday it was my big day," Sue said, her face full of pride and her story colored by emotion. She continued with frivolous details about the way John, her fiancé had proposed to her. I heard little of those details, my mind busy trying to find an excuse to pull away, as we shook hands goodbye.

My kids came around.

"Oh! Hi boys!" Sue greeted my children, smiling. "Look how tall you are! Long time no see, huh? How old are you now, boys?"

"Daniel is seven and… Michael is eight," I blurted, having no patience to wait for my boys to answer.

Perhaps Sue noticed my impatience. She looked at me and said: "Well, I think I should let you go, Dee. But, please, listen to this… last one, and I'll then let you go." In despair, I slid my hand out of hers, patting her heavy shoulder with my other hand saying:

"Let's talk about this over the phone, Sue. I think Paul is anxious to leave," I uttered, happy to finally find an excuse to escape the talkative woman. But in my mind, I knew that it will never happen — I'll never call her back. I have always avoided answering the phone when I have noticed her name on my call display. "Well, diplomacy is not a sin," I quieted my soul.

I continued smiling at Sue, assuring her once more that we would continue her unfinished story over the phone. She uttered something else, but I paid no attention. Then, I grabbed my kids by the hand, heading toward Paul, whom I assumed was waiting for us in the lobby. On the way, the strange feeling, which had washed over me during Dr. McCarthy's sermon flooded my soul once more. I squeezed my sons' little hands, in an attempt to calm my cranky soul. It was like a squashing sound. I felt nervous, but continued to move slowly along with the rest of the crowd, emptying the auditorium.

Looking around, I spotted a group of young people socializing in a corner of the main foyer, and I also noticed the new musicians there. They were surrounded by a group of noisy girls, eager to get the young men's attention.

"Look at these musicians," an old woman whispered near me. "Do you call this a decent way of dressing for church?" I turned to see the woman. She was talking to an old man. Both were close to me. Realizing that I had never met them, I turned away and continued walking.

"Well... the musicians, actors, artists, all these people of art dress strangely, I heard," the man said.

"But in the house of Lord, Bob?" the old woman replied. After a short silence, she continued: "Churches these days have an aspect of anything but churches, I'm telling you, Bob," adding: "I'll bet, if they were invited to the White House, they'd put on the best suit they ever had. Is the President more important than the Lord?"

"Well, dear, as the pastor says, there is a new trend enveloping our church, too. Who cares about our strong belief? ... Bigoted old people, as they called our generation."

I wasn't interested in the couple's chat, and I didn't even care if they were related or not. I continued inching along the aisle, dragging my children along, as I tried finding a niche in the crowd in order to get out faster.

"Are these musicians paid by the church, Bob?" The old woman started again.

"I guess," the man answered. "Hmmm!"

"Well, think this way! Professional musicians might double the number of our church members, which automatically means higher salaries for the pastor, music director, secretaries and janitors. So, they won't be forced moving from one church to another, running for better pay," the man said.

"What about the missionaries' salaries? You didn't mention them, dear," questioned the woman.

"Perhaps, their salaries won't be affected. Most of the world is made up of Christians now."

"Who needs to know Christ these days?" threw the old lady. It seemed that the man caught the woman's ironic remark. He said nothing, but sighed deeply instead.

For a moment I was under the impression that the couple followed us, but I immediately realized that they only took advantage of the same niche formed by the crowd and rushed out. I tried for the second time to depart from the couple. I didn't like their discussion. I found it too controversial.

The same peculiar feeling hammered my soul again. I tried to ignore it.

Suddenly, a sharp pain rolled over inside my abdomen.

"Oh, dear!" I said to myself. "This is my period." This thought helped me to calm myself down every time that peculiar feeling bothered my soul.

With my chin up and face smiling, I approached Paul who was entertaining Mrs. Reed, one of our good friends. The middle-aged woman was giggling, as my husband gesticulated. When my kids noticed their father, they rushed toward his open arms, wrapping their tiny arms around his body. I hugged Mrs. Reed and kissed her on both cheeks. That woman was the type of person who knows everything and everybody and is always aware of what was going on in our church. I have used her influence and connections many times. "This lady can bust me up," I've encouraged myself when I have been in difficult situations, especially after I had no longer been aloud to use Mrs. O'Neil, my former mother-in-law's contacts. And indeed, Mrs. Reed's strings have pulled Paul and I up on society's platform again. I've found little pleasure chatting with that woman, I have never let her noticed that. Diplomacy at work again?

Her masculine voice associated with her fully detailed and boring stories have always irritated me, but I have never let it out. Both Paul and I had appreciated her undisputed power, capable to produce wonder in my life. After my divorce, John, my first husband as well as Mrs. O'Neil, his mother, had been more than convinced that I would never survive without their connections. Aflame with delight, the mother and son had thrown me back in the arms of poverty. "The place where you belong," they spat in my face. And in the arms of poverty I would probably had been for a long time if it wouldn't have been for Paul's support and later, for Mrs. Reed's contacts. I have never said a word, complaining about the time Paul spent with Mrs. Reed. On the contrary, I had been the one encouraging him to be her alter ego. He has entertained her with the latest news and jokes, and she has liked that and being agog for news and good jokes she always has made sure she hasn't lost a chance to see Paul.

"Have you watched Diana's funeral, dear?" Mrs. Reed asked me without introduction.

"Of course," I answered promptly. "Poor, thing… What a shame!" And looking at Paul, I added: "We both watched. Actually we didn't miss a thing. I think the media covered almost everything. I really feel sorry for this girl… what a piece of luck she had…"

"Isn't that sad, my dear?" Asked Mrs. Reed, staring more at Paul than at me.

"Mom, let's go home," Daniel begged me. "I'm hungry."

"In a minute, my love! In a minute." I whispered, cuddling his black hair. "Did you watch Mother Teresa's funeral, too?" Threw at me Mrs. Reed with one breath, ignoring Daniel's bothering plea.

"Oh, yes!" I replied, staring at Daniel while trying to make him quiet. Paul and Michael showed signs of boredom, making me understand that they, too, wanted to go home. But Mrs. Reed was so caught with details about Diana's funeral that it was impossible for me to interrupt her.

As for me, I should admit that Mrs. Reed's latest news regarding Diana's death kept my interest. So, we spent a few more minutes detailing all the major events linked to the princess' death and funeral, including of course the sturdy Mercedes crushed like a flea in the Paris tunnel, and the enigmatic white car blamed for the entire accident. And the tears mixed with millions of flowers spread over the place where Diana had lived and died. We mentioned Mother Teresa's funeral, but we didn't spend dwell on it. Her life wasn't that exciting — a simple life, but a dull topic.

Seeing that I had no immediate intention to leave, Michael and Daniel found play partners, right there in the main foyer, running and laughing with their friends. Paul found a partner in Mr. Reed; they were talking about the crisis in the Middle East. From time to time, Paul's glance caught mine, suggesting it was time to quit chatting and go home. I caught his look, but ignored it, playing for time.

Mrs. Reed would have kept me there with her news for a long time, if Paul hadn't gently pulled me away from our friends. He wrapped his arm around my shoulders, and smiling at the couple, made me walk towards the exit. But Mrs.Reed didn't want to give in. She moved closer, uttering:

"Say, dear! Do you think that Camilla Poker will marry Charles now?" "Parker, Mrs. Reed! Her name is Camilla Parker," I corrected. "I don't know if they will marry or not. What I know is that Diana's death is a big blow to her two kids... Au revoir, Mrs. Reed!" I forced my French, rushing to catch Paul and my two boys. Exasperated by Mrs. Reed's insistent manner, they left me with her and her husband and headed out to the parking lot. They waited for me near our car, greeting people around them. Heading in their direction, I intentionally walked slowly, in order to make people in the parking lot noticing our brand-new Mercedes.

People were chatting in the parking lot. The preacher approached Paul. Seeing him, my heart was full of delight. "Good thing!" I thought, staring at him. "As you can see, my brother... we, too, own a Mercedes." Dr. McCarthy threw a short glance at our car, though pretending not to see it. I caught his look, and I immediately leaned against the car window, pretending to remove a leaf — indicating that I was the car's owner. But Dr. McCarthy ignored that, too.

After the preacher's blessing, we moved around the car, talking with people. We flashed smiles all around us, proud of ourselves, proud of our children and the car. We watched for our smiles to be returned, like golden crowns upon our stately heads. I thought: "We belong here. Yes, we belong. Our positions were bought and paid off by my lies, struggle and influence... But it was worth it... It was worth it."

Suddenly, my body stiffened, my stomach hurt. These were the same symptoms I'd had before, followed by the same need to cry. A new thing I discovered this time: the whole manifestation, which periodically enveloped my soul, seemed to be linked to meditating about my life's conduct. I stared ahead, overcome with emotion. That strange feeling came precisely at the same time that my desire of keeping myself in a pretend world of the elite was at its climax.

Every time that peculiar feeling came, I was impulsive and gloomy. Paul noticed my mood.

"What's wrong?" he asked, as we made ourselves comfortable in the car. "Nothing!" I replied. The same uneasy feeling bashed my mind again.

Paul looked at me. "You're sure?"

"Yes. I'm sure."

Two of the most important church members passed by our Mercedes. Noticing us in the car, they came to the window. We opened the windows and smiled at them. They "ooh-d" and "ah-d" over our taste in the new car. I liked that, though I didn't let them notice.

With a final wave, we pulled away from the rest of the people. Looking at my watch, I realized that we spent more time worshipping statues, possessions and ourselves than we had in worshipping God, spending more time outside the church than inside.

We didn't talk much during the drive home. I was staring out the car window. Mixed snapshots caught my eye: colorful flowers adorning people's yards, in contrast with the faded colors of some poorly dressed pedestrians, or elegant cars rolling on our poorly maintained Hwy. 75, passing old, outdated cars occupied by people with weird faces.

It was a beautiful autumn day. The leaves had just started turning red and gold. The sky had that intense blue color which September displays in Michigan.

The boys' giggling from time to time interrupted my contemplation. I looked at Paul. He was quiet, perhaps not in the mood for talking. "He's hungry," I thought. The kids giggled again. Paul smiled, looking at them through the car's mirror. I turned and stared at the three of them and laughed.

PART ONE

POST-CHURCH SERVICE ROUTINE

CHAPTER 2

SUNDAY ROUTINE AFTER CHURCH SERVICE

At home, I completed my household duties for lunch, and after we finished eating, quickly isolated myself in our master bedroom. Actually, before going up, I made a short attempt at watching "The Man From Left Field," a comedy with Burt Reynolds and Reba McEntire. Paul spent a short time outside in our backyard, flipping the pages of The Detroit News. Then, he came inside and watched the movie to the end. Michael and Daniel crouched on the sofa beside him, but not for long. Not interested in the movie, they went down to Paul's office, fighting over our computer. Resting on my large bed, I could hear the boys' yelling and giggling through the bedroom ducts. All of a sudden, an annoying rustle attracted my attention.

"Get down to Daddy, Lori", I yelled at my dog that was scratching and pushing her rubber frog against my bedroom door, begging me to let her in. "Get down, I said. Mama is resting, you silly. Go!"

The dog insisted for a little longer, whining and scratching, and realizing finally that she couldn't overcome my stubbornness, went down.

I relaxed about an hour, lying on my back and staring at the ceiling. In my mind paraded thoughts, ambitions and projects for the future. My mind was working noisily — like a turbine. The moment my soul exalted at a good perspective and future new connections, suddenly the same bizarre feeling came out of the blue, overthrowing my plans. Minutes went by without me noting their passing.

The dog came up again. Her scratches at my bedroom door forced me to go down to the living room. Paul was still there, resting on the sofa. The boys came up later, when they heard me talking with Paul. Lori grabbed her chain from the chair and pushed it into my arm, reminding me that it was time for us to go for a walk.

We all went out, but not for a walk. We visited the Canterbury Village instead, a small place with craft and antique shops. After we circled all over the huge Always Christmas store, buying nothing, we went out and walked around the castle, admiring the Tiffany Wisteria windows and life-like animation characters greeting visitors. Then we headed for home, abandoning the idea of visiting the nearby shopping plaza. But I couldn't wait to get home, and my husband noticed that.

"Are you sick?"

"Not at all," I answered… a little indisposed, I guess. We kept quiet, while the car sped along Hwy. 695.

"I think my period is giving me trouble this month," I broke the silence, whispering towards Paul's ear.

"Hmm… You're unusually quiet today. Even the kids noticed that," Paul whispered back.

"Well… it will go away. Don't worry!"

But it didn't go away. On the contrary, the same sad and eerie feeling, torturing my soul for hours struck repeatedly, making me skeptical about the real symptoms of my period. I tried to make sense of these feelings, to work out my good reasons and connect them to my experiences during the time I had given birth to my sons. But I concluded that I had never encountered such experiences; it was my soul in pain, not my body.

At home, I spent a short time working around the rooms and preparing things for the next day. I wasn't interested in watching TV, or spending much time with Lori, as I normally do every night before going to bed. Paul noticed it, too. He looked at me as if he wanted an explanation regarding my mood.

"Nothing," I replied with one breath. He stared at me for a while and then continued patting Lori and watching TV.

Paul had been always aware of my moods and of times when I wished to be let alone. He always respected that time. That Sunday he again respected my feelings. My children spent a little more time in front of the computer, and later went to their rooms. I, too, went up to my bedroom, taking a magazine with me. I changed my clothes and lay down on the bed, flipping through the magazine. Princess Diana's smiling face was portrayed on almost every page. Not hearing Lori's scratches at my bedroom door, I assumed she was with Paul in the living room.

The phone rang out of the blue. I let Paul answer it. I pricked up my ears. "Oh! That woman again," I said to myself. "She calls us almost every Sunday… Well! You can entertain her, dear." I was sure that Paul knew better how to socialize with Tina, one of his former classmates' wives.

Outside, the leaves murmured in the breeze, and their rustle mingled with Paul's chatter on the phone with Tina

"Oh! No. She is fine, Tina. I'm sorry we couldn't make it," I heard Paul saying. Perhaps we'll see each other by the end of next week. Well, I'm glad you had a good time. How is Tom?" Paul was silent for a short time and then he added: "Oh! I'm sorry to hear that. He should see a lawyer for that. It could get ugly." After a short break Paul spoke again: "Well, have a good night, both of you… I will. Yes, Tina, I promise." Paul burst out laughing. I smiled. Tina was known as a funny and talkative person, but I found her snoopy.

Silence again. My bedroom door opened widely. Paul entered the room, tiptoeing across the rug.

"Tina, dear. She missed us this afternoon and wanted to know why we couldn't make it to the show," he whispered.

"Right! She missed us. She only wants to have new data for her chatter," I mumbled irritated, covering my legs with the bed cover.

"You're unfair to her, Dee, she's a good person, but misunderstood. Well… anyway, she wished you good health."

I mumbled again, but Paul ignored my words. He approached instead and knelt down near the bed, trying to embrace me. He moved his lips close to mine, but backed down when he noticed me being uncooperative. He looked at me as though he was about to ask why.

"I'm sorry, Paul, I know Tom is your friend, but I don't like his wife's impudent way of nosing into other people's affairs."

"OK... OK," he said, attempting for the second time to kiss me. I pushed him away. He stared at me in surprise.

"You're acting strange, Dee," he whispered. "I'm not."

"Oh, yes you are, my dear, and it's not only today I noticed, but for the last few weeks."

"Are the kids in their beds?" I changed the subject.

"Why you're doing this to me, Dee?" Paul grumbled, searching my eyes. "Doing what?" I uttered. My eyes lodged protest.

"You know what... changing the subject is not an answer."

"I'm not changing any subject, Paul. I only asked a normal, decent, human question. I just want to know if my kids are in their beds... That's all!"

"OK, Dee! As you wish... Yes. Your kids are in their beds," Paul retorted, not looking at me. He got up, intending to leave the room.

"Get down here, Paul, and don't be silly!" I requested, ignoring his intention. "It's enough, one moody person in our family. Get down here! I want to have you right beside me," I said, tapping the bed cover with my hand. Paul obeyed.

I lied. In fact, I didn't want him to sit down beside me that day. I didn't even want him in the bedroom. I needed to be let alone, so I could talk to my soul. Unfortunately, our desires clashed dreadfully. Paul hungered for love; while my heart was full of ambitions and aspirations, leaving room only for a programmed, calculated love. My mind was full of plans, ideas and great deals heading in one direction only: upward toward the glory. Penance for this sin wasn't an issue for me, though I have refused seeing it as a sin. Chasing contacts was a habit of mine, mimicking my former mother-in-law, Mrs. O'Neil. That woman with minimum education was capable of moving mountains when connections were essential in her life; connections able to thrust her and her precious son upward into the bosom of the elite. The elite had surrounded her, and she became "the queen of the fiesta," rubbing elbows with famous and influential people at their famed parties. I had been an accident in both her and her son's lives, and they had had no remorse throwing me out of their lives at the precisely convenient time. I learned my lessons from this ruthless creation, and even from that humble place where I had been thrown; I had carried my head high, seeking a new path, climbing to "the ultimate glory".

Although I loved my family dearly, imagining no life without them, I have always been a very private person. It has been my own way of protecting my soul, as "a cat in a jungle" as Paul used to say. That Sunday was an unusual day for me, and all day I felt myself being pushed away from the mainstream by an unseen hand. It was a confused state, which tried in the last few weeks to drag me back into a certain part of my life. I couldn't adjust to that. That made me suffer and this made Paul suffer, too.

Complying with my invitation, Paul came back, sat on the edge of the bed and stared in silence at my face, waiting for me to start talking.

"Can you clear up this mystery?" He broke the silence, losing his patience.

"Oh, Paul, you're right! In fact, I did feel bad today, and also for the last few weeks," I whined, trying to clear up the air.

Paul grabbed my hand.

"But you said it's your period, is it true?" He whispered.

"Well, yes... Yes, I remember saying that. Perhaps it is my period, but I have another bizarre feeling. Oh, Paul, I'm so scared," I said, whimpering.

"Scared of what?" He wondered.

"For months I've been vandalized by some strange thoughts."

"Vandalized... Strange thoughts? Like what?"

"No name, no definition! There is a kind of remorse melted into fear or something like that, Paul," I replied. "I really don't know how to explain it." Paul's eyes became wider and wider. "It worries me, hon. I've never experienced anything like that in my life. Even during the time I was under Mrs. O'Neil's thumb, I never felt under such distress."

"Have you seen a doctor?"

"No."

"Then?"

"Then what?" I asked back.

"How long do you want to wait?" Paul was evidently puzzled by my strange behavior.

"I don't know what to say. I'm afraid they'll find me having one of those weird illnesses, like cancer or. …" Paul laughed. "Don't laugh, dear. Who knows which one of them is devastating my brain right now, while I'm talking with you." Paul laughed again, clamping his hand over my mouth.

"Come one, Little Cat! Don't be silly!" He relaxed. "You're too beautiful and strong to be attacked by those 'weird illnesses'."

I protested, pulling my hand out of his. "But, Paul…"

"Say nothing!" My husband uttered, grabbing my hand back. "One year from today, you'll be forty and I heard women start having menopausal symptoms early in their lives. Maybe you have some of those pre-menopausal symptoms, dear. Consider that, and don't torture yourself with such thoughts." He kissed my hand. "Clear up the mess you have created in your mind and carry your head high! This is the girl I want to see, my Little Cat!" For no reason, I felt my face burn with embarrassment. I attempted to say something, but Paul stopped me. "I know what you need to chase your thoughts away, you need my love, Little Cat. How about right now?" He said bending over me and moving his lips close to mine. I immediately pushed him away, saying:

"You're crazy!"

I panicked when seeing Paul's look.

"Cra… a… azy?" Paul's bulging eyes scared me.

"Oh, Paul! Not today… I don't feel like having anything, perhaps tomorrow night. Please, try to understand me, dear!"

"This is not just anything, dear. You'll see… you'll feel better," he insisted.

"Paul," I threw back. "Be reasonable!"

"Reasonable, you're saying… Reasonable, huh! How reasonable do you want me to be my dear? Don't you think I have been reasonable enough for weeks?" He waited for an answer. I showed him a smile. "Honestly, my dear, you have avoided me for nights in a row, each night you came with a new excuse. I had enough of me sleeping on the sofa in the living room. The kids may…"

"Oh, stop this nonsense!" I jumped, interrupting him. "Kids… kids, always kids. Kids are kids! That's all!" I tried to bottle up my emotions. Paul noticed that. It was an awkward time for both of us. He grabbed the corner of the bed cover and flipped it back and forth between his fingers. Whispering, he came straight to his point:

"Have you seen John?" His unusual soft voice moved me to tears. I could feel the pain my ex-husband's name inflicted on his heart.

"John?" I jumped, pulling the bed cover off my legs. "John? What's the matter with you, dear? You know very well, as I have told you many times since the divorce that I had never seen him, not even once. Bear this in mind! And stop torturing me with your annoying jealousy!"

A deep silence filled up the room. Paul continued playing with the bed cover. That irritated me. He caught that and stopped playing.

"You're very jealous, Paul," I broke the silence.

Quiet again. Then, with the same soft voice, Paul started:

"I love you very much, Dee, and you know it. I can't imagine my life without you."

"I love you, too, Paul, and you know it as well. Don't torture me!"

Paul came closer to me, saying: "You have no idea how much I have suffered for years knowing you in the arms of that man instead of mine. And I had seen you together almost every day. Think about that!"

I stared at his pale face. Snapshots from the time when both men had courted me invaded my mind. After a short moment he added: "I have had moments when I have wanted to put an end to that suffering, and…"

"Shush! Don't be foolish!" I threw under my breath. Paul didn't pay attention to my words. He continued:

"I've loved you the first moment I saw you walk into our classroom… Grade ten, remember?" I consented, but my pride kept me from enjoying my husband's enthusiasm. "You never had eyes for me, Dee. I had lurked in the shadows, and you knew that very well, but ignored me. I went crazy every time John paraded you on his arm in the school hallways." We looked sadly into each other's eyes.

"Paul, please stop this! I'm really not in mood to replay all those moments now. I need quiet."

"I only wanted to make you understand why I'm so jealous," said Paul, searching my eyes.

I bled for him.

"Oh, come on, Paul! You know that sick marriage is history for me now. It is another painful experience in my journal. A foolish experience that made me cry out with rage and pain. That's all!" I said, avoiding his look. I pulled the bed cover with my legs, extending them under the blanket.

"Painful years... maybe, but not sure forgotten, Dee. Your actions, ambitions, and maneuvers to regain the favors of your former mother-in-law's rich and famous gang scare me. I have never said a word, but this doesn't mean I'm not eaten inside by what I saw or heard around us."

"Heard?" I repeated, gazing at him. "Saw?"

"Yes, Dee, heard. I heard some not very pleasant words describing your manipulations and strings. There are no bounds to your ambitions, Dee. I want to..."

"OK, Paul. I had enough of this discussion. My heart feels empty today. Please, go down and check on kids!"

"Another excuse to get rid of me, my dear," murmured Paul. I knew he could read me like a book, but I pretended not to notice his uneasiness.

Paul got up and left the room the same way he came in, saying nothing. Lori followed him downstairs. "Perhaps I was a bit below the belt with my man," I thought, hearing Paul's footsteps. I wanted him out the room, but not cast out like that. "Well, I'll mend my manners tomorrow," I encouraged myself, getting off the bed.

"Oh, my gosh! What is it now?" I exclaimed, feeling dizzy and having a sharp pain crossing my head. It's not only the soul, huh? It's the body too, I guess! Poor me... Just like that, huh?"

Losing my balance, I grabbed the bed and sat on its edge. With my chin in my hands and the arms propped up on my knees, I stared at the painting on the wall. It was a copy of Paul Chabas' "September Morn" painted in oil on canvas by a contemporary artist. I tried to identify myself with the naked girl in the painting, staring alone before a vast universe. But I wasn't able to concentrate long; another sharp pain flashed my head again. I panicked and wanted to call Paul this time, but abandoned my impulse the moment I felt better. "Perhaps, this is my period... or the migraine announcing it," I concluded. I waited, continuing to sit on the bed's edge. I grabbed the magazine, flipping its pages. Princess Diana's smiling face stared at me. Some of Dr. McCarthy's sermon mingled with words from magazine stories, describing the Princess' life and death. Out of the blue, a fear of death rushed over me, followed by a compulsion to cry. I panicked again and rushed to the door to get Paul. I reconsidered when I realized that not one sound came from downstairs. "Perhaps he's sleeping," I thought. I listened again, trying to guess what he was doing. "Well, let him sleep," I said to myself, though surprised that he didn't follow his usually nightly routine of watching the news on channel two, WJBK-FOX and the Canadian weather channel.

I picked up some of my misplaced clothes, returning them to my walk-in closet, and looked at the clock on my night table. It was past midnight.

"Darn! It's time to get ready for bed… and look at me! I'm circling around the room like a mad dog. Gosh! What a day I have tomorrow!" I started toward the mirror.

A sudden noise played in my ears. This strange music sound conjured up a vision of the sea. "Gosh! What's this?" I only calmed down when I realized that the sound was in fact a vibration made by the wind, blowing against the glass of the window.

I spent a few minutes in front of the mirror, studying carefully each little line on my face. "I should do something about this, I might change my face cream," I contemplated, following a deep line showed in the corner of my right eye. "I shouldn't sleep only on my right side," I thought, pulling out the brush from its case and vigorously swept my long reddish hair, until my scalp hurt. I threw the brush back and took off my elegant robe. Naked, I rushed to the bathroom, but not before I spent a few moments in front of the mirror, comparing my body with the nude in the Paul Chabas painting. I spent long time bathing then went back to the bedroom. I rubbed my face, legs and arms with different creams. That job took me longer than usual. I grabbed my pink silk nightgown from the headboard and put it on. It was a gift from Paul during our trip to Paris. I stepped back in the front of the mirror. After admiring myself in the mirror for a few more minutes, I moved close to the window. I knelt down in front of it on the Persian carpet, attempting to pray. It shouldn't have taken more than a minute to say my prayers. Noticing my own image reflected in the window, I abandoned for a while my thought of praying, staring instead at my figure.

"I'm still very attractive," I thought. "No wonder I get men's attention. I'm beautiful," I murmured.

The color of my nightgown didn't show its pink in the reflection, but an ivory white; so did my hair. "I look like an angel," I marveled, staring at my figure. My hands, clamped in the prayer position, complemented the whole harmonious look of an angel. And the sound of the wind rustling outside in the leaves added more mystery to the entire scene.

Through the glass, I looked up at the sky. Without warning, a bolt like thunder pierced my body from head to toe followed immediately by the same ache on the right side of my head. I shivered, closed my eyes and waited a few moments. I could hear my heart beating like a bird fluttering in a cage. Then my whole body palpitated with terror. The same compulsion to cry came over me. It was like having an invisible being press me down with one hand, while with the other suffocating me — leaving me gasping for breath. My first reaction was to get Paul's help, but my legs felt like lead. I watched my reflection in the window. I examined that reflection, starring with my head. "For sure, I have a tumor in my brain," I thought, "maybe a cancerous tumor. Oh, Lord! Have pity on me!" The pain in the right side of my head was hammering each cell of my brain. "No! It's not my brain," I calmed myself. "It's my soul. My soul is in fire and takes it out on the body."

I kept staring at my image in the window. "Paul is right," I whispered. "There are no bounds to my ambition, and I'm paying the price… But I'm still young," I revolted. "I was created ambitious. This is not my fault. People made me ambitious… Mrs. O'Neil pushed me to become ambitious… Life itself created this ambitious product." I turned my head and looked at the clock. "Gosh! It's very late. It's almost one o'clock. I'd better get to bed." I stood up, dragging toward the bed. "Wait!" I said. "I didn't say my prayer."

I knelt down again, put my hands together once more, ready to pray. But, I couldn't. Tears fell on my nightgown, while my ears were bombarded with words such as: "Soul in fire… Soul in fire," repeated over and over like a broken hurdy-gurdy. I watched the tears come down the face of the static image in the window.

"What is it, my dear soul?" I quarreled with my inner voice. "Do you want to squabble with me? I am the way. I set my own way in life. I can't live this nuisance life according to my conscience. I want to live it according to my own style. I struggled to create this new 'me'. People are intimidated by my presence, and that makes me an auspicious person in this self-destructive world. Let the consequence of my work fall on my own head."

Silence.

Still kneeling with my arms across my chest, I prepared to talk to Heaven. "Oh, my God, I don't want to repeat the same 'formula' to thee. Teach me a touchable prayer, Lord!" cried my soul, lamenting loudly. "I forgot how to pray, my dear Lord. Please teach me!"

I leaned over the window ledge, stroking the area around my temple to ease the persistent pain. Staring at the sky, I hoped to find inspiration for my prayer. For a while, I cherished Heaven's canopy.

"God, I am in love with your sky," I whispered. "How marvelous is Thy Creation! How great is thee and how insignificant I am — a bit of dust in love with a Star".

It was a perfect night, neither hot nor cool, and the stars were amazingly bright. The moon was majestic, pouring down its light. "How come I have never had time to see the nature?" I wondered. "Oh, God! How many splendors have thee created, and I've never looked at them… No time, my dear Lord!

I kept staring at the sky. Thought after thought tormented my mind. It seemed that some of Dr. McCarthy's words imprinted on my brain. The thoughts were spinning through my mind, and every time one of them surfaced, overcoming my conscious, I fought it back. The struggle made me tired. But every time I closed my eyes, intending to let all my thoughts go away and go to sleep, Dr. McCarthy's words replayed in my mind, moving me back to Russia, my native country. "I shouldn't listen to that hypocrite," I said to myself. "He's like all of us in the church. He runs after wealth like every human being in this world. I owned a big mansion in Sterling Heights, he owns one almost the same in Rochester Hills, we owned expensive cars, they too have expensive cars. Afterwards, he is not below us in any way. So, what? Most Christians live in America, not in Cuba or Russia. God gave us wealth."

Still gazing at the sky, my mother's childlike face appeared, and I visualized her talking to me and describing once more the struggle Russian Christians had faced in their communist country. "… Your grandmother took me to an underground church service," mother's words echoed in my ears. "They were never intimidated by our atheistic government; on the contrary, they were always at their open-air church services, even though they were poorly dressed and fed. They lived their lives as if their Lord would return in any moment and gave no reasons to the church's opponents to call them hypocrites. They were of absolute simplicity, but bathed in love."

I was almost smothered by a silent flow of tears. "Why have I gone so far away from the real love?" I wracked my brain. "Why do I cheat my own soul? Oh, God, have mercy on my soul!" I couldn't make peace with my soul. I started to cry again, holding my face in my palms. My face, hands and elegant nightgown were full of tears and sweat.

Through my fingers I could see the face of Princess Diana, smiling at me from the magazine. I smiled back, asking her: "Where are you now, dear Princess? Where is your love and fame?" I kept gazing at her smiling face, tormenting my mind with numerous questions about life and death. It was clear to me that the Princess's death and the side-scenes linked to that made a great impact on me. It shook my soul, making me lose the real meaning of life on this planet — holding me back from the impetus of my ambitious life.

Shivers of horror went up and down my backbone. Trying to calm myself, I got to my feet and grabbed the Bible from the night table. Psalm 121 caught my attention: " I will lift up my eyes unto the hills, from whence cometh my help... My help cometh from the Lord, which made heaven and earth... The Lord is my keeper, the Lord is thy shade upon thy right hand. The sun shall not smite thee by day, nor the moon by night. The Lord shall preserve thee from all evil: he shall preserve thy soul." I flipped some more pages, but didn't read more lines from them. I laid the Bible on the night table and looked at the clock. Noticing how late it was, I urged myself to go to sleep. As I've usually done every night, I grabbed the hairbrush and combed my hair once more before putting it up with some hairpins. I laid my head on the pillow and made myself comfortable in bed, ready to sleep. But I couldn't. Numerous images stormed my brain. It was obvious that my foolishness compromised my mind and body's natural rest. I felt sick and weak.

After about an hour of tossing and turning, I switched the night lamp on and grabbed the Bible. I flipped the pages again, reading from

First Corinthians: "... and though I have all faith, so that I could move mountains, and have not love, I am nothing. And though I bestow all my goods to feed the poor, and though I give my body to be burned, and have not love for others, it profiteth me nothing."

I put the Bible back on the night table and I let my head drop to the pillow.

My eyes were full of tears. "Oh, Heavenly Father, I'm not a bad person. On the contrary, I am ethical, reliable, honest, prompt, all the good qualities you invested in me... but I don't know how I ended up making a mass out of my soul. Please Lord! Preserve my soul! Oh, my poor soul. S... o... oul!"

CHAPTER 3

DEPARTING FROM THE REAL WORLD

I startled as an invisible alarm went off in my head. I sprang up and frowned at the alarm clock's flickering light. "Damned clock!" I sulked. Twanging morosely, I closed my eyes, trying to take advantage of a few more minutes of sleep. All of a sudden, another stray sound whizzed close to my ears, this time. Not quite awaken, I sat up in the bed and took the hairpins off my hair, intending to get down and scramble to the routine of breakfast and getting ready for work.

It was the last Monday of September. Staring through the half-opened blinds, I noticed that the sun rose above the horizon. I immediately grabbed the bed cover and pulled it off my legs, willing to get down the bed.

"What's this…a bad joke?" I shouted hysterically as the entire room became flooded with a brilliant light. It was like having the sun removed from the horizon and placed on the ceiling in my bedroom. I shrieked in disbelief and horrified, I was about to spring out the door.

"Paul…Paul!" I yelled, but instantly I remembered that he had promised me the night before to take the kids to their school in his way to work. "Where is Lori…Lori…Lori, come to Mummy!" I continued yelling, calling the dog. I pricked up my ears. "Where is she? She must be scratching at the door by now." Although still tangled, I managed to come close to the door.

"What's that now…why am I freaking out?" In panic, I deepened my face into my palms, but I couldn't feel its skin. The fright urged me to run, but I couldn't do this either. "Oh… Oh!" I twisted around. "Oh God, help me! I am hanging loosely!" I screamed, feeling my body suspended a few inches above the floor, swinging to and fro freely — no gravitational pull. "Oh, my Lord! What's going on with me?" I screeched at the ceiling as if seeing God there. "God! G…od!"

Groaning, I moved my arms around, trying to hang on something.

Shivering, I rushed to let my dog in. I progressed fearfully towards the door, intending to grab the doorknob. All of a sudden, I heard the dog's scratches, but they mingled with queer whispers. They sounded like leaves rustling in the breeze.

Although my mind was clutched by fear, I was determined to take the bull by the horns and clear out the mystery surrounding me. "What a heck! I'll see what's there." Bumbling nervously, I turned the knob around, ready to open the door. The door didn't open. I was petrified. I shrieked, as loud as could. Then shut up and tried again, moving my hands hysterically all around the stubborn door.

Staring dreadfully at the door, a sinister thought crossed my mind. "How about being held up by strange beings, playing tricks on me?" This thought made me hysterical again. I paced left and right near the door. Suddenly my mind rejected sternly the thought. "No. I don't believe those gimmicks with people being abducted. I never did. People believing in this must be crazy." Encouraged by my thought, I appealed to my good senses. Therefore, still staring at the door, I let my mind struggle organizing data and make sense of the ordeal I was experiencing. "Yesterday I had that bizarre headache… today I'm having this alien experience. I'm sick, no doubt about this. But way am I thinking so lucidly if I am that sick?" The fact was that my poor brain tried to keep on a string. I calmed down a bit. "I'm sick… very sick. I should get in bed, and stay there till Paul returns," I pondered, turning around and facing the bed. "No, I'd better call 911…and do it fast till I'm able to sound a word."

However, my intention was in vain; I couldn't move from there. It was like a puppeteer's unseen hand stringing my body up and playing with me the way he wished. I screamed over and over, calling my husband and kids' names, even Lori's. Kneeling beside the door, I blustered confusedly throughout my wailing.

My groans mingled with Lori' scratches at the door. Then, I curled up near the door like a fetus in his mother's womb.

CHAPTER 4

FIGMENT VERSUS FACT

I didn't remember how long I have spent there, resting crimped near the door. What I remembered instead, was I running towards the main entrance, and bursting through the glass doors leading to my office. All of a sudden, a strange poster caught my eyes. It showed a beautiful black woman holding a bunch of white flowers in her arms. At the bottom of the poster were the words: 'PEACE AT LAST!'

"Who posted this here?" I wondered, gazing at the sign. "It wasn't there Friday, when I left. I bet it's Mrs. Dean's idea."

As I dashed through the doors with my arms full of papers, I looked down at the skirt of my long, white dress.

"How did these dungy spots got on my dress?" I gasped, pushing the office's door with my elbow. I rushed toward my desk, threw the papers on it, and began scratching at the spots with my long, red fingernail. The door clicked shut behind me. Seeing that the spots refused to fade away, I dipped a piece of paper towel into a glass of water which I'd left on the desk the week before, and tried to wash out the spots. Some came off, but only to surface again, even bigger. After a few more attempts I gave up, grabbed the papers and fell into my chair. Outside I could hear people buzzing in the corridors. Despite the fact that I was being late, I didn't bother letting my boss know I was in. "I do well in all my work. He knows that." I calmed my own consciousness.

Still in my chair, I looked around my office.

"Hey! What is this?" I wondered, eyeing a bouquet of huge white flowers that I couldn't recognize. "Who brought them here?" And rolling my eyes around, I noticed that similar flowers were spread all around on the either side of the room. It looked like a funeral home. Shaking, I sprang up my chair, trying to touch those flowers. "I can't believe my eyes…what's this? Are they for real, or what?" Some flowers were in big, white baskets, others in small, pearly vases.

The sun fell on the petals and made them glow. A strange fragrance seeped from them, which reminded me of dried thistles. Cold chills meandered up and down my spine. "Is my mind playing tricks on me? Where am I? This isn't my office! Oh, my Lord! Oh…oh! Help! Help!" In despair, I bit my arm, but no pain. I bit it again. I felt nothing. Then, I bit the other hand…then I pinched the leg. "Who is behind this?" I screamed, thinking that someone might hear my yells and rush to my help.

Seeing that nobody showed at the door, I moved around the desk, trying to make a sense of what was going on with me and around me. As I paced back and forth the office, I noticed some flowers pinned on the walls beside a big picture portraying President Clinton. "Wait a minute! This is for real. This was here for a long time. I can see the dead mosquito on it. I smashed the bug Friday… on this glass. Then how come this is real and other things aren't …Oh God, what is this? Am I dreaming? But why can't I wake up? Am I dead? Why is my heart beating then? Look…look it's beating! And… how come I am dressed in this white outfit and wore these white shoes? I know…I know well the day I'd got them — that raining day in Paris…in France. And why is everything white around me?"

I wanted to cry, but I had no tears. Only my chest and stomach were in spasm. The eyes could not cry. I attempted to make some sounds, but I couldn't hear them. Even my screams were circling inside my head. They couldn't be spat out.

I kept staring at the President's picture. "Wait a minute! Where is the picture with Paul and my boys? It was here on my desk Friday. And why so many pictures with Clinton? I wondered. The President is not the most important person in my life." With my eyes widely opened, I stared once more at the President's face. "This is not Clinton! This picture looks like him… blond, tall…all right, but yet, he's not Clinton. And why do I have this man's pictures lined up all over my office's walls?" I moved along the wall. "Hey! This is not the First Lady!" The person portrayed in the picture looked more like an old Greek peasant woman, wrapped with a black kerchief around her head. There were Mrs. Hillary Clinton's features, but she was strangely dressed — all black. "Why is the President's finger pointing at the sky?" I wondered "And why is he surrounded by all these poorly dressed people? Oh, my gracious Lord! They all wear black! Oh… what's this?" White and black people were holding flags of different countries.

I stared over and over at the pictures, trying to make sense of them. Trying also to make sense of I being there, caught in all those bizarre surroundings.

Every time I attempted to clear my mind, new experiences burst with severe impact, making me more confused and breathless. When a beam of hope just showed in front of me, a new disillusion immediately struck.

Suddenly, there was a knock in my door, followed by voices. "Dee… Dee…Dee!" The voices called, whispering. There were many voices —midgets' voices.

"Oh! Finally!" I breathed with relief. "Somebody at last comes to my rescue." My heart tossed — there was joy. Blissfully, I scuttled towards the door. It opened by itself. "Hmmm!" I uttered, looking discreetly around. "Hmm! Nobody's at the door," I said. "Who called my name then? I heard it clearly. Oh, God, don't let my brain explode!" I paced around cautiously, looking in all directions.

The bank was jammed with scantily dressed people. They looked disoriented and melancholic. I unexpectedly felt the rush to help them, though I didn't know how. Despite the fact that I've hold for years a higher position at that bank, never being forced to deal directly with customers, in that moment I decided to work as a simple teller. I moved around trying to ease the strain of other tellers.

There was a feverish excitement in the bank, loud voices, and people rushing, pushing and yelling at each other. Out of the blue, Mr. Troy, my boss, entered the bank's doors, heading toward me. He has rarely visited our bank; I had been always in full control there. Seeing him I began working even faster, making customers moving at a rapid pace, like videotape in fast-forward. Mr. Troy stood at the end of the line with a huge green paper in his hand. I assumed it was a bank check. I wondered why was the check so big, but continued working feverishly, listening to snips of conversations buzzing around me:

"I think a serious problem is going on in the Middle East these days…you see…is not a joke what is happening over there…"

"Israel is in trouble…"

"It can't affect us here in America…" "Oh! This is a safe country…"

"Don't be so sure. I've been born in Europe and Europeans thought the same way and…"

"Who cares? Live and be merry…"

I threw a short look at the crowd; it became larger and larger. The bank was full over its capacity. My hands were moving fast, like a machine. In front of me, a small girl tried to reach the counter. I bent over to grab the paper from her hand.

"My father left us last night," she whispered, staring at my hands. "He is in the army," her mother intervened.

"Hmm!" I sounded.

"I have no job or a secure bank account," the woman whined, petting her daughter's hair, while holding another child in her freckled arms. I smiled at both of them, while inviting the next person to move forward.

All those conversations made me feel good. They supported me believing that everything was normal with me and around me, even though I couldn't make an elucidation of the unfolding of that occurrence.

When it came Mr. Troy's turn, I mumbled some words and looked at the paper he placed on my counter. I lifted it up and tried to read it, but I couldn't do that. It turned instantly into a newspaper. Huge letters lay scattered across the page like giant frogs. I looked for an empty space on that paper, intending to find a spot where I could put my signature. I eyed my boss. It seemed as though our roles had changed; I was giving my stamp of approval to my boss's paper. My benevolent attitude made me smile at him. Still smiling, I picked up a black marker to sign his paper, when suddenly…a screaming whistle shrilled through the air.

Everybody felt to the floor, a common practice during a hold-up in the bank. As I hit the floor, I frantically pushed the security button.

The screaming blast continued, but there were musical notes within the scream. Notes like the call of a trumpet, urging solders to war. People were roaring, crying anxious to find out what was going on. Some stuffed their fingers in the ears, running aimlessly. Others pulled their shivering bodies along the hallways to find a piece of furniture, to hide behind it or to protect their heads. The sound screamed higher and higher, even louder and louder like wailing horns. And then I heard vibrations like unintelligible words beating through the noise. Some people around me tried to escape the noise by running out the bank; others kneeled close to the walls, screaming at each other. The outside whistling muffled their shouts. Their bulged eyes were searching for safety, while their mouths were gaping in grotesque shapes. We looked like caged wild animals filmed in a horror movie. People bumped into each other, pushing and staggering toward the glass doors. Whereas people on the outside were pushing against the doors desperate to get in! I scratched, pushed and kicked my way outside. All I could think of were my boys. I burst towards the parking lot. My body felt light — a flake carried by the wind.

Outside, the noise was even louder. It basted my ears, trying to beat the horror that blocked out the normal life around. My heart shattered out a heavy rhythm and the noise shrilled in my ears.

People sardined themselves in the street, while the sun soared gracefully over the sky, unshaken by the swarm under its rays. Cars were scattered all over the streets, blocking each other. The police cars were blocked too, while the policemen, dressed in unusual uniforms, tried hard to have control over the entire chaos.

A bag lady hid her head under some plastic bags. Though rushing, I threw a short look at the woman. Her large body was covered in a ragged, red dress, while her soiled fingers clutched a dirty plastic bag. Crouched beside her was an elegant young woman, trying desperately to use the bag lady's body as her own protection; she covered her head with the bag lady's filthy dress, shaking wildly. They clung together, screaming for help. The contrast was striking, but I had no time for them. I continued running towards my car.

Despite the fact that the parking lot was not too far from the bank's main entrance, it took me a longer time to get there. "Where is that damned parking lot? I lost my way for sure! Oh, my goodness… it was there Friday!" Baffled, I turned around to find the place. A stray dog followed me, running and panting with me. He looked dirty and disorientated. "The lady bag 's dog... I guess," I said to myself, throwing a short look at the frightened animal. Throngs of birds soared aimlessly on the sky. Still panting, I eyed the sky, yelling: "I'm alive...I'm alive. These flying birds are proving it to me...Yes, I'm alive."

Staring at the sky, I suddenly wondered: "Where are these come from?" I shouted, eyeing the large and unusual clouds rising up on the sky — from the north. Their strange colors made me stop and sifted their gently descend. "Dark gray clouds... I've seen many times, especially in Texas, but strong red and grass green clouds... Never! Strange! Strange bloody particles!" The darkness they brought with them added even more fear and evil. "Wait a minute! Are they clouds? They act like clouds, but don't look like them."

Frightened, confused and lost, I mingled with people swarming around me. Even the dog left me. My brain almost blew up inside my skull. The ambiguous circumstances, fallen like stones on my head, crippled my normal life. Though full of fear, I looked at the sky and shouted:

"Alas... My God! Where am I? Why me in this ordeal? Am I dead... when did I die then? Am I alive? Why then wandering in these bizarre surroundings? What's going on with me?" My groans suffocated me, though still running and quarreling with God.

A thought flashed through my mind: "I should run straight to my kids' school. Oh Daniel! Oh, my dear Michael...I must see you both? God, they need me and they need me now... they must be frightened, panicked... I need my kids! I'll do the impossible to get there!" I stopped for a moment, thinking: "But what if I don't have children? I don't know who I am any more...I don't know if I am married. I don't know if this is another person or I...God I am confused. Where am I? Please, help me, God!"

I kept going, but lost my direction. I passed houses, stores, buildings; some I recognized. Those made me gain confidence in my brain again and kept me going, aiming my kids' school. The clouds multiplied themselves, forming a large blanket covering the sun totally. "Dark at noon?" I wondered.

In a flash, the parking lot came in my view. I stopped, staring at it. "What is this? Am I in another world, or what? How come I know this place? Is this a parallel world? No! It cannot be… I'm sick! I am sick for sure, and that's why my brain mixes facts with visions… but how about all these desperate people flowing around me? Are their brains playing tricks on them, too? And, how about this dust that I got on my shoes, or these spots splashed on my dress by these passing damned cars? These are facts…How come I hear people talking, birds twittering and cars' wheels running on the roads? This is not my imaginative mind, this is for real… so where am I? Where am I, God? Who am I? Who brought me here, God… and why? Who benefits from this tormenting ordeal?"

Deluded, I started walking again, searching for my car in the parking lot. An old couple clinging together against a tree gazed at me in terror. As I reached my car, the couple staggered towards my car. "Get out my way!" I screamed, showing them away; I immediately regretted my gesture. "They can lead me to a reasonable answer for this bizarre ordeal," I thought, and instantaneously turned my head to fix my mistake, but the couple vanished.

Hoping to see my car it was like meeting again a missed friend. Hurrying and shivering with the keys in my hand, I approached the spot where I expected to find my car. "Ah, there you are!" I shouted, but my first reaction was unbelief. "Eh! This is not my car!" I shouted again, backing down and rolling my eyes over in search of my car.

"Sh…u… u! Sh…u… u…u!" I was running from one car to another, trembling and panting, though pushed violently by the crowd. "Oh, my gosh! What kind of cars are these? They look strange…I've never seen such design before! People look strangely dressed, too. I've never seen such style either! What's going on here?" With a short look I examined my dress. "OK, this is my dress… I recognize it, and the shoes, too… even the purse I recognize. It's a gift from Paul. But why am I dressed differently than the people around me?" I bent over to view my figure in a car's lateral window.

"A…ah!" I jumped back, screaming and staring at the wrinkled face reflected on the glass. "Whose face is this?" I yelled, pointing with my finger at the figure. "What kind of joke is this? I just saw my face last night in the mirror…and my window, too."

I cautiously paced closer to the car to have a second look at the reflected image on its window. "There are my features, all right, but it couldn't be my face…I'm young. That's old," I shouted while bending over and forcing my bulging eyes stare over and over at the strange figure. I tried to scratch the glass of the window using my fingernail. "Is it a real thing or a deception?" I wondered. But I was instantly pushed away by people, squeezing themselves between cars. I threw a swift look at people swarming aimlessly. "My God! I'm so lost and dazed, and nobody gives a dime that I'm here. 'Here'? What this 'here' means to me now? What world is this? I can't recognize it! It's not the same world I've been in the day before…where am I? Who am I? Am I the person whose face I saw now reflected on that car's window, or the one I've seen last night in the mirror? God, please…please, have pity on me! Give me a clue! What's going on, my dear Lord?

Silence.

I sat down on the asphalt and held my head down in my palms. "Where is Paul…where are my kids? I need them." I cried, but had no tears, only pain. My soul was in pain. I couldn't move. A huge muddled crowd, surrounded me, but yet I felt lost and alone, thrown in a cloistered world.

Everything was a closed book for me — a mysterious book.

Still baffled, I turned around gazing at the crowd, trying to copy their intentions. Some were able to get in the cars, others freaks were fighting each other to get in one. Cars squeezed to and fro the parking lot's driveways, but most of them skidded. People slalomed in and out of the spaces between cars or other obstacles. I followed them, trying to find a way out of that parking lot, determined to walk all the way up to my children's school.

"Am I circling around?" I wondered, realizing that I marched over and over the same alleys. "I am getting nowhere… Oh, Lord! I want to get to my kids, please, get me there!" I swiftly turned around, heading towards another alley, but came back to the same spot where I've been the first time. "Ah! I can't take it anymore! I'm frightened…and I lost my sense of life. I don't know if I'm dead or alive… and even if I am male or female, old or young…married or single. Boohoo…boohoo!" I cried my eyes out, but no tears — a painful buffer. "Where has my family vanished…where are my beloved ones now? What's going on with me, my dear Lord?"

Though still circling among cars in the parking lot, I racked my brain, torturing my mind to come up with new solutions. "If I'll take this alley… no, I've tried that three times already. No! I'll pass that car and turned left…and going that way I'll perhaps escape the people's crush. All these hysterical creatures swarming like burned ants around me! Wait a minute! Are these people for real…and is this sky full of threatening clouds for real? Is this killing sound existing as fact? Are all these manifestations a part of the background, added as a decor to my agony? G…o…d, answer me!" I roared from the bottom of my lungs at the terrifying sky. "G…od, where are you?"

Silence again.

Still staring and yelling at the sky, I stammered over a construction sign and felt on the asphalt. There, on my knees, I cried, screamed and cried again. People coming from all directions hit my crumpled body, but I didn't rebelled. By the contrary, I wanted to have any type of ache, or to be in any physical pain; I needed to assure myself that way that I was alive. People in their feverish passing jumped over my fallen body. Still lying on the asphalt with my head in my palms, facing the ground, I heard a sound coming up the earth.

"Earthquake!" I yelled hysterically. "Earthquake! Hey…stop!" I yelled at the crowd this time. "There's an earthquake…Get down, you fool!" Nobody listened; they kept running aimlessly allover the place. "Run…run, you fool, if you wish!" I roared, forcing my ear closer to the ground, while horrified at the earth's whine.

"Boom… boom. B… o… o… m…m!" Strange sounds busted one after another, amplifying the previous sounds. Panicking, I scrutinized the place in all directions, like a periscope. I slowly got up, while still staring at the ground as if expecting it to crack and swallow all of us in a twinkle.

"Who pushed me in this jumble? What is the hubbub? Is this the United States of America? Is this America I knew? Am I still living in this country?" Everything around me looked surreal "Oh, Paul! Where are you? Have you ever been part of my life…have I ever been married to you? Oh my sweet babies, would I ever be able to see you…to hug or kiss you? "I stampeded over and over asking God the same questions that tormented my soul. "I was in love with life… you know that God. But, where have I been pitched now…and why?" I was stunned. One side of me wished to vanish, to die, to become nothingness, while the other feverishly desired to live as before, and to find the kids and husband I have always known.

"I'll find a way to get back to normal…I'm strong. I've been always strong. I'll fight my way to my kids' school." I yelled at the sky. "Oh… God, just watch me! I didn't put my arms down yet!" A warm, rather emotional feeling invaded my spirit.

A high building came to my sight. People rushed in its direction, I too hurried in the same direction, but I suddenly found myself in the center of a huge plaza. Impressive highways surrounded the place. There was a hasty motion on them; cars were running back and forth all over. "Hey! I know this area…I'm in Troy. Oh, yes…yes, Troy! Oh…my mind can function. I can recognize places. Oh, thank you Lord! Oh, no doubt about it! This is Troy! I am home!"

Happy, but still perplexed, I stood up there in the middle of that plaza, forcing my mind to remember all the details linked to the place. "I know that building with smoky glass windows and that store…and that street…and…wait! This must be Oakland Mall. That's yet…Oakland Mall! Hmm…it doesn't look quite like it. Hey! There's Sears and the Theatre…but wait a minute! Their entrances look different. Sears has never had those pillars in the front. Oh! I'm so confused!" Still standing in the middle of that plaza, I looked around, trying to put the puzzle together. "Let see! I am in Troy area… Fine! I recognize that street and that one… and that group of trees there I remember. Oh, look! I know that huge building…oh, my Lord. Oh…oh…my brain works! My brain works! Let see again! So, I'm in Troy area and this is Oakland Mall. At least it supposed to be, though it looks larger and different… but why are these bustling people so strangely dressed?"

Nourished by hope, I wandered around the plaza, passing more frightened people and abandoned cars. It was neither dark nor bright. It looked like those late afternoons in December, even though I knew it was only September. The grayish shade dominating the atmosphere, the bizarre hue and cry accompanied by eerie sounds, as well as the general chaos around me made the little hope aroused in my soul vanish away.

"Oh, my Lord, if I could wake up to the life I have lived before… why can't I, my dear Lord? Where should I run next…and for what purpose? At least let me know that," I simply said, murmuring at the sky.

I looked steadily at the place, attempting to recognize the sites. Feelings of bitterness invaded my soul. A faint flash colored one of the stores' windows. I moistened my lips with the tip of my tongue, and with a quick motion I forced my body move there. I walked quickly from the spot where I spent quite a time contemplating. While walking without hesitation towards Sears, I could hear the harsh breathing of people passing by me. Their breathing sounded like the hunting dogs' gasps. Fearful sounds, women pushing baby strollers, old men rushing their partners and also young people slaloming or shoving people aside, created mostly the general upheaval. "At least I am not the only unfortunate who 'benefits' by all these changes. They too are in turmoil," I pondered, still walking. "Neither of us knows the way out this situation," I said, looking at the panicking people. "I could either go with the crowd or wait here in this plaza to see what's next in store for me." With this thought in mind, I paced slowly, being undecided which way was better for me to take: continuing to walk towards Sears, following the crowd, or wait outside in that plaza. I stopped.

Neither threats nor dread had any effect on me any longer. Therefore, I decided to submit myself to the unseen hand, which I found responsible for the entire outbreak in my life. I sought to ease my tension by pacing instead of running, also by pretending not to hear or see the uproar around me. I concentrated upon the entire experience, though trying not to be at my wit's end with this encountering. By the contrary, I helped myself find a realistic explanation of what was going on with me. I even planned my way out of the situation. "If I could concentrate more…if I could find a reason of what's happening to me…I might be able… Hey, lady, don't push!" I yelled at a woman, who bumped into me, but no riposte. The woman kept running, dragging a big plastic bag. "Was she hearing me?" I wondered. "Hey…you! Hey…lady, I dare you…!" I screamed, louder and louder, pulling and pushing people around. "Nobody hears me! But I can hear my voice, how come they don't? How come I can hear their lamentation, panting, roars and shouts…and they can't hear mine? Oh! What's going on? Where am I? Am I crazy?" I was stricken by panic again and with my hands up in the air I tried to stop people.

"Please, sir, can you hear me? Lady, please look at me…am I alive? Are you real? Am I real? Mister, please, stop! Look at me! Dear lady, help me!" Nobody paid any attention to me. They simply continued passing by my shivering body. "Oh, over there… Ah! I know that little leather store…I'll go there. No! I'll better go inside the Mall." I paced to and fro a number of times, and finally decided to enter the Mall.

Turning left near the Sears building, I found myself face to face with huge and outlandish military vehicles.

"War…war…war! War? Tanks?" I panicked. My ears were buzzing, my eyes horror-stricken and my mouth shaking. "Since when we have war…and what war is this? It was peace yesterday when I left the church!" I tried to go closer the barricades, where military machines were precisely aligned one beside the other. "So, there is a war going on. Oh God, help America! Help my kids…my family! Oh, my sweet Lord, have pity on us!"

Many military cars surrounded the tanks — they looked like cats in front of huge elephants. They all were painted in a strange earth-bluish color. Solders wearing the same color of uniforms were swarming all over inside the barricades. "I've never seen helmets like those," I said to myself, gazing at the solders' heads. "These look more like gadgets than helmets," I thought, "and the solders are talking to them. My goodness, they seemed to belong to another era. My Lord, were am I? This is not America for sure!"

I examined my palms. They were full of sweat and make-up, blended with dust and street trash. A warm feeling soothed my spirit. I cried and then yelled: "I'm alive…I'm alive! Hey, people I live…I'm not dead. I am here in this bloody place, all right, but I'm alive. Look…look! I'm dirty, as you are. Look, my dress is full of street's dust. Thanks God, I'm alive!" I forced myself closer to the barricades. Suddenly, buzzing sounds, followed by unclear voices filled the air.

They came from the military convoy. I moved closer, but an officer's hand made all the people depart.

"Sss...s! Boom! Bang." A detonating sound whistled around. The ground shook frenetically. "Bang!" Another explosion erupted. Then another one— louder this time. The air was vibrating and the ground trembling. My teeth were chattering and cold shudders ran up and down my jarring body.

Everyone felt to the ground. I, too, lay down, covering my head. There was a mass of people spread allover the Mall's huge parking lot. From distance, more detonating sounds were heard, matching each other.

Beams of different colors furrowed the sky. I kneeled down and looked up. "My goodness, what are these? Laser beams? ...My g...o...o... d... ness! I can't believe this! What is this? What! Are they communicating among them? It looks like. No! It couldn't be real... it's only my imagination." In spite of my fear, while still closer to the military convoy, I kept wondering at the beams, trying to make a sense of their signals. "Are we invaded...but by whom? Creatures...but where are they? I only see human faces around me. Oh, my Lord how puzzled and desperate I am and nobody cares...not even you. Where are you God?"

"Your children...your children! Find your children!" The same inner voice tormented me once more. "My children...oh, my children...but do I have children?"

I stood up, being even more determined to reach my children's school, but plunged down again when another booming sound traversed over my head.

"Oh God, I would never be able to get out of here!"

I had no hesitation of getting up again. For a few moments no other sounds were heard except for the people's panting and rushing. Following a large group of people, I moved closer and closer to the Sears' main entrance. "Oh, Lord, how this could be? I've just been here yesterday with Paul and the kids... but how come Sears' entrance looked different now? What happened? Sears never had such majestic entrances." I dared to enter Sears, accompanying the crowd.

"Keep going," the inner voice commanded. "Mew...mew...mew!"

"Hey! What's this...a cat? A cat... here? Where are you, fool?" I bent down, looking through people's legs.

"Mew...mew...mew...mew...m...ew!"

"Ha…a! There you are! Come here!" I managed to grab and clasp the little white bundle to my chest, when suddenly I was about to throw it back on the floor. "Eke! It feels like glass wool! No bones?" I stared at the cat, shrieking in disbelief. "Are you real…or this is another gimmick in my ordeal?" I clasped tightly and tightly the poor animal, but the more I squeezed its shriveling body the more I concluded that I was holding an image of a cat. "But it mews!" I revolted. "If it mews…it's alive, and if it's alive…I am alive too." I pushed the animal tighter against my chest. I wanted to feel its heart, to convince even more myself that it was alive.

"Mew…m…ew!" The cat tried to climb up my shoulder. I stopped walking and took the animal off my shoulder. I could feel its bony, little paws struggling to get up. People were rushing in all directions, ignoring pure and simple that I was there with the animal in my hands. The cat was desperately mewing, but nobody cared; people didn't even bother to throw a look at us. I was almost to feel the cat's heartbeat, when suddenly another booming sound made all of us plunging to the ground. The cat vanished.

"I lost'm! I lost him! Oh, my… I lost the cat and he was the only hope I had. Oh, my bad chance! He could help me find the truth in this ugly misery! Darn! If I only could feel his heart beating, if I only…" I looked in all directions, but people's movement blocked my view. "Hey…where are you, bloody fool? I lost you…lost…lost!" Still on my knees in Sears' main hall, I looked all over to detect that cat, ignoring people's legs that hampered over my hands. "Hey lady, move aside!" I yelled at a young mother who was hurrying and pushing a baby stroller. The woman didn't hear me. She kept rushing, bumping into my legs. "No pain?" I stared in disbelief at the stroller and then at my legs. "She hit me…and I have no pain? How could it be?" Annoyed and puzzled, I stood up and continued rushing with the crowd, abandoning the idea of finding the poor cat.

"Keep going!" My mind stimulated me again.

"Keep going, huh? If at least this would lead me somewhere," I said to myself, thinking of a solution to escape the ordeal. "Let see! There is a war out there…I don't know who is fighting. I even don't know if this war is for real or not. I want my family with me. Oh, how much I miss them! I have no other hope. But find them. Darn! How am I getting there? 'There'! Where 'there'?" I was baffled. Too many peculiar encounters, running at a swift pace one after another. Human minds are not programmed for such a speed of data. No wonder my mind is acting awkwardly.

I stopped walking, trying to concentrate instead: "This is not good! I shouldn't have entered here... I should go out and beg someone to take me to my kids' school, or Paul's work. Yes! I'll go out! It must be there a good soul willing to help me get out of here." I circled around for a while, not decided which direction to take. I paused and pondered a few moments.

While watching attentively the crowd, a sinister thought crossed my mind: "What if I have no family? What if that old face I saw reflected in the car's window is indeed mine...and I'm not young anymore and the family I had died...and... Paul... dead? No! It couldn't be...Paul is strong and young, I'm young too, and have two beautiful kids and ...and...I'm very alive. But where am I? Why am I lost here? Why... am I in this turmoil and war? War? Why me in the war? It was peace yesterday...Oh God, I'm so frightened...so scared and I see no end of it!" I rushed back to the main exit. "No...I'm sick...for sure! There is no war and nothing of this is going on here. I'm not 'here', I'm conceiving mentally everything. I'm in my bed, dreaming. It's only my sick mind, imagining scenes and loosing the real trucks. But how come I feel this damned floor I'm walking on and how come I smell and hear...and panic and feel my own heart beating...and all of these people panting, pushing ...rushing...why? Why is that? Am I encountering an adventurous expedition through the unknown? Then, why me?

Why at this time? Am I living in the past... am I living another life? Had I lived another life before and I am coming back to it now? No! Absolutely, not! I don't believe in reincarnation. This is a deceit... a farce. Then what is it?"

Affronted with puzzled questions, my mind refused to decide on my next move. Therefore, I went out, waited there for a few moments, and then rushed back through Sears' main entrance. But before entering the massive doors, a sparrow felt from the sky right near my legs, sliding over my shoulder.

"Bad luck!" A strange thought crossed my mind. "But I am having already enough bad luck, " I replied to myself. I picked the bird up, but couldn't quite feel its body in my palms. It felt like a snowflake, ready to melt. I freaked out: "Ugh! It's no real!" I immediately dropped it in the petunia flowers, found in a huge ceramic pot. "It wasn't real…I'm sure!" I thought, shaking my body in dismay. way.

Though, back inside the mall, I wandered a while around, cutting people's way.

"Keep moving! Go on all the away!" The inner voice encouraged. It seemed that it purposely beseeched me to move ahead, to journey onto a predestinated path. I didn't know why. My only wish was to get out the ordeal as quickly as possible, yearning to beat it before it would strike me even more violently.

I advanced, though not rushing. I paced along the isle, letting people around me precipitance and bump into each other. "They went berserk!" I thought, throwing them a look, while seeking to find a safer corner to hide.

I entered a pet store, but soon realized it had been a bad choice. Scared cats and puppies were whining in huge cages—some longing to get out, others to abscond. Birds were tossing their jerky bodies in fear. "They are alive…they suffer…they're scared and are crying…mewling like kids. They are alive…it's not a tricky joke. So what is it with this strange world around me? Oh, if I would find an escape I would…" I instinctively moved my arm, wishing to pet a scared cat.

"Hey, what kind of cage is this? Cages are not to be sophisticated gadgets. A cage is a cage! Look at this! It closes and opens up by itself. Oh, my goodness, what more should I encounter?" I pushed once more my hand into the cage's enclosure. "Nothing! Hmm!" I tried again, wondering at the cage and the frightened animals, but immediately jumped back: "Eek! This is a charade…bad joke! How come I can't touch them? People touch pets in a pet store. I looked around me; nobody was in the store, except for the pets and myself. Outside the store, there was a continuous hubbub, while inside everything was in disorder. I moved closer to the huge cage again, examining it carefully. "They don't notice me…they either can't see or ignore me," I thought, gazing at the terrified animals. "A…a…ah!" I screamed frantically, jigging back and bursting through the doors.

A huge cold-blooded reptile, rolled up near the cage made me dash out. "Ba…boom! Ba…boom!" The throb of my heart deafened my ears.

"Ba…boom! Ba…" I felt something choking me; it was like a giant's hand pressing down my neck.

With one hand covering my chest and with the other stamped around my neck, I walked aimlessly along the main isle. Instinctively, I looked up at the impressive glass ceiling. Swift lights running like bright celestial bodies all over the sky came to my view, making me even more alarmed. "Oh God, how long do you want me to endure in this impalpable world? If you wish to kill me…then kill me! But don't push me farther into this limbo! I can't take it any longer…I can't take it! You took the wonderful life off me…please, give it back, my sweet Lord! I can't recognize this world, please…Lord! Please! Boohoo! Boohoo! Oh Lord! You took even the feeling of weeping away from me. Oh, what's going on with me? Where am I?"

The sound of murmurs coming from the fountain, placed in the middle of the main mall's foyer, attracted suddenly my attention, making me for a few moments overlook the tumult around me.

"Rest here!" The inner voice demanded. It seemed to me that I was shunted from one place to another like a hollow doll by the puppeteer's hands.

I moved closer to the fountain, staring at the water. "And what, pray, may that be?" I exclaimed, gaping at the water's unusual waves. "Waves? Here? Is this water or jelly? It looks like shaking jelly and I wonder why?" I kept staring at the trembling water in disbelief, neglecting again for a while the total chaos around me. The on and off multicolor lights pointing at the water added even more mystery to the entire scene, making my eyes run at the light speed from one area to another in that immense mall, every time descrying more peculiar things. "Everything is acting strange around me…and in this mall…and…there is…"

"A war…" The inner voice continued my initial thought.

"There is a war…Fine!" I repeated morosely. "I'm trying to understand that, but what, pray, does it have to do with me? I've been thrown here… I've been uprooted from an astounding life, beloved family…stripped off my youthfulness and thrown here…although I don't have a clue what this 'here' means. I'm 'here' breathing, rushing, crying, wandering and panicking…though nobody gives a dim that I am 'here'. Here! Here! H… e… re!" I yelled, pounding the ground with my leg.

Every time the electricity went off, screams and more panic arose and when it went off, only murmurs and dragging feet were heard. Bewildered, I moved back to the edge of the fountain and looked at its shaking water. "I look old indeed!" I exclaimed. "But how come I look like that? Is that I? No, is not! Yes, it is! Oh my gosh…I look horrible!" My face was unrecognizable and my hair disheveled. My white dress was full of spots and torn in many places.

Wondering at the reflection in the water, I tried to make a clear distinction among the other reflected faces seen in the same water.

"Keep going!" The inner voice said again. "Where?" I thought.

"Follow the crowd…" The voice urged. And I followed the crowd, rushing, panicking and panting with them.

"Mrs. Death is never tired…Mrs. Death is never…Mrs. Death…Mrs. Death…" The inner voice kept repeating my grandfather's words describing the calamity of the World War II. His words invaded my mind and the smell of death engulfed my entire body, frightening me even more. Suddenly, I notice that the air was putrid. An evil stench erupted from nowhere and swirled around us. People were running in despair, covering their noses. Many felt on the floor.

Death struck unexpectedly. Mothers lost their children and orphans were wandering all over.

"Oh! God…my children," I deplored. "I want my children with me…I must get out of here immediately. I'll get to their school even if I should crawl there."

"Go there…go there," the voice inside of me snarled.

"How?" I pondered.

Outside most of the people were on their hands and knees, crawling in the dust and staring glass-eyed ahead. Military vehicles multiplied like mushrooms after the rain. "Poor souls!" I cried, horror-stricken by the scene. "Oh, our poor souls! God is shaking our bodies…our earthly houses…our frail houses!" The only well-organized people were the military crews; they acted like robots. This frightened me and tried to run as far as I could from them. It was something inhuman in them. Even when they helped people around, they did that following orders not as a humanitarian act. They treated people like animals, pushing them to safety or throwing them out, especially when one happened to find refuge among their machinery.

"God, please let me find my kids…you know this is essential for me now. Don't turn your back on me! I need my family, God!" With my hands up and knees bent on the parking lot's asphalt, I prayed and begged God for a long time, never minding the panic around me. "I have fear of death and…I see death all over here. God, don't let me die… don't let my beloved ones die. I'm not ready to meet my mother and my father…and I'm not prepared to meet you, God! Please, give me more time! I'm still young…I don't want to die!"

A loud creaking noise came out from the ground, then another one followed and many came after that. Horrified, I stared at the impressive, gray glass building across Highway 75 and swiftly eyed the others around it, as if I expected all to crack down like domino pieces. It didn't happen that way; they continued to stand tall.

Rushing, and together with other people I reached and crossed Highway 75. As expected in such confusion, the road was packed with cars. Strangely, most of them were able to run, chaotically of course, but nobody cared about transportation rules. I wasn't bothered by that either and not even by the peculiar aspect and design of the cars. Even booed, frightened and lost as I was, I learned to accept the strange, 'new world' around me, but never abandoning my goal of uniting with my family.

Wandering around the commercial places and some apartment buildings, I saw people racing up and down, like rats caught in cages. It seemed to me that people around me ran faster and noticed that as much as I wanted to keep up with the young people, I was still at the pace with the old ones.

"There're people up there," I said. "I'll beg one of them to take me to my kids." I rushed towards one of the building's parking lot, hoping to find someone to give me a ride to my children's school. "Awful thing to ask in such panic," I thought. My enthusiasm was cut short when discovering that nobody bothered to answer my plea. I roared like an injured animal.

My mind froze, horrified by my surroundings including the gun metal sky, the unbearable stench, the cracks in the ground, crying children and desperate parents, the bloody wounds and the corps, some floating on the small, man-made lake, others rummaged on the roads. Some small buildings collapsed one after the other, taking their occupants under with them, while diverging pieces of metal and wood through the air. Dozed with horror, seconds seemed like hours. "I'll be better off waiting here for the end of this nightmare," I pondered. "I can't be in charge of my life anyway." I backed up a few steps and then stopped.

"Mrs. Death is never tired…Mrs. Death is…never…tired…" My grandfather's words pounded again and again in my ears. I walked ahead. Suddenly, I stumbled and fell face down into a bed of marigolds and petunia flowers. Their sweet cinnamon smell wrapped me like a shroud. I inhaled their fragrance with great deep gasps. My frantic heart began to beat slower and still, I rested there not thinking, not seeing. I couldn't get enough of the fragrance — sweet cinnamon and death. I yearned to stay there, to melt there, to become one with those flowers — to die there. A baby sparrow squirmed beneath me. I pulled it out from under me and dropped it in the flowers, though not felt much of its body. It lay there limp and frightened.

A silent shroud of tiny white flakes came down from the sky. "Ash," I said to myself, looking up. "Ash," I said again. The sky had turned blood red. Flame shot up the 'Sunoco's gas station. Explosions split the air. The flame burst higher.

"What is this?" I screamed at an old man running past me.

No answer.

"What's burning?" I screamed at a lady standing on the curb half-naked.

"The end," my inner voice whispered.

"The end?" I yelled. "The end of what?"

"The end," the voice repeated.

All over me was Hell–Doomsday. "God, help me get out of here… help me find my kids," I screamed at the sky. "Oh God, you abandoned your Creation and let somebody else took over!"

Dragging my exhausted legs and racking my brain, I departed from that parking lot aiming to walk towards my children's school. From that place where I've been for a quite time to my children's school, there was about five-mile distance towards Flint. "If I'll take the short cut among houses and commercial buildings I might be able to shorten this distance," I pondered, rushing in that direction.

Panting, I approached an apartment building, placed alone in an empty field. Out of the blue, I felt beleaguered by a bright light and immediately struck by something sharp on my neck and head. I instantly felt to the ground. I attempted to touch my neck, but couldn't move my arms. I tried to move my legs, but I couldn't feel them either. Something warm came out my nostrils, stinging my lips with a metallic taste. "Blood?" I panicked. I tried to touch my lips, but my arms didn't respond in any way. I tried again, using my tongue this time, but I couldn't move that either.

"Help…help… somebody, please, help!" I groaned. No one answered. No one helped. I tried to crawl, but I couldn't move. I waited… and waited, weaker… and weaker…

CHAPTER 5

THE BOUNDARY OF THE UNKNOWN

"…Black…all over…black and nothingness! Oh…oh! A…a…a…ah! What's this? A…a…a…a…ah! No! No! I don't want there…No!… Not in that nothingness! It's too black…It's nothing…It's only dark… Dark! I'm scared…scare…! Ah! Ah! I'm passing through… I'm passing through! Oh God, please, don't let me die… I don't want there! It's black! It's not…life… Life! Life! Shuuuuu! Sh…u…u! Ah! A…a…ah…ah! Oh God, please, stop me! Shuuuuuu! Push me back… Shuu! Oh God! No…no…no! Mother…Mom…where are you? Mom, be with me…. Help me! Come to me! Oh God, where is my mother…Oh! Don't let me flow into this dark…dark…dar…k…k… I feel dark, I feel…fe… e…l… A…a…a…a…"

Silence…a deep, annoying silence.

"My name is Dee-Anna Turner…" I murmured slowly, quizzing my intellect. "I have been born and baptized as Ana Kazlovsky…in Russia… and we had moved to America at the 'diapers stage'. My father's name is Iuri Kazlovsky and my mother Olga Kazlovska. Both had been born in Kiev, Russia, and both are dead now — my father of a heart attack and mother, weeping after him. I'd had been married to my high school sweetheart, John O'Neil, whose mother had helped us terminate very soon our evil marriage. Later I've married another high school classmate, Paul Turner… and have now two boys, Daniel and Mike….and also a mother-in-law, who is very ill and alone. Paul is an important man, an executive director for a big corporation, and I also hold an important position with one of the well known banks in America." I paused. "Wow! My mind works! I'm alive…alive…and feel better. I'm not dead… I'm …I'm…me…I…the same I…I, Ana…A…na…I mean…Dee-Anna, Dee- Anne Turner…married, kids… I'm an American and believe in God, His Son and Holy Spirit…and I'm one of those convinced churchgoers. Oh Lord, has pity on me! And let me go back to my life…to my good life, oh God! This is misery for me. Don't kill me, God! Not now… I'm smart and full of life, please let me live! Let me go back to life!"

I wasn't moved back, I was forced to progress into nothingness instead, but I didn't react, though I felt liberated and light —very light. Instantly, I was pushed upward through a dense fog, seeing nothing around, but haze.

"I'll be all right again…yea…all right!" I murmured. "Oh, please… God, help me be all right. What is this brume now? Brume! I'll be all right again. But why am I … in the fog? I'll be all right… Oh God! Help me get out of here! I want to kiss my kids and hold Paul again. They need me, Lord! I am moving through…moving…mov… A…a…ah! A…a…ah! Help! Where am I going? A…a…ah! I don't… I can…not… A…a…ah! Stop! Oh God, take me o…ut…out, please, take me out of here!"

I wasn't taken out of there. By the contrary, I was dragged deeper and deeper into it. I felt like being a "nothing" floating into "nothingness" — neither smell, nor sound. There was no dark or bright, and also no forms or matter either, only total void.

"Am I nothing like this nothingness… am I really dead?" I panicked, trembling like jelly. "No, am not! I'm alive… I can think and suffer… No! This is I, the one I've always been. The same ego…the same me… the same, the same… I am I. And yet, I think, I'm dead…but why did I die? What is the cause of my death? People die of something. People have just surrounded me. No! I'm not dead. I'm just out of thoughts. That is all! Perhaps, my brain has a blackout… Oh Lord! Help me! Who am I? Where am I? I am dead, isn't? But why…why? And where are the others? Where are my mother and father? There are dead…and if I'm dead, they must be with me here, welcoming me, isn't it? No, I'm not dead, because…I don't want to die. I'm young and healthy… I can't die.

And yet…I'm dead. No hope left for me!" I felt like being dropped down in an ocean, while bathed and carried nowhere by the ocean's weaves. I gave up hope, waiting instead for the unstoppable fate to carry on with the end of the end.

The moment I decided to let things go their way, a sudden, overwhelming peace enveloped me. I accepted being dead. I made peace with death. The only thing that puzzled me in that moment was my new existence — my existence as a new form. Although, being in the same time too frightened to think about my own death, or that I was indeed dead.

◀ ▶

I tried in vain to reach the ground, though I pushed hard my feet against the soil. I jumped and bounced, but nothing made me feel the force of attraction between my body and the sole. Still jumping, I bumped into a body, which was lying down on the street's asphalt. "It's mine," I yelled. "It…is…m…mine. Wow! I'm there and here… I… myself… in two places. Wow! How could this be? Still standing up, staring at the body on the asphalt, I moved my arms around my form and with a quick action; I bent down, trying to feel the flesh of the dead body.

"Nothing! Nothing! I can't feel it… I can't! That thing is not there. It's only an illusion… an illusion and nothing else. Being here…it is also an illusion, and that thing lying there is another illusion. Perhaps a joke…a trick…a tricky ordeal. That's all…a tricky trial! In fact I'm not here… I'm in my bed, in my mansion in Rochester Hills…in Michigan…in… United States of America. Oh God, who is tormenting me…and for what purpose? Am I indeed crazy, God? Is that thing there I? How come there is no head attached to the body? Why is there a body without a head? I see legs, hands…but no head. Oh God, am I indeed dead? And that thing it's my own person? Then who am I now? I feel having arms and legs, but I can't see them… I feel like walking, but no soil under my feet. I feel like being dressed in something, but I can't see what is it… Oh, my Lord, take me out of this torture! Who is that thing there? Have I lived in it and have I in fact died? Where? Last night in my bed or there on the asphalt? Oh God, I'm so confused and nobody is here with me to clear up this mess! If I am dead then why I still feel so baffled…and why am I thinking the same way as before? I see no difference between 'I' then and 'I' now...so the suicidal people solve nothing, huh? They're left in the lurch, huh?"

I moved closer to the body and tried to examine it, but something drove me to look up. I stared at the turbulent sky and said:

"Of God, how come I'm not an angel now...which I've always thought I'll become when I'd die? How come I am not an angel now? How come I'm the same ordinary human being as I've always been since I've known myself?" I looked again at the body, kneeling down this time. Its knees were bent up against the chest, curled inside, the arm was holding on a bag. I bent over and examined the scars on the neck. Some I recalled as being from a fight I had had with John, my first husband. "Oh, how young I died!" I pondered, but instantly an inside urge made me have a second look at the corps there. "That thing there might not look young," I thought, "but I've never known myself old either."

Without warning, I was pushed away from the scene and moved beside a bus stop booth, which I recognized it immediately; it was a new one, placed right in the corner of the street where my kids' school had been before. "But this looks old and ruined...how come is not new anymore? It was in a perfect shape Friday when I took my boys from school."

I moved around, wondering at booth, when suddenly, a group of pursued people passed by me like flies in a storm. Some cars drove by in hurry. "No...I'm not an illusion as I thought," I said to myself, "I can see people...I can see these cars moving and their frightened occupants inside." Why? Why, am I here...why in this war? Why this cataclysmic tribulation? And why becoming two bodies? One lying there and one standing here."

The same unbearable atmosphere took over the surroundings. The sky became even darker and the sounds of blast and sorrow filled the air.

"My goodness! I can see better now...I can see the entire surface... Wait! I can even cover the entire surroundings with only one look... Wow! Wow...I can see everything at once... I can see that and this building and...I can... Oh my...I...Oh!" The entire area came to my view at once. "The same panic, the same distress! Oh God, you're done with America! America the beautiful," I murmured, rolling a swift look around. "America...the beautiful..."

In spite of the tragic view offered to my eyes, I felt much calmer and in the same time alleviated though still confused. It was like waiting for the next thing to happen — good or bad.

More people came in my direction, but they only passed by me — not seeing me nor hearing me.

"Hey, mister, please stop! I want to talk to you," I yelled at a young man, but he rushed right through me. Petrified, I touched my form. "Am I a floating vapor? People are passing through me like passing through the air. Am I nonexistent? But how come I feel their pant...how come they can't notice me? Oh God, take me out!" I kneeled down, imploring God's mercy and waited there on the asphalt for a long time; I was not sure where to move next.

Noticing that I waited in vain for a good thing to happen to me, while witnessing nothing, but panic and turmoil, I decided to move along the street. I followed a group of people, heading in the same direction, and I hoped to finally reach my children's school.

Outside it became darker and darker, but that it didn't affect me; I was able to clearly see like in daylight. Only people around me were affected by the dark; they hampered, yelled and cursed. Passing some billboards, I instinctively threw a look at the commercials. Everything displayed up there was unknown to me. It looked very futuristic as in science fiction movies. It was nothing like I've ever seen before; every picture seemed to nod. I progressed along the road, still staring at the billboards.

"Do they belong to the year 1999, or what?" My thoughts gave up on me.

I couldn't make any correlation of the time. To top it all, just when I thought having a tiny clue of the situation, a talking picture struck my eyes. I shrieked in disbelief. It was actually a slogan, repeating like a marionette: "Go Americans! Go my sons! America, America! Save America, boys!"

"Save America? Of what?" I wondered. I looked puzzled at the people panicking around me and again at the talking picture. "What's that? What's going on in this strange world? Which America are they talking about?"

Perplexed, I progressed along the road. "If at least this were my own enigma." I thought, continuing moving ahead. I panicked again while noticing how quickly I moved around, avoiding with the use of a simple thought the unknown places, and how swiftly I moved among the familiar ones. I watched attentively each building from the street. Suddenly, some familiar sites came to my view. Trying to locate the school's building, a sinister thought crossed my mind.

"How about being only an image, and not being able to be seen by my kids!" I was petrified at the idea. "Oh, God, wake me up…make me come up of this… Escape me from this nightmare."

I wasn't helped out; I was forced instead to progress along the same street, wondering at the building and billboards.

"Hey! I know this man… its Mr. Klass…yes, Mr. Klass, our customer, who comes regularly to our bank. Hey, Mr. Klass…can you see me?" I yelled at the frightened man. "No…I don't think he can notice me," I whispered disappointed. "He looks so scared…poor man, he's dead scared. Mr. Klass, look at me…here…here," I waved my arms in front of his eyes. "No…no…it's in vain! Oh, Mr. Klass, how badly I need you to notice me," I murmured, staring at the man. Once an elegant man, always displaying an alluring charm, the poor man was now sitting with his legs bent on the dirty asphalt, beside an abandoned car. He looked old. "What is he waiting for?" I wondered. "What are you waiting for, Mr. Klass?" I yelled. "He's staring at the sky." I looked in the same direction, staring at the same scene; there was a dogfight among some kind of laser lights.

Mr. Klass followed in horror each ray's movement. "Maybe he knows more than I do," I pondered, still staring at the sky, but moving ahead in the same time.

There was a general panic; yet people moved along the street. "I won't go anywhere from this street, unless I find my boys' school. They must be very close… I can feel their presence…they're somewhere this area," I thought, examining each site I passed.

"Pasta House…Pasta House here? Since when is this store here?" I wondered, noticing the store's old building. Though still very elegant, the building was vividly lightened by the rays' motion. "The boys' school mustn't be that far," I said to myself. Instinctively, I looked at the store's window. "Where am I? How come I can't see my face reflected on this?" I turned around to see the tree reflected in the store's window. "How come this tree can be seen reflected there…and I can't see myself there? How come I see these cars…people…all their reflections are there on the window, but I? Where is my figure there? I am an illusion…that's yet…an illusion, " I murmured, turning around and back and forth for a number of times, eyeing the store's window. Miserable and confused as I was, I decided to abandon the site and move ahead.

"What, pray, is this?" I yelled, trying to push the leaves of the tree away of my face. "Are they passing through me…or else? Oh, my gosh… Ugh! Annoying tree!" Frightened and confounded by the experience, I forced myself out of the tree's crown. "How many tedious adventures must I encounter till I get to my kids?" I asked, moving back and forth near a parking lot.

As I was dashing ahead, a drumming sound, like a horse's hoofs, made me startled. Though still moving, I looked up towards the direction of the sound, blinking in astonishment at the approaching scene. Some type of air vehicles filled the sky. Instinctively, I attempted to throw myself to the ground, and hide inside its cracks, but I couldn't. I immediately wove my form into an opening formed by the corners of two buildings instead. At the sight of the aircraft, people roared and ran for safety. I, myself, stared in disbelief at the horrifying scene. "Are these monsters fighting with the lights? How could this be? Are these planes and lights brawling? I can't believe this! Look…look…these monsters mouse the lights and the lights strike back." I swung my eyes back and forth, from the sky to the frightened people around me; they looked like a horde of mice faced with a hard working, morose tomcat. "Wow…wow…these lights are chasing people…who are dead scared. Oh, my God, I hoped they… Oh! Oh…" I shouted, realizing that the rays were shooting at the terrified people. "They're shooting at me, too…oh my Go… No… no…I must get out of here… Oh……A…ah!" I yelled, bursting myself forcefully out of my hiding spot. "Wait a minute, they can't shoot me …I have no body. My body is not with me…is there in the street…or in my bed…or God knows where…but they can't shoot at me." I came out my hiding place.

Instantly, I found myself in front of a red scarlet building. I immediately recognized it as being the beggar's lodging and one of the former, famous factories in the old times in America. "As a matter of fact, this is very close to the school," I thought. It shouldn't be that far away from this place."

Under a cloud of terror, dark, danger, uncertainty and death, the surroundings made me even more confused about the real location of my children's school.

"Where that damned school could be?" I cudgeled my brain, noticing that I was moving around and around the same red building. "I'm getting nowhere… and I've just been here Friday afternoon. I parked right there, over that spat…" I said, staring at the parking lot meters, placed close to the factory's building. "It's that buil … Where is the school now? Oh God, where should I move next? Where to find my kids? There I am… close to my kids' school…and the school is nowhere! Oh, my! The lights and their gnashes made me crazy. Oh God, when… when would you put an end to my misery?" I revolted at the sky. "With each move I made, you make me discover how nonexistent I am… Why, God, why? Am I indeed nonexistent, God? Am I imagining all? But I can feel…I can smell… walk, panic and fear…hide like all these harassed, poor beings, swarming around here. Is death all it is, God? Will I ever be able to walk away from this tribulation, or I am predestinated to wander forever between strange worlds? Which world do I belong to? Which world do I find you?"

CHAPTER 6

ROAMING INTO NOTHINGNESS

Out of the blue, an incandescent glow lingered around me. I felt being spied by it. I hid. The light followed me; no sound, no luster, no words. It just stayed put there. I hid again, sucking my form from one place to another. But, the light was after me giving me no rest and making me instead depart from the street that I hoped to find the kids' school.

"What do you want?" I yelled frenetically at the light, which was tightened up itself in a bundle of beams. I received no answer. "Are you alive?" I asked again, but I had no reply. "Are you protecting or scaring me?" I attempted. Silence. "I need you…please, be my help," I desperately yelled. "I need to…" My words were cut short by a blow, which struck the light in pieces. "A…ah, my Lord…what's this?" I screamed, terrified, eyeing an aircraft, which was shooting a bunch of rays at the light. I almost felt and smelled the metallic body of the weird aircraft. It came very close to me, so I could perceive the dull blue color of its interior as well as parts of is machinery.

"No pilot…no person guiding this monster?" I wondered. "What, pray, makes it move? It looks like an airplane, though it's not a plane," I said. "It has wings, all right…but it seems not to need them." The inside and outside color of that vehicle was the same as the color of the solders' uniforms and their machinery, seen before around that huge mall. It was a blue-green color, which was blending with the surroundings — one time becoming dull blue, while the other an intense sky blue color. It was an optical phenomenon similar to the pimpernel flowers, which close on cloudy days.

Back up...back up!" I heard. "Don't go closer...move back!" I was commanded, the moment I was about to come very close the craft. The voice that commanding me didn't sound human, coming out of the vehicle instead of its interior. "If nobody's there...who talked to me then? Hey...sir...where are you...who are you?" I dared.

"Move! Move! Leave the place!" The voice commanded again, more imperatively this time. A tingling sensation in my limbs made me move unwillingly.

"How come he saw me...and nobody else could see me? Who was that guy? Is he in the same world with me? Or this is my illusion again? Oh God, please, illuminate my mind," I pleaded. "If I could be able to get Paul with me...or maybe a doctor...or perhaps some good pills would put my brain on the right path again. Oh God, come on now...I had enough of this misery. Don't let me stay a prisoner of my own mind any longer."

The sound of feet running and crawling, cars' creaking wheels and building's cracks made me come back to the reality of the new world, which I've been thrown into.

"No! Unfortunately I'm real," I said, disappointed, "and live in a real world with real problems. Why am I here? I don't know, and have no clue of how to get out of here either. There is a 'hand at work' here, and I am its victim...for, God knows, how long."

Some how, I came back to the same street I've been before, assuring myself once more that it was the one capable to guide me to the kids' school. I wondered a while along the street, witnessing again the same horror, fight, screams, panic and death — only trees and plants were calmly living their undisturbed lives.

"Oh my...how come I didn't notice the school?" I asked dumbfounded, discovering the school's playground. "I moved around that strange looking building numerous times...where are my senses? What senses?" I rushed to the main entrance, but I immediately stopped. "Oh, poor kids...oh, my... They're frightened. It's normal...Yes, normal. They're only a few...It's also normal.... Oh, poor kids...oh, my kids!

Michael, Mic… Oh, Daniel…" A few children were gathered around two adults, shivering and bewailing, while the adults tried in vain to confront them. For a moment, I forgot my own sorrow and offered to help, but nobody noticed me. I scrutinized for a moment their cloths. "Why these strange uniforms? I wondered, staring at the students' white and blue unusual uniforms. "Since when did this school impose uniforms?" My kids never wore uniforms." Still marveling, I left the spot, heading to the door.

"My kids…I must get to them…but, how? These people are in my way…I'll check the other entrance. Huf…f…f! Huff…f…f!" Panting, around the building, I tried to find the entrance I have always used. "It must be something wrong with this building. It didn't look the same before! Maybe this is not my kids' school. No! I'm sure it is…the main entrances the same alleys. Yes, this is the one. But how come is so huge now? It was a small school before… 'Before'? 'Before' what…when? Oh God, where am I again? I'm a mother and I need my children now. Please, show me the way to them… Please…please, dear Lord! I can't stay this confusion … Hu…f…f! Hu…f…f…f!" I was breathing hard and quickly as I was moving from one door to another and from window to window. "Their classes should be in the east wing…where is the east wing now? The structure and the bricks are the same, all right, but where, pray, are the two wings now? They were here Friday. This is tormenting… really tormenting! Aha! A door…I'll use it," I said and sprang through that door.

"No children here," I said to myself, "where are they? Look! A caretaker…sir, I'm looking for my ch…i…l…please, stop! Sir, I beg you…stop!" He passed through me, rushing towards the door. "What am I going to do…what am I go…i… Oh Lord, have pity on me! If you want to punish me…do so…but, please, don't take my family away from me…and don't take my mind away. It's unbearable to be confused… it's unbearable to be insane and make no sense of things around. Have mercy on me, dear Lord!"

Bewildered and desperately looking for my children, I searched each classroom. Although I was in big rush, some classrooms' walls attracted my attention. The pictures displayed on them belonged to time unknown to me. "Year 2019…21…22 and even passing the year 2046. What's that?" I questioned, staring at the newspaper clips, hanging up on the walls. "This is year 1999...why those years? Maybe the class had a special history lesson," I thought, trying to make sense of what I saw.

Still puzzled, I crossed the main hall, passing the school's main office. It looked different, double the size and very elegant. Nobody was there either. In the gym room there were a few older students, hiding under a plastic cover. I rushed to talk with them. "Hey guys...can you tell... me... No! They can't see me. Listen, guys, I want to..." My insistences were in vain. After staring a little longer at the frightened students, I turned around, heading towards the exit.

"VICTORY TO THE HAWKS! Said a slogan, hung up on the gym room's wall. "See...I'm not insane, that thing was there since I know this school...and was there Friday too... Daniel had gym Friday, last class, and I've been here to pick him up...I spoke to the gym teacher. The inscription was there on the wall in the same place... where am I? Who am I?" I screamed frenetically. "What's going on with me? Where am I thrown? How come one thing is real, though others are so strange?" Bursting out like a bird freed from a cage, I shouted: "Hey look... look! Look... there is the school's cafeteria. Oh, yea! Here...here... here! My kids must be here for sure," I shouted, forcing my form towards that place. "Yea! My kids might be gathered...right here!" I was so anxious to get inside cafeteria that it seemed to me the short cut towards there took forever.

Neither students, nor cafeteria workers were there, except for a huge, gray cat. The poor animal was desperately mewing, running baffled from one corner of room to another, passing even through my legs.

"Eeeeek!" I screamed and jumped aside letting the cat snick out, passing by me.

A water pipe broke. Its content was all over the cement floor, causing the water to abundantly extend over a huge area. I walked through that water, but didn't feel the sensation of getting wet. I bounced, but the water remained calm — no weaves, no splash. I looked at the cat. The water was splashed all over the room, while the wet animal got crazy running aimlessly.

"I must get out of here...out...out...Oooooh! All these things make me crazier than I am... where is that door?" I yelled jumping back and forth over the water. " Aha…there… good… there's the door!" But that door didn't help me out; I found myself in a strange room instead.

"What's that now? Is another classroom or… what? Dried flowers, broken jars and tubs…dead reptile…notebooks? Why are they lain down all over? Science…sciennnnnce room, I gueeeeess!" My lips, jaws and the entire body were shaking like jelly. On the front wall there was a sign saying: DANGER! KEEP OUT! "Danger? Hmmm!" A sarcastic thought flashed up in my mind, but I wiped it away. My only wish in that moment was to get out of there as faster as I could.

Looking in all direction, trying to find that door, a cracking sound made me startle. I instinctively jumped aside. A lateral wall collapsed spreading its cement blocks over the desks and experiment tables, taking also with it the door that I supposed to use for bursting out. I rushed instead through the piles of debris in order to get out.

"Eeeeek…eek!" I sprang up, screaming while seeing a bunch of frogs crawling on the floors under the debris, and I screamed even louder, almost hysterically, noticing two hands appearing from under a broken desk. A blond boy showed his small face and bulging, blue eyes. I stared at him, with horror as if seeing a ghost. He looked through me — at least he seemed to.

"Get out…get out immediately!" I yelled at the child, trying frenetically to make myself heard by the feeble boy, perhaps grade one or two. He was crying and screaming, calling some names. I moved around him, hoping that I would develop some kind of energy or vibration that he would be able to sense, finding that way comfort in me, he couldn't notice my presence. He crawled instead, getting under another desk, weeping in despair.

I left the school's building and in my way out I looked again at the faces of the students, gathered in front of the main door. Shattered and desperate, I moved aimlessly along the school's front alley. I felt a strong compulsion to cry and I perhaps cried in some way — a new manifestation anyway. "Oh God, where are my kids? Where to find them…where are they? Paul…Hey, Paul took them," I whispered. "How come I didn't think about that until now? I'll go home. They must be home. Yes, home! Home! I must have a home! Oh God how come I never thought about going home?" While still sipping my words, I forced my form out the school.

I rushed to get out the long school's alley. My eyes ran at light speed from one corner of the building and backyard to another, and I was almost out when suddenly, a tall, metallic pole came straight in my view. It was proudly weaving a huge American flag in the air. The outside dust and anomalous dark made it looked black. Through that dust I noticed some human silhouettes. I stopped.

"Hey, what's that boy doing there?" I pondered, noticing another silhouette stooped near the huge metallic pole.

A strange feeling pierced my mind. "Maybe is one of my kids." I thought.

I scurried there. "I don't know this boy," I murmured, "I've never seen him before…and why so strangely dressed. Oh, that ugly uniform… what kind of uniform is this anyway?"

The child seemed to be dead. His arm was in a cast and kept upwards. All around the white cast, there were names written in black. I etched a smile like that of a mad person. I didn't know what to believe. "Kids dead…kids in pain…kids lost…kids wandering on the ravished streets. How more should I witness? And way me? Damned souls…damned me! We all are damned souls! And I was so ill inspired as to have come searching for my kids here… in this strange school… everything around here is a gimmick, intended to snag me. Nothing, but a gimmick… and I pushed in the middle of all this mess. Someone wants to scare me. That's all! Yes, to scare me to death. Perhaps my kids are dead…maybe Paul is dead too…I'm also dead…and all over Mrs. Death mows more damned souls."

Although, all those thoughts waylaid my common senses more and more often, I tried to strengthen my fears, stocking my capabilities and get home by any means. And I immediately rushed towards what I knew being my home.

CHAPTER 7

INSIDE THE STARTING PLACE

Perhaps my determination was well appreciated though my wish was instantaneously solved. From the school's alley I was mysteriously zapped right near our backyard hedge, though I had no clue of the transporting method or time used.

"Home…I'm at home…my home… my home," I yelled. "Oh God, thank you for bringing me back home." I was so blissful for recognizing my home that I forgot for a moment my strange condition and circumstances. "I'll go straight inside…yes inside!" I said, very determined to pass over all obstacles to get inside my dearly house.

"Gosh! Where is the alley now? Where is that lovely alley? That's not my alley…this is not my house! What? What's going on here? What's that construction there? We've never had a glass sunroom on that side. Sunroom here… since when? No! It's not a sunroom… it's something else… something out of this world anyway. My goodness, how am I getting inside… I'll call Paul. Paul! Pauuuul! Come here…come outside! Daniel, my love! Come out to see Mommy! Oh, my…where am I again?" I yelled hysterically. "Ssshu…s…sshu!" I forced my form move around the house, breathing with difficulty. "Ahhhhhh! Where am I? It's all right!" I tried to calm my frenetic soul. "I'll be fine! If I would at least get inside, then everything will be solved. Oh, God, only if I would be able to get inside. But how could I get inside? Paul! Paul, are you at home? Paul! Please answer me!" I yelled, trying desperately to shake the window and break its glass. "Wait a minute! My keys…my key! Where is that key?"

Then silence — a deep silence. "Lori, my baby, come to Mommy!" No sound or movement I heard. "This house is mine — and yet it doesn't look exactly like it" I pondered. "It looks old and deteriorated…and why these bricks? They were never in the front of my house…this is not my house for sure!" I moved swiftly near the window to look inside. "Wow, I'm inside, " I slurred. 'Inside'? What moved me inside? What's that? Who transports me all over? Why am I so mysteriously flipped? Could it be possible to be 'translocate' without sensing anything?" I cautiously paced along the hallway. I recognized nothing around. Strange things appeared in my view.

"Something is not all right here…is not right! Is strange, very strange again…" I whispered, moving with fear along the main corridor. "These windows and walls are telling me that I'm in my own house, but everything else around here looks different. I've never had this table, these chairs…and what's this machinery? I've never had such thing… it looks like an ambulant laboratory, not a household thing! Oh, my… oh, my Lord, have pity on me!" I noticed a paper posted on the side of that thing. "A note? Is it mine? It looks like one." It was in fact a 'do things' note. I read in my mind: "Phone Linda…Dentist…Paul's test… Call Mike…Driving test…" With my eyes, I followed up and down each item from the note. "Driving test. Driving test? What…whose driving test is this? This writing is my writing, all right, but yet, I don't remember writing this note!" I moved my eyes down the list. "Call the mechanic for the 'Dingo machine'…Dingo machine? Could this monster be the Dingo machine…and what, pray, that machine is used for?" I wondered, approaching the weird gadget. "What are these buttons for? And why so many knobs and switches…and so many lights and funny doors! What are these tiny doors for? What is this machine used for?" I attempted to touch a switch, and then another one, and another, but I couldn't feel them. I tried again and again, moving my arms from one tiny door to another. I couldn't touch or open them. It was like trying to smell or rip a flower, shown on the TV screen — no fragrance, no matter. "Oh God, you surely clapped me in a such complicated mystery. Am I crazy indeed?

Am I pacing into my own mind as I'm suspecting? Who's laughing while entertained by my torture?"

Still standing in front of that bizarre device, occupying almost the entire wall, I continued to read from the note. "Call the vet for Puffy… Puffy…who is Puffy? It sounds like a cat…or dog's name? Lori… Oh, my gosh! Lori… exactly Lori, my dog can help me solve the whole mystery. Lori…where could Lori be? Her cushion must be here…in front of that door. Oh, my…door, my door… that's my bedroom door, for sure. But, how come I didn't see it first?" I rushed there. "Lori! Lori! Come to Mama baby! Looori!" I waited, but no response. I moved a few steps ahead. "Wait a minute! Where is the big painting I have had right there on that wall in the corner? This is not the one I have had here before…and where the rest of the pictures are? Where are my kids' pictures? "Where is my wedding picture? And what pray are these funny things hanging up on the walls? I've never seen such things…they look more like framed mini-computers than framed pictures."

The whole bizarre encounters as well as the objects and futuristic decoration in the house defeated me utterly. And not only that, but my entire attitude changed. My experience made me slowly understand that I was under an imposed type of trial or assay and that I had been chosen for that, involuntarily of course. Why? I didn't know. Why me? I had no clue. I felt like being somebody's guinea pig. For what purpose I've been chosen? I had no idea. Maybe there were hundreds and hundreds of people like me, but who dared sharing or talking about such things in those modern days?

The more I tried to understand the confusing situation the more I fought to calm myself down — accepting somehow the strange situation, acting somehow more rational. I felt like a bird caught inside a huge vacuum machine, clasping firmly on the wall of the rotating shaft, while waiting as quietly as possible for the machine to stop. I couldn't recognize my own feelings. Were those a state of confusion, despair, and uncertainty, fearing of the unknown or regretting the 'sap' of life or all these mixed together. One thing was sure; they tormented me, but I unexpectedly gained more inner strength.

I used that inner strength to make peace with my mind, I rather say to bargain with it, or even to pull the rug out from under it — 'I show you more calm and understanding, you give me elucidation and release from the ordeal'.

So, I tried to put my best foot forward in attempting to go straight to my bedroom — the starting root of my entire ordeal. I had a feeling that the solving key of the whole mystery was in that room. But I wanted to play it safe and open the door cautiously, as if expecting someone to be on the other side of the door. I attempted a number of times to approach the door, pricking up my ears and racking my brain to find a way of opening it.

It was silence, an utter stillness — deep serenity and dark. This annoyed me. I preferred to hear something — anything that could cry life, not that morbid silence. I could even take those terrified 'booms' and 'bangs' from the outside, or the nature's unrest, in order to escape that frustrating tranquility.

"Pop…Pop…bang!" A loud popping noise made me somehow happily hurried back downstairs in the kitchen room, right near the monstrous machine. I felt like somebody answered my wish.

"Oh, no! Poor me!" I shouted, shivering. "What is this now! Is someone here? Hello! H… e… llooooo!"

"Bang! Slam!" The same noise again.

"Is somebody here?" I yelled, but my voice vanished into the air. "Why am I all the time on a blind alley, not getting the result I want? No matter how insistent I am." I pondered. "I mess up everything I tried, I'm up to the neck with everything; I rather die or live." And after a few moments, I thought: "But I am dead, am I? Oh my God, I am so confused and alone in my own house, or at least what it seems to be 'my own house'."

"Slam! Bang…B… …ang! Clack…bang! Click! Click… click!" The noise came very louder this time.

"Ah!…Eek! My gracious! Who is this? Hey! Who's there?"

No answer. A little white puppy, a Puddle, came in yelping and limping. I couldn't utter a word. The animal smelled around, tracing something in the air while staring in my direction and then ran away yelping, as if someone was banishing it away.

"Hey, you…fool! Where are you going…Hey! You…what's your name? Are you Puffy? You must be! Yes, Puffy! Hey! Puffy! Come back here, silly creature!" I was moving around trying to get the dog back, but it was nowhere to find the animal. Alas! Alas! What should I do…what should I do? Shall I burst outside this spooky house, wait here or what? But my bedroom must be here… and I desperately need to get inside it. Who's making all these naughty jokes? Was this dog real, or some kind of coarsely humors! Maybe I, myself, am a suggestive joke and not meant to be here in reality. Perhaps I am in my bed in my bedroom…in my real house, in another world… perhaps another planet, surrounded by my family. Maybe Paul is trying in vain to wake me up, while Daniel and Michael are desperately weeping beside my bed. Yes! I can visualize the scene. Or maybe an ambulance is in front of my house while the paramedics are trying in vain to help Paul waking me up. And I am left in the lurch here in this bizarre house, wondering how to wake up from the dreadful tribulation — to live with my family again a pleasant life." I suddenly stopped my thoughts. "No! This is craziness… it mustn't be real. What kind of foolishness is this… what am I thinking?" I looked up, yelling from the bottom of my lungs. "This is not a life!" I waited a moment and yelled again, repeating the same words. "My bedroom," I shouted. "My bedroom…I must get inside my bedroom. I must gain my life back right from my own bedroom. I probably must get right inside the room in order to be able waking up. Yea," I pondered. "Inside, fine… but how? Maybe this is the trick: I should struggle… I should fight to get up there. In fact everything stared there, and that is the place I supposed to be in order to get back to the reality. I must immediately get up there!" And up I went — fleetingly, not by my own move, but with the help of unexplainable stimulus.

    Determined to throw caution to the wind, I approached the familiar knob of my bedroom's door, intending to gush inside the room. Jolting nervously, I rushed to the doorknob and turned it on forcefully — I felt nothing. I tried again, repeating the same gesture over and over. Each time pressing more firmly on the knob and using different tactics — all failed.

    "Open it…Open it!" I roared, striking the stubborn door with my legs. The callous door continued to remain closed, defying each time my desperate attempts. I yelled and cried, begging it to open. I even called Paul and my kids' names and also Lori's, but nobody answered my dashed cries. My own fear and desperation ravaged me. The lamentations and tormenting sounds coming from the outside scared me no more — perhaps, not even heard them.

I didn't know how long I was waiting there, in the front of my bedroom door. Embittered and hopeless, I let myself at the mercy of fate. Did I cry a lot in those moments? Yes, a lot — painful mourns, but no tears. Did I yell and curse? Probably! I didn't recall. But I vividly remembered what happened to myself after that moment.

Still kneeling on the floor with my head squeezed by my knees, while weeping and sobbing, I suddenly felt overwhelmed by a sensation of being mysteriously transported away.

"Gosh! Who did this?" I yelled hysterically, rolling my eyes around, hoping to find an answer to my unexplained translocation from outside the door to inside the bedroom. I popped up enraged.

"What am I? Whose puppet am I? Oh God, why are you abandoning me, letting my in the craziness' arms?" I had no time for more lamentation. Suddenly, my bed came to my view. My dear bed… my dear bed! Oh, how I missed you!

I'm home! I'll be all right again! I'll wake up now. Yes! I knew it… I knew it. "Oh, thank you, my Lord!" I burst loudly, weeping like a child, while staring at my king size bed, covered with strange linen sheets that I couldn't recognize.

"Wait a minute!" I panicked. "This is not my bed. No… no… no! No it's not! A gimmick again?" I gabbled, gazing at the strange bed, while boosting my form up. The same frightening feelings tormented me; one side of me mind begged to storm the bed, while the other asked for caution. I gradually advanced, mastering each of my moves. But the more I proceeded the larger the distance between myself and my bed became.

I stopped. I felt as having an unseen hand pulling a string in front of me, while holding my bed by one of its ends.

"God, please don't let me be tricked! Why this struggle? Who is dragging my bed away from me? I feel like a cat allured by a child's string. Who is mocking me?" I stopped moving, waiting instead. I cried, bulling my fists at the white bedroom's ceiling, which was slowly melting like a snowball on a hot kitchen range.

"They're melting…they're melting my ceiling," I screamed, bulging my eyes, while seeing the bedroom's walls evaporating right in my view. "All around is disappearing…where are you taking them? Who are you? Why are you messing with my bedroom… and messing with my life?" I roared from the bottom of my lungs. "God! God! Please, make my nightmare go away and let me go back to my real world…my real home!" I stuttered. Yelling and running from one corner of the disappearing room to another, I tried clutching on the existing objects placed meticulously in that room. They too were dissolving into the emptiness.

Wheezing and staring with horror at the vanishing walls and objects, I noticed a tiny glowing light like a Ping-Pong ball appearing in my sight. It seemed that the entire bedroom including its walls and objects were sucked into it. I gapped in disbelieve at the ceiling and the rest of the room as they all dissolved into the light. Everything became light around me, I felt even myself overwhelmed and hypnotized by it like a bird by the serpent's eyes.

It seemed that the outside war's horror was sucked into the light, as well. A deep silence overcame the place — terrifying and fatiguing silence. I couldn't move, yell or even think. I stood numb in front of the light, bewitched by it.

"Don't give up!" Something slurred in my ears. "Step ahead… take this way!" The same voice instructed me.

"Where? Where?" I mouthed panicking, while feeling the radiant glow engulfing my form. I threw a swift look around my body. "Wow! I'm crystalline…I can see through me! I look like a curtain… a transparent curtain." I jumped full of fear, trying to back up.

"Go! Go! Gooo!" The same voice urged, interrupting my sudden excitement.

"Where?" I startled.

"Ahead! Go!" The voice indicated.

"As far as it goes?" I slurred, eyeing suspiciously the volatile path, which separated myself from the light's epicenter. No! No…no! I won't go any further! Enough…enough…enough! I want to go back! I want in my bedroom… bring me the bedroom back!" I shouted, staring ahead as if seeing an authoritarian power. I felt being stormed by its power, all over me — entirely dominating me. My submitted servility did not help me at all. By the contrary, it made me became a vassal to its intentions, adding even more misery to the fearful circumstance — shallowness with many-sided facades. No! I won't go! I'll wait right here!" I murmured, my foot striking on what was left over from the disappearing bedroom's floor. I stared into nihility.

And wait I did — not for a long time, though. Without having a little chance of defending or protecting myself, the same power, defying my wishes, sucked or rather inhaled me into the void. A void which abstractly thinking could take a form — something similar with the nothingness surrounding a flying bird or space ships. I expected the void to take form — carnal or celestial. It didn't happen. I was sucked deeper and deeper into that gruesome void. Then, suddenly halted.

CHAPTER 8

UNDERGONE INTO NIHILITY

Paralyzed by frightful thoughts, I didn't realize that I was descending into something — bathing into a vivacious atmosphere. It seemed that the air was actually an entity, ready to keep in touch with me — coercing me into obedience, imposing gruesome thoughts on my mind. I thought: "If I would at least be able to burst in tears… Who knows, I might be able to impress 'the Thing'? I broke. I felt sweating some kind of moisture every time I was pushed to pace farther into the scary atmosphere. I felt chased until my last breath. I knew I was capable of distinguishing colors, but there were not colors. It was like walking into clouds or fog, but even fog is colorful — different shades of white and gray. There was like walking into water — gaseous water. Everything around me was without color or definition. It was nondescript. More morbid thoughts poisoned my soul.

Keeping my form stock-still on the edge formed by what was left over by the vanishing bedroom and the 'infinite' ahead of me, I tried to overcome those thoughts by finding a way to communicate with the 'void'.

"Are you a star? Or a light?" I dared. Nobody answered.

"Are you alive? Who are you?" Nothing sounded.

"Am I going to die? I mean really…really die?" I insisted, staring into the void and shivering horrified. My mind purled, my thoughts echoing like shallow streams over stones. "Am I already dead… or wandering into my own mind?"

The silence was unbearable.

I screamed hysterically — louder and louder. I wanted to break that silence in one way. Seized by the fear, I swiftly turned around, jumping back to the previous spot, behind what I knew being that 'unlocked bedroom door'. "I don't want to go ahead… I don't want to go ahead… I don't want there! That's a gimmick… a gimmick meant to annihilate me. No! Never there!" I forced my form back into what ever I saw being left over from the imagine of my bedroom "I'll stay here and wait. I want to live. I don't want to die. I'm still alive… I can breath… I can walk… recognize things… I think rationally anyway. I mustn't be dead… I mustn't… I couldn't. Oh God, get me out of here… please… please, God, don't destroy me!"

Nothing happened to me for a moment. Only the bedroom slowly and peacefully vanished, fusing into that atmosphere, like icicles melting into the sun's rays. My first intention was to grab everything around, stopping things from disappearing, but I went through them instead or them through me — we interpenetrated each other anyway. I felt like having somebody melting the things around me, forcing me this way to move ahead.

"No…Oh, no! Please, don't kill me!" I yelled over and over the same words, for God knows how long. I kneeled down, practically on the air, and with my hands together I prayed: "Lord, please don't let this happening to me. You created everything around us and also inside us. You have created me and set a destiny for me. It is beyond my control what's happening to me. Don't let my destiny end up with a lonely death and an irreversible annihilation. Please, don't let my soul be killed. Here is no life. This 'here' scares me. I don't want entering this 'here'… I'm scary… and what's happening to me is very strange… oh, God! Oh, God help me out of here!"

I kept silence for a while —tormenting silence — perching my ears for possible sounds. Nothing sounded, nothing moved. It was quiet —morbid stillness.

"Have I not been a good companion to the world?" I dared again. Have I been created only to procreate and then miscarried out the world?

Who? What… and where should I beg for life?" I yelled and implored — cried and talked loud, until I finally realized that every attempt was in vain. I felt like a dried leaf, trying to teach the wind how to gently blow it to safety. I became more convinced that everything happening to me through the entire ordeal was predestined — meant to and decided upon. Like a fetus that has no control over its forming in the womb or choosing the conceiving couple and its date of birth.

Everything was sucked away into the void, leaving nothing surrounding me, except for that indefinite void. Although, magnetized by the absorbing void, and also being unsure of the own safety in case of leaving the spot, I decided to wait. My resisting attitude prevailed — but not for long.

◀ ▶

"Where am I?" I screamed, moving my arms in all directions in search for something to hold on. I had similar sensations as being snatched out my bed and thrown into eddying waters, while still trying to wake up. "What happened to me?" I yelled, striving to grab anything I possible could to sustain my form on. I moved my hands all over my form trying to identify the face, neck and the rest of the body.

"Eeeek! What in the world is that on? Is this 'me'? It's not fabric? Yes…it is! Oh, gosh! It's not! It's not leather… I'm sure. But what is it? What is it then…and who are they? Who are you?" I tried to grab by the arm a lady who was pacing next to me. Excuse me… who are you? I'm Dee… Dee-Anna … I'm Dee-Anna Turner," I introduced myself. Who are you? Are you alive?"

The woman didn't answer. I didn't give in. I rushed near a man, yelling at him:

"Hey, sir, where are you heading…were are we going? Who are you? Who are these people?" Silence.

"Say, lady, what's all this about…where are we? Why do so many people surround me? What is this crowd?"

I tried to hop upwards to examine that crowd surrounding me, but I couldn't bound it with my eyes — no boundaries in any of its corners. It was out of all proportion. Staring at an ocean, one can see at least the horizon line. The view of that crowd had not even that. It was like a mass of indefinite, swarming bubbles. And I was able to see it in all direction, as if having eyes in all four directions of my head. I couldn't move my eyes from that crowd, though extremely terrified. "Why am I into this crowd?" I panicked, shriveling uncontrollable. It seemed that they all progressed forwards, but there was not a 'finish' line, no chatting either. Only sounds — humming sounds! Frightened, I tried to back down. "Back to the drawing board, Dee-Anna!" I encouraged myself. "If you wish to live, go back… and do it fast!" I urged myself, turning my head in searching for that 'back' line. "This crowd is an illusion…a phantom, a specter ready to submit you, dragging you into nonexistence." I cogitated for a short while, staring at the weird faces around me, and promptly turned, and pushing people aside, I tried to move backwards. I achieved nothing. It seemed that each member of that weird crowd was conveying into each other like licks of fire. I felt somehow being part of those licks. I forced myself, jumping upwards again. Susurrus flowing like singing waters move like waves, dancing over my head. Nobody seemed to be bothered by my insistent jumping upwards. "But, there is not sky above," I marveled, "and is not ground beneath either…no earth, no sky's canopy. Nihility only…and we're swarming into it." Despaired and puzzled, I gawked toward neighboring faces. "Are these people mute? Am I swarming into the 'land of mutes'?" I pondered. "Why are you murmuring?" I asked a woman, moving next to me. I stared at her lips. "Nothing! They 're stock-still!" I said to myself. I stared at other lips. I turned around, examining more lips. The same stone faces with stock-still lips. "Are these moving stones…vibrating marbled stones… humming marbled stones?" I didn't know what to believe. "Maybe, I look the same…maybe they see me being the same." I instinctively moved my hands all over my face, arms and legs, attempting to discover similarities. I paced ahead, keeping the same languorous cadence. I didn't know what else to do. I had no choice. Nothing that I tried worked. I even wanted to shriek into their ears, to wake them up. It seemed to me that they were part of the past, some kind of déjà vu. I wanted to provoke them in same way — I wanted to see them alive, to see them living. I whispered instead, moving my lips close to a young blond man.

"Sir, what's going on here? Where are you coming from?" I waited, staring at his face for an answer — nothing. "Please, sir, answer me" He didn't answer. He continued to pace impassible. "Is this the earth?" I then turned to a lady who gave me the impression that she was staring at me. "Is this the earth, miss?" I insisted — no answer. "Perhaps she was staring through my form", I thought.

People did not look at each other; they all moved in the same direction, staring fixedly as if they were viewing something inside their minds. But they did not look like lunatics. I tried to approach some other people around me, each time using different tactics and questions — nothing worked. I found myself in the same puzzling situation, having no clue where I was, why I have been thrown there and where I was heading or how to escape from there. I felt being the same 'I' as I always remember to be, but into an 'unknown', strange world in a bizarre surroundings — indisputable horror.

Resigned, I moved forward with the mob. "Who knows, maybe they have the key to this slow pace. Having said that, suddenly my first impulse of fighting docility and prostration came back.

"No! I can't go with them… I want to go back! I can't follow them… they are not real. It's a trap…a decoy. No…no! Take me back! I want to be sucked back! Up…down, wherever my earth could be. Put me back on my earth! I want to be back there!" I roared hysterically, moving my arms in all directions, while trying to push people in that bizarre crowd away from me. "Oh Lord! Why are you abandoning me?"

I felt pushed ahead. "No…no…n…n…o!" I roared over and over. "No, please…no!" I yelled stiffing my form to the volatile ground and pushing it against a knot of a man. He passed listlessly ahead, oscillating through my form. Stunned, I rapidly moved my hands all over my stomach and chest as intending to stop him from leaking out my body, while puzzled like never. "Eyes, heads, legs…arms…all a human body needs…and made of. Still this creature vanished through me like sinking sand. Just like that! Eeeew!"

"Baaaboom! Baaaboom!" My heart turned crazy. Still stunned by the bodies' ingression effect, I kept eyeing around. "Normal faces…normal people, but still lonely. Shoulder to shoulder, but still secluded. Spiritless faces with forlorn hope!" I paced calmly for a while, meditating. "Do I look like them? — Perhaps. Oh God! Please let me see Paul and my kids! These are dead people and I feel alive. I am trapped among dead people... me a living being." I felt a great compulsion to cry — my eyes couldn't tear.

Eager to make a sense of all those bizarre things around me, while hoping to find a solution to my ordeal, I concentrated to assay the people's faces and movements. I tried comparing their faces with some familiar faces, even with Paul and my kids'. The idea became a stimulating hope. I said: "Perhaps this is a trial, intended especially for me...perhaps to learn from it. Maybe someone is monitoring me right now...checking my reactions and responses... a trial with a purpose...a trial with meaning. Maybe my arbitrator is right here... part of this crowd... perhaps looking at me, pleased to see my agony." I frowned at the woman next to me. "Is she tested too? Are all these hopeless faces judged?"

"Baaaboo! Baaaboom!" My heart was tossing inside my chest. "Wait a minute! Did I say 'judged'? Then this must be the judgement... the great one...the great judgement!" My heart deafened me. "No! It couldn't be! It doesn't look like that. How do I know? Have I seen one before? Hey, lady! Is this a trial...I mean the judgement... I mean the great, last judgement?" I waited, seeking for her answer. "No! She couldn't see me."

I continued pacing, not sure of the real meaning of that momentous adventure. Thought after thought tormented my mind — one thought revoking the other. "If this is the last judgement, then where are Paul and my kids...where is Papa and Mama? Where are their parents...where are my ancestors? Why have none of them come to greet me?" I broke out annoyed.

"Oh...o...doomed world! Oh...my lost soul!" I yelled, hoping one of those faces would make a move — respond in one way. But I only strengthened my fear instead of helping my soul.

Still, I didn't want to give in, thinking that insisting I might get something. Therefore, I threw a waspish look at my neighbors again, as if ready to sting them, forcing them this way to react somehow. Nobody mimicked a gesture. Not even moving a finger, a lip or an eyebrow. "Dummies!" I revolted, yelling with passion. "Boneheads!" I repeated, continuing pacing. I withdrew — but not for long.

Examining even more attentively the faces of people pacing next to me, a sinister thought crossed my mind: "What if they're ghosts?" I yelled hysterically, ready to scuttle away. "No! They can't be! Their eyes and lips look full of life…they are alive. Their skin is pink… the blood is circulating through their bodies. But how do I know, I have never encountered a ghost…never seen their skin's color." I stared again at their faces to convince myself. "No! They're not ghosts…their eyes shine and lips are red like all living people have. But who are they? What kind of beings are they?"

Affronted by the same turmoil, I turned around and pushed against a young girl's chest, intending to stop and make her aware of my presence. She literally evaporated, passing through my shaking body. I stood agape in horror, but still tried the same thing with another person — an old man this time. I was agog for an explanation, a real one — an earthly one. I thought: "Alien to all my knowledge — physics and physiology together."

I frowned at the mysterious faces capable of penetrating each other's bodies. "Am I like them?" I babbled. "Am I flowing through people's bodies like these creatures?" I jumped ahead, pushed by the desire of trying that interpenetrating effect on me, then stood still, letting the flowing crowd advancing through my body. "Wow! " Mixed feelings of fear and curiosity made me stay put. That worked better for me than pushing people around in order to escape to the back. I thought: How about waiting here, while letting all these people passing ahead through my body? Being the last one of the crowd I might be able to run back to the previous place. It didn't work as planned. I lost the sense of time waiting in vain. Realizing there was no way for me to see an end to that 'passing through me' crowd, I decided to progress ahead with them, no matter what.

The crowd's headway and humming sound made me feel outcast on an ocean, pushed back and forth by the huge, living waves — rolling and crashing waves.

After a long journey that way, I lost my sense of time and place. I had no idea of how long I walked there — no idea where I walked, either. I felt no exhaustion, no hunger, no thirst and no need for sleep. I was progressing incessantly into and toward an indescribable and indefinable void. I couldn't tell if it was day or night. I only knew that I was moving ahead. Either side I turned, I saw nothing — there were no other forms around me but that milling crowd.

I felt tied by an invisible harness and dragged like a mad cow to the slaughterhouse — I rebelled no more. I just let myself moved with the swarm.

CHAPTER 9

SWIFT JUMP FOR CATCHING LIFE

"Where is the crowd" I startled, though whispering. "Where is that woman, pacing next to me just a few moments ago…and that short man in front of me…and that black young girl? Eeeeek! What's this steam around me? What is this now?" I yelled, eyeing the foam around me, while it changed color and radiance in contact with my form. Instinctively, I reached out to grab some of that materialized 'nothingness'. Where am I going? Where is that mad crowd? Who makes me float into this? How come am I always alone? Who is torturing me this way?"

Fear anchored me to the spot, although it wasn't a solid spot. Nobody pushed me ahead. I contemplated for a while, like a mouse inside a labyrinth, trying to find the hole out. I tried to apply my common sense, but no logic could answer my questions. "And now what? Which way to go?" I assayed my strength: "I could move…I could think…suffer… panic…yell… but not get out of there." I waited.

Suddenly, a bank of unusual clouds opened up in front of my eyes like a gigantic screen. I tried to banish my fear. "Living clouds? It can't be!" My own words were swimming with my thoughts. "These clouds are making 'Ping-Pong' leaps all over the place. Oh, my gosh! They're lining up now. Either way, the clouds were mushrooming together or penetrating each other in an absolute order.

In a twinkling of an eye, my form was sucked into a large group of those clouds, practically navigating among them.

"Aaaaah! I want back…down…back! A…a…ah! Let me there!" I blubbered, trying desperately to hold on something and propping unsuccessfully my legs into the air pockets. "Darn! Would I ever be able to escape this mess?" "Never, I think! I'm gone…gone forever. I'm going deeper into this 'beyond' instead of going back to life." I freaked out. " Dee-Anna… dead! Oh God, don't let this happen. I'm still young…and love life." I whispered, while staring petrified at the nothingness sucking my form into. "Mom…Mom…where are you? You gave me birth… where are you now? No! No! Don't push me there! I want back… back… move me back!"

Nobody pulled me back. On the contrary, I was pushed ahead even faster.

Still hurling into the abyss, a perfectly boundless, shinning line materialized in front of my eyes. It looked like an immeasurable laser beam — no starting or ending angles. No horizon or sky canopy either, only a pure and simple straight strip of glowing light emerging with a deceiving appearance.

"Life…life… life… l… ii… fe… life at last!" I yelled, forcing my form forward. "I'm going back…I'm going back home! I'm going back to life!"

"Baaaboom! Baaaboom!" The wild heart's tossing shook my entire body. "This is a sign of life. Yes…yes! My heart is assuring me that I'm alive. Oh God! How can I get into that light faster? Push me there faster! Suck me there! Help me there…there…there! I need there…there… back to life." Pushing myself while running ahead with my arms stretched in front of me, I kept begging Lord for help and intervention. "I knew I was not dead…I knew I had nothing to do with that scary crowd. Yes! I knew it." I repeated over and over, forcing to get faster to the enlarging light. "I knew I was alive…dead people are with dead people. I was caught by accident among those scary figures. Yeah! Yeah… that's way I didn't see my mother and father. Look! That's life… that line there is the blessed 'life'! Yeah! That's 'life'… I can see its welcoming arms drawn out toward me… and I'll be soon swallowed into it. I'm coming… coming… home. Oh God, pull me faster there," I yelled through my panting, trying rapid and giant strides. I couldn't define the kind of happiness that shook my entire form. I had never experienced such burst of joy — the joy of being alive. All my thoughts, fear and panic were washed away by that joy. Nothing counted for me in those moments, except for rushing back to life. I felt the euphoria breaking me in pieces.

The brilliant strip was motionless, and the quicker I moved toward it the larger it seemed to become. I had the feeling that my way toward that beam took forever, boiling my courage away. I felt like an exhausted swimmer who sees the shore departing in spite of his advancing efforts. I couldn't make any sense of the surrounding. It looked like an awkward environment from which I couldn't backtrack. Slowly, that bursting joy faded away, replaced once more by the same panic and fear. The backwash of each cloud's tremor left me even more scared. I wished to barge into that beam, to blend with it, but my frenetic strides did not help me much.

Far away, something that looked like islands came to my view. There were innumerable islands — small and large. All of them seemed to be engulfed in dense gray clouds, giving them peculiar forms. The unusual light made the islands look like marshmallow mushrooms, tossing and navigating in all directions, as if self-controlled. Perhaps, in other circumstances, that phenomenon might look to me quite fantastic, but during my ordeal it petrified me. I was not even able to discern my feelings. I was surprised, ransacking my brain for a logical answer linked to every strange thing I have encountered since I have been snatched away from family and thrown into that abysmal unknown — the domain of pain, grief and fright.

◀ ▶

I had no way of knowing about the length of time I spent abandoned there, in the vicinity of the light and living islands. The only thing I knew was my own nervous tremor while staring in horror at the flutters of mushroomed forms and movements, and also my fervent prayer. It was like an explosion — like thunder. I wanted so desperately for God to hear me. I feared that if He failed to listen to me, I'd lose my only chance to return to that light — to my life. "Will I be lost forever?" I prayed as I have never prayed in my life. Begging I let my words flow like a tumultuous stream out my mouth, imploring God for my last chance to be alive again — and I prayed with fervor. My entire form shook and my hands scratched the ghostly foam in desperation to climb up. I didn't mind the painful silence around me. My faith was greater than ever — I knew that I was watched, listened and monitored. I felt it in my soul. And that's why I yelled and screamed as never before. "God, don't leave me here…give me the last chance. Push me there! Push me back to life."

CHAPTER 10

BITS OF EARTHLY LIFE

I knew for certain that the glowing line before my eyes was actually my lifeline — 'grab it or lose it'. I hoped the mysterious line was there to make me wake up to life — to my real life. "I am alive…my soul is alive…all souls are alive in this universe." I rushed ahead, bathing in the materialized air; galloping and puffing like a wild colt — my eyes focused on the expanding line.

Suddenly, a mysterious peace came over me — terrifying peace —enveloping me like sun's rays emerging from a heavy cloud. It scared me, too. I panicked. I couldn't trust that peace. "It's a gimmick!" My mind yelled. Don't go for it!" My common senses admonished. "A mellow lure…silence before the storm!" There was a fight inside me — the peace was fighting with my precipitate soul. The peace won the moment the enlarging line came upon my body, swallowing me completely.

I felt naked. I panicked. I felt exposed like a nude model, watched from all directions, by hundred of busybodies. I moved my arms all around my form, trying to cover myself.

"I'm crazy," I uttered. " But a fool knows nothing about himself or things around him," I pondered. "I am aware of everything. I'm thinking and acting perfectly normal. I can detail each moment of my life… starting even with the time I've been about four years old. No! I'm not crazy! What's going on with me is not craziness... though it seems very crazy indeed. Oh God! How confused I am and nobody dares to help."

My confusion died like a sputtered flame the moment a beam like a sun's ray engulfed me. "Gulp! Gulp! Gulp!" Sounds like gas bubbles from a swamp accompanied that ray.

"Eeek!" I jumped aside a few steps, trying to kick my feet free from the ray's reflection. "Eeek!" I exclaimed again, jumping like a frog, while noticing that the ray was following my feet. To my stupefaction, the ray became larger and larger. At once, tiny and fragile traces of different life scenes made themselves visible in this glowing ray.

"It's beautiful," I found myself saying. "It can't be the earth, though! There is no horizon line... and no sky above, either! Wow! But... these are earthly views... Wow!" My eyes squinted and my fingertips burned as everything around me glimmered like candlelight. "Life! Life again... these are signs of life... no doubt about it. I'm back to life. God took me back to life. I'm home... Oh, God! You heard my cry. You answered my plea." I jumped, hopping like a baby, crying and laughing. "Oh! It's so lovely... so soft... so good to live again!" I inhaled deeply, repeating my breathing over and over like after an asthma attack.

Suddenly, one of the scenes enlarged mysteriously, right in front of my eyes. It seemed that it came to me like a person, trying to introduce itself. My wild joy died abruptly. I had been part of the scenery. I stepped carefully, although curiously, examining everything around.

An old tree, whose leaves reminded me of a willow, hung over a crystalline spot of water not too far away from where I was standing, or, who knows, maybe crawling. Curious but still terrified; I moved cautiously toward the water, hypnotized by that tree. The water shone in the morning sun, which also danced on the leaves. The scene was unreal and earthly at the same time. My first instinct made me want to burst in admiration of every little detail of that sight, but a worrying voice hindered my emotions.

"Hush! Don't make a sound!" Came the advice. Instinctively, I swung around, trying to detect the source. My mind puzzled while discovering that the sound was actually a manifestation of my own thoughts.

"This is evil!" I thought, groping to get away from that tree. "I'm bewitched," I thought horrified. Out of the blue, an eerie sensation warmed my entire form. I didn't have time to react. It sprang away like a scared gazelle the moment I spotted a face reflected on the water's surface. I froze to death. I had no words to describe my fear. The tears in my eyes blurred my vision. I unsuccessfully rubbed them with my palms and bowed down for a clearer view. I boiled with curiosity, eyeing the childlike face, smiling at me.

CHAPTER 11

BRINGING BACK MY CHILDHOOD MEMORIES

"Could that be mine?" I jumped, still gazing. "It's me... I, I... Ana. That face is mine!" I said with one breath. "That face is the face I had as a child... yes! Yes! I'm not mistaken. That face is mine! Mine... me... 'I' as a child." I stuttered, staring around as if expecting someone else to accompany that 'I', the child. 'But... but... but,' my lips and entire body were quaking. "But how come... the two of us in the same place?" I slurred, touching my lips, head and face trying to convince myself that I still existed. The girl was lying down in the grass, near the tree, playing with a wild daisy. I approached carefully, staring at the girl's playful fingers, when suddenly I bounded energetically, noticing that the girl actually was lying across a woman's legs.

"Grandma!" I yelled ecstatically. "Grandma!" I yelled again, jumping toward her, ready to join both. Then my instincts stopped me. "No! It mustn't be real! Another lure... vivid, but still a lure! I'd better get out of here. This is evil again!" I stepped back, still staring curiously at the two. In fact, it was a real sight and the two of them were interacting like any rational human beings. The only baffling thing about the view was my incapacity of interacting with them — not even touching them. Disillusioned and confused, I remained still, standing a few steps away from them, witnessing their chatter. For a moment I envied that chatter, that enchanting affinity. My mind tried hard to recollect that moment, and like seeing in the fog, mixed and feeble feelings caused me to relive the moment. My grandmother's trembling hand was caressing the girl's tiny face. I felt it on my face too. I relived the moment as it had originally happened many, many years ago when I'd been a child.

"That girl is I… the child is 'I'… 'I'… 'me'… no doubt!" My eyes were frantically tracing each of the girl's movements, and I couldn't take them off her face, either. Without realizing, I moved forward and examined attentively both faces. I was so caught trying to capture their words and gestures that I didn't notice that the entire scene was gradually fading way. The more my eyes devoured the sight, the farther the scene moved away, until it became a line again. It disappeared as it came, leaving only a linear trace. I remained still, my eyes straining as it faded.

I didn't have time to panic or react in any way. Bursting like fireworks, reminiscences after reminiscences of my childhood soared around like soap bubbles while following an invisible route. They reminded me of ants swarming over their hills. One scene dissolved into a new one, leaving me no time to focus. Episode after episode paraded in succession, revitalizing my forgotten memories. They integrated me completely into them. If one particular episode attracted my interest more than others did, it became larger and detailed and immediately sucked me into it, making me relive it once more and remembering every detail of each unveiled moment. I was indeed part of the scene, but I felt like a bubble of air — existing, but not touchable.

PART TWO

REMINISCENCE OF MY CHILDHOOD MEMORIES

CHAPTER 12

'I' THE CHILD VERSUS 'I' THE ADULT

"When I was a child, I spake as a child, I understood as a child, I thought as a child: but when I become a man, I put away childish things. For now we see through a glass, darkly; but then face to face: now I know in part; but then shall I know even as also I am known."

(Recited by Mr. Tony Blair, England's Prime Minister, from I Corinthians 13:2,3,11 at the funeral of Diana, Princess of Wales, on Saturday, September 6th, 1997)

"Buuuut... I don't want to go there... I'm scared, Mama," I heard somebody saying. I twisted around to locate the voice. Suddenly, a tiny, little girl and a young woman came in my view. I saw both from behind.

"Go out there... I said, girl! Don't be afraid! It's only dark outside... you've seen dark before, haven't you? Now be a good girl and bring Mama that copper basin. Don't be a chicken, girl."

"Mama! Mama... my mama!" I said, rushing around to see her face. "And 'I' again... 'I'... 'I', a little girl." I uttered, staring at the familiar faded, floral dress, which the girl was wearing.

My confused thoughts mingled with my mother's and the girl's quarrelsome words. Shreds of the conversation caught my ears while I remembered all of them very well. My heart tossed, my form trembled, recognizing my mother's young face. Reliving the scene made me once more forget the fact that I belonged nowhere, being purely and simply in limbo. I moved close to my mother, longing for her attention.

"Mama!" I whispered. "Mama!" I expected no answer and expected not to be noticed. No person encountered during my sinister ordeal had showed signs of noticing or sensing me. That moment proved again that I was right: my whispers came back to me unanswered. In the same time, I didn't want to lose the chance of being with them. It was true that I'd pleaded God to make me go back to life. And I was moved back to life, even though it was 'a prior-lived-life'. My thoughts were interrupted by the girl's burst of tears.

"But I don't want to go out there... The Big Monster is there," she insisted, crying, yelling and kicking the floor. My mother turned her bulging eyes toward the girl.

"You're a liar... a big liar. There isn't such monster. You're making it up!"

"Mama, I've seen it... I've seen it right there in the bush... with big horns... and... and... and a big snout... like that... and... Yes, Mama... a... a... there, over there, believe me, Mama."

"You're such a liar, Anushka! You've seen nothing. You're a liar... a coward-liar. And these little lies you're telling now will turn into great... gigantic lies. Now go out and bring me that basin."

"No!"

"Go, Ana! Prove yourself now. You're always putting on airs... thinking you're a queen. Show me now you have a queen's courage, girl!"

I smiled. It was the first time since I'd encountered the mysterious ordeal that I smiled. That particular scene made me smile, and I felt good. I remembered that moment. I knew I had been a liar. I had lied a lot as a child and later on in my life. It has seemed normal to me to lie, and my mother knew I'd had that habit. I used my lies as tools of convincing people, including my Mama and Papa. Reliving that moment kept me smiling. I remembered the struggle that had taken place inside my heart — the child's heart. My ambitious nature had fought over my childish emotions, and the first had won. My eyes followed the girl as she reluctantly kicked the flimsy wooden door and vanished out into the dark. I smiled again. My mother smiled, too. That was a fact that I'd never known before. I enjoyed seeing it now. At the time, I had never known my mother's real compassion for my normal, human fear. I'd seen her as a spy, ready to unveil my lies in front of Papa's eyes.

My first reaction was to follow the girl outside, and I did that. I burst through the open door outside into the dark. Amazingly, there were no 'outside', and no girl around either. I was completely stupefied. The girl vanished, as if never there. I was alone in an indescribable dark 'nothingness'. I turned around. The door was still temptingly open, as if inviting me inside again. I did that. I gushed inside as fast as I sprung out. My mother was still there lost in her own thoughts. She was sorting a huge pile of dirty, discolored clothes. I eyed the pile, and instantly recognized some of my childhood clothes — things long forgotten. I bent over, trying to touch a pink-and-white dress with small, green dots. My hand went through the pile, as if squeezing my hand into a pile of air bubbles. I repeated my gesture — the same result. I then stared at my mother. She looked back at me, but I was more than convinced that she had no clue that I was standing there. I lost my patience.

"Mother... Mother! Look at me!" I yelled, grabbing her by the shoulders. She passed through me, or I maybe passed through her svelte body. I couldn't tell.

The motion was so swift and unexpected that it was impossible to make sense of that strange inflow. Baffled, I turned around her, trying to grab her by the back this time. Again, our bodies passed each other, canceling my hope of being sensed. I let her carry on with her laundry, dragging her heavy slippers across that gnawed wooden floor — a sound that had been so familiar to me. She was dressed in her usual apron, worn by a battalion of women — chewed by time. Its floral design erased long before, no strings or buttons to close it, some rusty safety pins performed that job. Her hair stood on end like bristle and her face was unusually pale — almost gloomy.

The creepy noise of my mother's sloppy slippers boxed my ears. I looked at them. I knew them very well. They were Dad's shoes once — his only good shoes worn on Sundays and holidays. With a brisk move, I was back near my mother, staring closely at her slippers. They reminded me of the discussion my parents had had over them. "Woman, these are my only good shoes," I remembered Papa furiously revolting, noticing his mutilated shoes. "What have you done to them?"

"Oh, come on, Iuri!" My mother had jumped. "In a few months we'll be out of Russia, thank God... in America they don't wear such ugly shoes. Be realistic, man! Wear them as slippers for a while!" And sneaking near my father on our old sofa, fawning like a child, my mother had added: "Oh, Iuri, I can't wait to be in America... America, full off goods, rich and famous people. Oh America... America! Such a blessed place!"

The memory of that scene vanished as fast as it came, taking with it the pile of clothing, my mother and her slippers. But the room remained there intact and so did some of the objects. It was like an invisible hand changing stage designing. I, the spectator to my own life's play, remained to contemplate the moment.

I struggled in vain to remain calm.

I thought I was meant to stand over there — waiting for the next stage to unfold like a path — the tail of a comet. I had nowhere to go, anyway and no target to reach, either. I stood and waited. I was afraid to move, think or ask to go back again. My assumed future scared me more than those traces of unfolding memories. I had known people claiming to be exposed to traces of their past lives, but never heard anyone claiming to retrace the scenes as I had.

I looked around, examining the room. On the kitchen table there was a tiny basket with three eggs and a bunch of small marbles of different colors. I tried to grab one of the marbles, but my hand went through them, the basket and even the table, leaving me only with a sensation of touching things, not a true physical contact with them. I was not deterred. I tried again a few more times, each time squeezing my palm tighter, attempting to get the same feeling that I had had as a child while playing with them.

While still trying to grab the marbles, I felt inexplicably transferred. No feelings of motion, no sounds — only an eerie sensation of belonging to another place. I wondered if I was the one standing still, though the stages moved around me, or the one moving around places. Something like lying down on a sofa in Detroit, while actually walking with a parade in New York or witnessing a bomb attack in Israel — and all making sense. The same thing happened to me. Places, events, people and things were brought to me, making me actually part of everything, except of touching or grabbing them. I kept all my emotional capabilities intact and just a few physical. I could walk, run, move, even cry, suffer and panic, but couldn't be noticed or sensed by any of the figures, familiar or unknown, during the ordeal.

◀ ▶

"Oh, my... oh, my... ohhhh... h... grandma! Grandma is here! Grandma... gran... d... and there's Mama ... Mama... ma... Papa... and ... Oh! All the family is here," I exploded happily, at the same time scared and confused. A big crowd surrounded my family. I panicked. I said to myself: "What am I doing here? I am an adult now, not that five-year-old child. 'I', the child, is there with this crowd where she perhaps belongs, and 'I', the adult must be back there in my bedroom with my husband and kids. We're here together, but living in different worlds... and different times. Oh, God, how confused and desperate I am... how lost... inert... forgotten in limbo and nobody is here to help. Why? Why all this?"

My eyes moved rapidly from one person to another, foolishly hoping to be helped by one of them. I thought: "They look full of life... they might be able to drag me back into life. At this desperate moment, I even don't care which time... which stage of my life. I want to live again. I want desperately to live again. The state I'm in now is not life... is death... death in a veiled form, in a foxy form — death served in a fancily wrapped box, tied with a red ribbon. A lunatic cage — a rueful destiny."

'I', the girl, was standing glued to my mother's black skirt, as she looked from one person to another and sharpened her hearing to make a sense from the adults' conversation. My instinct and oddity pushed me to chiefly examine the girl. It was 'I', the adult versus 'I' the child. I eyed the little girl, dressed elegantly in harmony with Russian fashion at that time. And I vividly remembered that dress and the shoes, and also where my Mama had purchased them. I felt good — very good, I should say. I trusted my memory. It proved that I wasn't crazy. It strengthened my thoughts, thinking that what was happening to me was pure and simple an accident, not my own insanity. Suddenly, my instinct pushed me to embrace that girl, or more precisely, to go back in that tiny body again and live the life a second time.

I scanned the crowd, staring particularly at my grandmother's face. Tears flowed down it uncontrollably. I vaguely remembered her. I then looked at the two young women supporting her arms, and consoling her. I didn't recognize them. I assumed they were related to my mother, perhaps her two young sisters. My mother sometimes had talked with me about them. My grandmother was sobbing while the two young women were trying to calm her down. Tears also washed their faces. My mother was sobbing, too, caressing my grandmother's face with her gloved hand.

"Take good care of her!" my mother whispered, pleading with the two young women. And all four women burst in tears. The men, too, were soberly wiping their tears. I looked at the crowd, attempting to recognize some faces. I found no clue to the identity of those people, and I didn't recognize the man standing beside my father, either.

"Adieu, comrade Vania!" I heard my father addressing to the man. "I'll send you words about us… soon!" he continued.

"Don't write me… you know… the… government," the man whispered into my Papa's ear, looking cautiously around.

Papa smiled. "Thank you, comrade… you're been a very good friend to me all my life."

What struck me the most, though, was the fact that the majority of people in that crowd were blond with blue eyes — kind of northerners. They formed a circle around my father, mother and the little 'I'. It was obviously that we were the center of their attention. For a moment, I forgot my state of wandering among the worlds, letting myself involuntarily mingle with the crowd and in the same time reliving the moment. Staring around the huge corridor of that impressive building, I could notice people rushing back and forth, dragging their luggage.

Still wondering at the corridor's walls, I did not notice when the entire crowd, including my parents and little 'I' went out. I rushed to follow them.

"Airport! Airport… air… poooort!" I said to myself, marveling at the gigantic airplanes spread like mushrooms all over the vast field before me. "Airport… airport here?" The scene immediately sparked in my mind the event. "That's it! It's our departure from Russia… definitive departure, "

I whispered, recalling instantly that moment: the three of us, my father, mother and I had been slowly pacing toward the airport gate, with eyes full of tears and hands weaving at our sobbing relatives. I'd never visited Russia since, neither had my parents. My father had died with 'Russia' on his lips. As for my part, I had been too young when I left Russia to be able to fall in love with this country.

I followed the three, walking beside the little girl. I passed a number of officers, staring at us. The little girl's wide eyes caught an officer's attention. He smiled. The girl panicked. I passed through, along with my parents and 'I', the girl, an interminable hallway. To my stupefaction, the more I walked alongside them, the farther I seemed to be moving away from them, and slowly the entire scene faded, leaving me in nothingness and confusion again — black limbo this time. I felt sucked into a neurotic darkness. And I stayed there, stirred by fear for a long time — panic, yelling, pleading and without hope. It was exactly the opposite of the inexplicable calmness experienced before. I saw or felt no dimensions, no limits, only my existence.

"I need my life back, God… my real life… palpable life, dear Lord." I desperately cried out, weeping like a child. My panic and sobbing impressed none. Nobody cut my suffering out. I felt just thrown in between worlds and forgotten right there. "Cry and die soul, nobody cares!" A thought crossed my mind. I just lay there on nothingness, holding on to emptiness and crying to nothing. I felt desperately down, lonesome, rotten, abandoned and betrayed, and even wished for a few moments to vanish, as if I'd never been created.

"Relax," a conciliatory voice encouraged. "Relax and don't cry!" "Relax?" I echoed, pricking my ears up, while staring upwards, where my common senses hoped to find a kind of sky or canopy.

"God, are you there?" I whispered, whining. "Are you there somewhere? Why aren't you talking to me?" Silence.

"Are you seeing me, God?" No answer.

"Relax," my mind urged. I knew I was crying, but no tears came. I stepped back. Suddenly, a tiny bit of light came through, although it was still dark enough all around. In despair, I focused on the light, stepping and rushing through the air. The unbearable silence annoyed me, but I kept gazing upwards at the light.

"Pooo! Puff! Pooo! Pooo!" I felt my lungs heaving.

I stopped. The whole surrounding was vibrating — my form, too. I wheezed. A voice inside of me wheezed, too. I groaned. The voice also groaned. It didn't take much for me to realize it was my own soul that was weeping softly. Something inside made me feel defeated, even though my eyes were still nailed to the mysterious, frail light.

"No… I'll never be able to get up there," I thought. "Waiting in peace to be sent down there… in the fierceness… in the hell… that's meant for me". Perhaps I'm already in hell… and that thing far above me is the 'life' that had been taken forever from me. "Hell… hell… I'm deepening into it. No! Nooooo!" I roared, staring around with wide eyes, hoping to find something to hang on to. I was petrified by my own fear. No ground under my feet, no things around me, I was standing still sustained by nothing, like stars in the sky.

"Relax," said the same voice over and over.

"Pull me out of here," I screamed from the bottom of my lungs. "Let me rule my destiny… let me back in the bosom of my family, where I belong."

As I cried out, I was sent back to my family. Not to my kids and husband, though. I was sent back to my parents instead, witnessing again my own childhood memories.

CHAPTER 13

AMERICA – THE STARTING LINE

Mrs. McGregor, the government's representative, was pacing the platform of the city's airport without knowing that right beside her a group of flustered people were waiting for the same family to arrive from New York. It was one of those sunny days of autumn that makes the yellow leaves look like gold blades dangling from the trees. And I was part of that scenery, standing right there, beside the woman. I eyed her nametag, pinned to her dull jacket collar. Her legs looked stiff as a board, and her face gloomy. She was pacing back and forth on the platform. I waited close to her, watching her movements, certain that she was holding on to some mystery.

It was indisputably good to be back to life — indescribably good. I felt being an inhabitant of a world again. Chased throughout strange worlds as I'd been for a while, I finally felt like I belonged. Was I frightened? Yes, terribly. But I at least came to the point of accepting the minimum possible — bits of earthly life.

Mrs. McGregor rushed in one direction. I immediately followed her. The waiting group also moved forward, facing the same gate. The doors in the front of the check-in booth open widely. Two adults caring their luggage and a small child emerged from the shady corridor. I stared ahead, overcome with emotion.

"Papa… Mama… and me again. I just saw them before… moments ago… in Russia… at the airport… there… there. The same clothes… the same luggage. How come they are here now? Yea, the same Mama… the same Papa and the same 'I'… how could this happen? Oh, my… why am I so confused? Why me again? Where am I, in fact?" I felt like yelling, crying for my parents' attention. I received no consideration. Papa's high cheekbones and flashing smile appeared shining in the sun's ray. My mother's face could not be seen clearly. I remembered their modest clothing vividly contrasting with the stylish people surrounding them — and I remembered everything well. Still stupefied by the scene and wondering, I followed the group and my family, passing right under my nose. Thoughts invaded my mind like a mechanical cooing refrain. The ecstatic sounds accompanying my family's departure from Russia as well as their immediate arrival in America pumped vividly into my brain cells. Every detail was displayed freshly for me. Every detail that I remembered was there, including the smell of different perfumes and sweat — fragments of conversation, too.

The group and my family shortened the distance between them. I didn't move. I stayed on the same spot, close to Mrs. McGregor, not for a moment taking my eyes away from the girl. Recognizing again my figure, my clothes, and even my injured knee gave me a temporary joy, some kind of gaiety. I stared at the girl's face. I was familiar with that face, although I admired it every day in the mirror, taking care and washing it every day, all my life. My parents' tired faces came into view. I hung on their words, as if I remembered all they uttered while greeting the group — remembering their poor English.

"Thank you… thank you people, come… take us," forced his English Papa. He pushed my mother and 'me' -the girl - into the middle of the group. "She's Ana… our Anushka! Say 'hello' to people, girl. Hmm! She's five… and you woman, shake hands here with people. Oh, look people… she's my wife, Olga. My girl …English… study, you know, in … in… in…" and he turned, facing Mama and blushing, looked for the word in Russian.

"Kindergarten," Mama helped.

"Ahhh! Kinderguten," came out Papa's twisted translation.

The group politely smiled. My parents laughed back, evidently embarrassed by their poor English.

Mrs. McGregor made her way closer to my family.

"Excuse me... I'm Mrs. McGregor from the Immigration office," the women introduced herself, attempting to shake hands with my flummoxed parents. They tried hard to make their English work, minimizing it to intelligible sounds. Looking at them, I relived once more the same emotions as I'd experienced at the time. I hadn't had a clue about what was going on around me, a small, frightened girl. But now, noticing my parents' servile attitude I realized the important role the woman had played in our lives. At the beginning, our lives and well-being in America had depended on that woman. The government had sponsored our family and the woman was one of its representatives.

Suddenly, I felt the need to scrutinize the girl again. She was crying — embarrassed and mistrustful — not knowing where she will go next, having no clue where she was or what kind of world that airplane had brought her into. Not knowing even the mystery of travelling by plane, or what an airplane was — that never-to-be-forgotten airplane. So, there we were: 'I', the five-year-old girl, and 'I', the adult 'wandering throughout the eerie worlds, experiencing the same frightening feelings about the near future.

My parents and 'me'- the little girl stood in the middle of the group like strangers among strangers, everybody gazing curiously at them, like inhabitants from another planet. And there was a strong lack of communication. Fingers talked more than tongues. I also gazed at those people with the same curiosity. From their whispers, I could tell they were members of a church, oriented in helping newcomers, and that Papa had been the one writing them for help, while still living in Russia. I also noticed people's admiration knowing that my both parents had been highly educated, but disgusted also by the group's comments regarding my parents' 'bad taste' and 'old-fashioned' clothing. The girl attracted most of the admiration — a notable tribute to her charm and innocence. "What a beautiful girl," said an old woman from the group. "Unusually beautiful, I should say."

"Indeed," another one replied. "She reminds me of Our Virgin Mary," she added. My eyes stared at the girl's face.

"It depends," the first lady commented. "In my mind the Virgin is blonde with a long face, but I agree this girl has angelic features… and innocence." Ignited by the women's comments, I watched attentively each part of the girl's body. It was then I discovered that even though I was only five, I'd been indeed of an usual beauty: long, supple limps and fingers, perfect oval face with red, fleshy lips and light brown eyes, olive shaped and the most stunning smile. The beautiful features I had inherited from Mama and the svelte, tall stature from Papa.

Still chatting, laughing and commenting, the group departed, while my family was taken way by that matriarchal figure — Mrs. McGregor. I was about to follow the group. To my despair, I discovered that each person socializing around me a few moments ago was practically evaporating into nothingness. The only ones remained were travelers, swarming back and forth in that impressive airport's area. They had no idea that my family has just made the transition from the communism to capitalism, not even that they vanished taken by that government's representative. They seemed to care less that I existed, wondering where to move next — what bits of my forgotten memories I must witness next, and in what world. And I waited there, crying, revolting, and begging the 'unseen one' to reveal itself.

Then, slowly, the loud laughter , tears, noisy airplanes and travelers bustling around, the grandiose airport's building, all vanished like decorative floral patrons from a piece of fabric dumped into a basin with chlorine. I was left in dark — into the nothingness again. Bits of optimism burst inside my soul — the hope, the only friend that still endured along with me. "Perhaps that's 'my life to be' for me in the future," I thought, frightened by the idea. It was like suddenly being blinded forever by an accident, while desperately trying to accept and adapt to the new unfortunate condition. I felt alone — extremely alone. "If at least I could have another soul with me," I pondered. "One in the same turmoil with me. Perhaps no soul in this universe knows I'm tossing into this non-existence… or only my mind had been transferred out to some other parts of the universe. Who knows where my body descended, noticed by nobody." Hope took over again. "No… I'm in my bed… with my beloved ones. Only my mind is wandering into this mess… and it's temporary, I know it… and I am not mad, I know that, too. I am smarter than ever. But, I wonder, why am I visiting my childhood memories inside my mind? And for how long am I supposed to visit these? I'll wait." And I waited, thinking over and over of all sorts of solutions, suppositions and ways to escape all. I wanted to flee out of the mess as fast as possible, though a minuscule side of mine burned full of curiosity of roving into my precious memories.

CHAPTER 14

'I' THE HIGH-SCHOOL GIRL VERSUS 'I' THE ADULT

"So many years passed, Mama, and our life is nothing but tears, humiliation, shortage… rejection… and regret." I startled, recognizing the line, and I remembered vividly the conversation. They were my own words, my grumble. I had said those words, while quarrelling with Mama, years and years ago. Sounds of sobbing merged with sounds of clangorous dishes crowded into a sink." I pierced my ears as wishing to devour those sounds. I even felt an alien pleasure to listen to those sounds. I needed more like those to hear. The sounds became my friends… a needed fellowship — the only companionship that I had. "The only hard reward for Papa's and your hard work in this country is insecurity and misery," echoed the voice again, dominating the loud grumbles. "Even the tiniest portion of our happiness is always shadowed by uncertainty and fear… and you both are always sad. Our rooms in this filthy apartment look and smell like Salvation Army's stores… and we eat, sleep and walk on things that others had before. I'm sick and tired inventing lie after lie, while telling my school mates about my 'boutique-purchased clothing'… and…"

Shaking, I stood up, attempting to move toward the source of the sounds. "Mama and me again," I said to myself. And Mama and 'I' there were. "But, where are they?" It was sober. The conversation seemed realistic, but no image shown — no physical participants. I felt secluded — even suppressed. The tension became unbearable. "At least, I hear life around me," I encouraged myself. Suddenly, when I was about to convince myself that I'd become blind, out of the blue, a tiny bit of color surfaced right in front of my eyes as if it had been there for ever. It was like a slow-moving picture — a Polaroid photograph ready to unveil itself to the onlooker's eyes. The more the tiny color reveled itself, the louder the voices became.

No doubt in my mind that the girl whining in front of me was 'I' — the high-school girl, 'full of striking beauty and intelligence', as I remembered being characterized by others. "Mama I can't take this humiliation... this poverty any longer... I..." the voice came out louder.

"Calm down, Ana dear, there is going to be a day when our rooms will look and smell like Sears," Mama threw back.

I remembered the discussion, the fuss, the repulsive smell and also my mother's pain. I didn't need to hear more, but I needed to be with them feverishly. My thoughts mingled with their loud voices. "God," I pleaded. "Let me stay with them. If your will is to have me wandering around the worlds and eras from now on, let me at least remain at that stage," I implored, still staring at the girl's face. An unusual peace and tranquility that I've never experience engulfed me. That scared me. "It smells dangerous," I thought, but in one way I liked it. It was perhaps the blooming of my beauty, and the smell of the youthfulness. The two of them were still talking and protesting against the fate. I wanted to loose myself in that moment and forget everything forever, even that I had once existed. And all thoughts and feelings marched in my mind while the picture of my Mama chattering with me, the high-school girl, emerged from the void, becoming clearer and clearer. I let myself be absorbed by it. My eyes moved continually from Mama to the girl, firmly conscious that I could not be seen, sensed or touched.

"Mama, don't you see?" The girl uttered, "I excelled in my studies, Papa is the smartest guy I have ever seen... and you struggle so hard with that dirty job..."

"Cleaning job," corrected my mother.

"Yeah... cleaning job. What a honor for those toilet bowls at the factory to be washed by people with Master's degrees!" the girl erupted. "You humiliate yourself, bowing in front of all those bosses of yours who don't have even half of your education... only for the sake of their dirty money. And what do we have… except for that thrift-store junk? What's wrong with us, huh?"

My mother said nothing. She glanced from time to time at a scene portraying streets in Moscow — a painting that had been, and still was so familiar to me, which had hung for years in our apartment. I kept my eyes fixed on my mother's pale face. Her dignity was deeply injured. I then stared at the revolted girl's face, examining her attentively. I knew what was in her mind at that moment, although I remembered that scene vividly. Outside my parents' home my friends and acquaintances saw me as a beauty. I had considered myself a woman with 'perfect features', but having the bad luck to be born into the wrong family and wrong country. I'd always known that my tall, svelte body stood out among the rest of the students in my high school, and later college and university. My large, oval, light-brown eyes always communicated better than my voice, though I used my soft voice to persuade people. I never lost the chance to gain people's hearts and favoritism, using my candid look and voice. And my confusion had become greater and greater every day; one side of mine had seen my indisputable success. The other side had always come in conflict, while watching the struggle of Kazlovsky's family to keep up with American style.

The girl's plight brought me the same confusion I had experienced before.

"Oh, Mama… Oh, poor Papa… they both have done the best they could. It has been my stupidity and pride that never saw that," I thought, not moving my eyes a moment from the girl's crying face.

That scene reminded me of a time when my pride, ambition, hate and determination had started to bud. Coldly indifferent to my parents' struggle and humiliation, I had let those buds take over my life. Realizing that now, remorse took over my soul — strange remorse, never experienced before — regret without vindication. And that made me suffer — a burning pain tossing my soul. "I am judged," I thought. "Yes, judged… judged by my own life. I'm 'tête á tête' with my own life, and this unjudicious life is my judge. But… why? It doesn't make sense. No! It's not that. What am I thinking? The reality is that I'm sick in bed, at home … at my home, with Paul sleeping downstairs… and the kids around… and Lori wheezing outside my bedroom door. What's going on around me is unreal… all this is unreal. Oh, God… why this mystery… why this misery? Why is this happening to me? Is it a normal phenomenon… do we, human beings, all experience this at some point in our life? Is Paul going to go through this misery, too? Did Mama and Papa go to the same past?" Everything I'm seeing parading in my eyes seems perfectly real, but how come my existence is not real? Yes… there is Mama… talking… crying. I can even feel her warm breath. There is 'I'… me… flippant adolescent, beautiful and fresh like never. I can smell her cheap fragrance. All these scenes are real… real… real… real indeed. They are replaying as if they had really happened in my life, and I know that. What's surreal in all this mess I've been sucked into? "

I didn't expect an answer. I knew nobody would answer me. I knew they were only my tormenting thoughts — prisoner to my own thoughts. I felt chained inside a non-existence, sometimes hopelessly witnessing my own life's show, or other times panting in horror, being chased between worlds and times.

"I look awful with this long hair," I heard the girl complaining. "I want to shorten it. All the girls in our school have their hair short."

"Be different, girl… be different!" replied Mama. "Don't you see all the girls here look like sisters? No personality… no nothing. And what's that on you?" She startled, noticing my blue shorts.

"Shorts, Mama… shorts. What else could they be?" Replied the girl with a stingy look.

"They're too short, girl," my mother said.

"Shorts are supposed to be short, Mama. Girls wear these sort of shorts here… don't be absurd." Mama's wide eyes didn't impress the impudent girl. "Besides, I want to show my gorgeous legs to the world… I want to open the life's doors with these legs. I want to be the queen of the world… and I'm going to be one. Don't forget… I'm a Russian, Mama. Russians like to conquer… they have always wanted to conquer the world. I, too, want to conquer the world, Mama, and I'm going to conquer this foolish world soon." Mama couldn't say a word. She eyed the girl, dumbfounded. " I'll detach myself from those clutching dirty hands of humiliation and poverty." The girl raised her voice and looked straight ahead, as if the entire world was there in front of her eyes. "I'll be famous… a great, respectable lady… with people moving aside in my presence." Mama sat down on the chair with her knees knocking, her wide eyes staring at the girl's gracious body, walking like a queen in the middle of that humble room.

"Anushka... Anushka, dear... what evil made you think that way? We are poor by fate, not by choice, girl." The girl paid no attention to Mama. She continued with her ambitions.

Outside it was cold and foggy. The girl wrapped her shoulders and back in a large, floral shawl, and mimicking a Spanish dancer, she examined her skipping, slender figure, reflected in the glass of the window.

"I'll climb on the elite's ladder," she threw, " even if I have to drag my bloody knees and hands upwards." She turned around and pointed in my mother's direction. "Look at you... just look at you! What have you done with your beauty... washed the American floors with it, hah? Wash the feet of these arrogant bosses with it, hah... say it, hah? I am not doing the same with mine. I am going to use every fiber of my being in order to succeed, and I'll use all of them wisely... carrying them up society's ladder."

My mother was stunned. No guilt or compassion was seen in her daughter. The girl kept her mystic beauty wrapped like a precious stone and Mama noticed that.

From the spot where I strained to witness the discord, my soul tossed, ready to burst my form forwards, ready to ram my fist into the girl's mouth.

"Don't do that, Anushka!" I heard my mother's crying voice, thinking for a short moment that she was addressing her words to me. I immediately remembered that she was talking to the girl — 'I' the adolescent. And it was true indeed: we couldn't penetrate each other's worlds for sure. "Show the world your manners and intelligence, not your legs," Mama whispered. She frowned and then started to cry louder. My soul cried with her, while 'I' the victorious girl shrugged off my mother's tears with her typical indifference.

"Mama, you'll never come out your stupid world to see the reality... the dumb... austere reality. You're extrovert, Mama... I'm introvert. I have heard this recently... and I thought it surely applies to both of us. We're different, Mama... this means we're different, very different. We live in two different worlds. Extrovert and introvert... ha, ha, ha... ha!"

the girl laughed, weaving her long shawl under Mama's full of tears nose, tiptoeing and humming a Spanish melody.

My mother looked tight-lipped.

I felt charged with pain — indescribable pain. A weave of sorrow bathed my soul as if my mother's entire suffering was swooping over me. The invisible wall separating our times — our worlds — hampered me from leaping to my mother and begging for forgiveness. Hurting my own soul with remorse and harsh words and self-incrimination was all I could do in order to alleviate the pain I felt. I desperately wished to be a virgin again, to start my life once more, to begin right with that particular moment.

Mama was still on the chair, crying. The girl stopped dancing. She moved to the sofa and was indifferently flipping the pages of a magazine. Mama stared at her.

"Such a candid… tender child," she whispered, "transformed into… what… what, God… what?"

I moved closely and bent next to her. I kissed her hands, while staring at 'I', the rebellious girl who was busy, rubbing her neck and shoulders with a perfumed sheet from the magazine. Mama's eyes were full of salty tears. My lips were moving through her shaking hands, but I didn't care much. I continued kissing them, and I felt good. Oh, so good! While still looking and kissing the hands, I noticed that they were slowly fading, disappearing like trees into a dense fog, while another apparition came out the haze at the same pace, overlapping the first scene. It was like my thoughts were taking vital forms, forwarding the 'secretly kept' tape of my life.

"Eeeek! I startled, jumping up, frightened by the change. "What's this now?" Mama's hands virtually melted through my hands and new things appeared clearly in my view, while they, too, passed through my shaking arms and hands.

I remained stuck in the same spot where I've witnessed the other sight. It seemed that only stages moved around me. This time Papa came to my sight. I instinctively withdrew my form back in the corner of the room. A mixture of fear and respect overtook me — the same feelings I had always had in Papa's presence. I eyed his imposing figure.

"What's up, woman?" his grave voice filled the room. I felt sandwiched against the wall — a stranger in a hostile land. With her down-to-earth simplicity, Mama looked at him, replaying:

"This girl again," she said shifting her eyes toward the girl's bedroom. "We're losing her, Iuri… I'm telling you! Oh… yeah… we're losing our girl… and very soon, man."

"What… what?" Papa thundered. "Was she a bitch again?" My mother looked at him and nodded. "Slap her impudent face, woman, don't let her impertinence continue… or I'll smack her…"

I froze in my corner. First of all, I was a wandering soul — unseen and unnoticed. Secondly, I was forced to witness different stages of my life — scared, alone and without hope for a vital future. And finely, I was intentionally predestined to endure pain caused by my own actions in life.

I stared at Papa's tired face. I had always been aware of the fact that I've lionized myself, and I've never regretted it. Only my parents had been alarmed be my self-worshiping.

"Woman, don't look at me as if you don't understand what I'm saying," Papa rumbled, looking at Mama's hands as she was pouring his favorite borscht into the plate.

"You're crazy, man! They'll take her away from us if you spank her."

"They?"

"Yeah… they… the government. Who else?"

"Whaaaat?"

"Many poor immigrants lost their children because of spanking… parents have no right in this country."

"Bullshit!" thundered Papa. "Let her cry to the government as much as she wishes. These exhausted arms brought her here and this bent back slaves for her, not the government. Make her behave, woman, make her be a true Russian lady not a cocotte."

Papa's words made a real impact on me now. I had never known them then, even though he had intentionally thrown his words loud enough for me to hear. I had caught the threatening voice, not the words.

Mama didn't answer. Papa stopped threatening. Emotions flooded throughout my soul, staring at my parents with almost child-excitement. I wished so much to be seen or noticed by them. I yelled their names, and I punched the air with my fists, hoping to produce sounds like waves.

Nothing worked. My invisibility and nothingness scared me greater than the scene itself. I was aware that the scenes unfolding in front of my eyes were only copies of what had happened in my life long ago. What was going on with me in the present moment frightened me awfully. I stood hopelessly in my corner, but not totally despondent — not futile, either.

As for me, I was conscious as never before that I had been purposely placed there, but from two bad things happening to me, I chose the most vital one. I preferred being with my loved ones, even as we existed in different times, instead of wandering among scary worlds and lifeless figures. Remorse and fear, regrets and grief — feelings without hope. "Out of the real world, hope of the second chance died out and perhaps my life died with it," I thought. "Oh, my poor soul, encased in a mass of clay, created to fear and then die."

My parents' words and sighs diminished bit by bit as their bodies faded slowly from my view. I was left again in a scary darkness sprinkled with tiny particles of colored dust. They bothered me terribly, and I squeezed my eyes to examine them. Red, orange, green, blue and move, fluorescent bits of quarts bombarded my face, eyes and body.

"That's it... death... this is death!" I thought horrified, projecting my wide eyes on those particles. "That's all death is... I'm going to die... I'm dying... No! No... noooo! Nooooo! Please no!" Pieces invaded me like gushes of sand. "Poooo! Pooooo!" I felt like those particles bursting out my mouth after damaging my inside. "Yeah! Yeaaaaah! Yeaaaaah!" My arms were swimming all over the air as if gasping to surface somewhere, pushing the particles aside desperately. They were all over me as well as inside my body, bubbling aimlessly. They had no smell or taste, only bizarre, striking colors and speed.

"I don't want to die... no... please nooooooooooo!" I cried. "Send me back to those lives... stages... memories... what ever, but take me out of here! I rather relive my past instead of this dubious... scary present. Ohhhh... please help me! Help me... help me now! Bring me Papa and Mama here again... make me a child again, but don't kill me please... please... oh, please!"

It took me some time crying, pleading, screaming and tossing to realize that what was happening to me in that particular moment was a conveyance — a passage toward a new episode unveiling my adolescent life.

This new exposure portrayed me as a high-school girl again, squeezing my svelte body inside the school locker room. The girl was hurriedly rubbing her face and lips to take off the strident red lipstick, applied in abundance at the beginning of that school day in the same mirror glued on the locker's door. Down beside her legs there was a 'Walkman' cassette player. I recognized it instantly. I had had it for years. I even recognized the song; coming to me in waves. Schoolmates walked back and forth along the lockers hallway. Faces long forgotten paraded in front of me. I felt good. I had no words to describe how good I felt. Panic, panting, fear and confusion… all those forgotten for a few moments! To my desperate regret, that scene was shown only as a glimpse. Panicking again, I stretched my arms forwards, trying in vain to keep the scene vital, or to keep myself surrounded by that scene. None of my desperate attempts worked. I found myself surrounded by rushing pedestrians instead, swarming on the street that I instantly recognized. I'd had many memories linked to it — memories from my wild adolescence.

I stood, close to a school bus, full of noisy schoolmates. The only person getting off the bus walked gracefully. 'It's me… I… again," I startled, distinguishing my figure. I eyed that beautiful and willowy figure, and I liked her very much. I've never seen myself so attractive and full of grace.

"Hon, you forgot your lipstick today," was the bus driver's cunning remark sounded, as 'I', the girl got off the bus. The girl's arrogant look did not bother the driver. The woman shrugged with indifference. The girl took a tissue paper and with a swift move wiped the lipstick from her provocative lips. It was a moment in my life that has been forgotten. I couldn't understand why I relived it and why it was reopened for me in those wandering moments. One thing was pleasant for sure… seeing that street again.

From that street, without a bit of warning, I found myself in the previous darkness, bombarded again by those mysterious shining particles. The bits collided sometimes with shreds of scenes containing people, streets or events that I had once experienced in my life, or I was only imagining seeing them. In my panic and fight to keep the particles away from my sight, I couldn't see what exactly I fought against — the glowing bits or the bits effusing scraps of my life. In my brush with those bizarre, unexplained exposures, the only thing I knew doing was to call the names of my beloved ones, while whirling aimlessly into that darkness and gush of tiny particles. Each bit of light sucked me like a magnet, moving me swiftly toward it. The back and forth delusive run kept me there for a time I couldn't determine. I was in fear, I screamed, ran and panicked, while punching with my fists at those whirling particles. Petrified and alone, my heart still had the strength to know: "Run! Run! Run!" it said.

"But where?" I thought. There was a moment that I couldn't even inch forward or backward. In moments like those, the best I could do it was to sum up my entire bizarre situation. "Is there a 'next time' or 'next moment' for me? Is this 'that's all' for me? Is there something left in store for me? Is this death? Is it my own death? Is death practically a life without meaning... without aim? Oh, God... let me proceed from this mess. Clarify this for me... I want to know if I'm still living or I already died. Oh, God, let me find the path back to life. I promise... promise with all my heart... I promise I'll be good. I'll never be wrong again! I'll hurt nobody from now on. God, let me find my life!"

I immediately found my life, but not the one I begged for.

PART THREE

MARCHING ONWARD TO THE GOAL

CHAPTER 15

MARCHING ONWARD TO THE GOAL

In the corner of my bedroom, in my parents' shabby apartment, I noticed myself again. I gazed at the young beautiful girl and gorgeous than ever. I eyed my fingers, frenetically selecting eyeliners, lipsticks and mascara. I knew what she was thinking in that moment. I vividly remember her thoughts. They were dreams impregnated with rotten ambitions. Defeating the poverty while triumphing over the society's elite.

Suddenly, groans came from the other room. I knew they were Mama's. I spontaneously remembered the moment. Mama was in pain; it was one of her severe gallbladder attacks. I felt sorry for her, even though I knew that was only a copy of what had happened then. I had been bothered by it at the time — not because I had cared, but because it had interfered with my high-school prom. I had just gained my first husband, John's heart, and had been determined to be the queen of the night.

"Ana… Anushka… please call an ambulance!" My mother pleaded, crying. "I can't take the pain any more… please, go… please hurry!"

I couldn't see Mama, not even the contour of the other room, though I was determined to burst through the door and take her into my arms. I knew that there wasn't another room. The exposed scene was comprised only of a corner, a bed and a mirror inside a room — inside my bedroom. Agitated and baffled, I looked at I the listless girl, while she was pacing in dance's rhythm with the prom dress wrapped around her naked body.

"Anuuuushka... Annna! Come... come here, my girl!"

"Get an aspirin, Mama," the girl yelled back, continuing to ballet in front of the mirror.

"Ana... I want to go to the hospital... call an ambulance!"

Mama's panicking words did not impress much the girl. She tried to match the shoes with the dress this time.

"Ana... Ana... Annnna... Come here... I can't get up! Take me to the hospital!"

"Come on, Mama... what did they do to you there last time you're been there? You waited there for hours and finally ended up at home in the same bed, sipping your chamomile tea," came the matter-of-fact voice from the happy-go-lucky me.

"Come here, Ana..." begged Mama. The girl didn't answer. She leisurely put the shoes down the floor near the hem of her long dress and grabbed a cardboard box from the closet shelf, placing it meticulously on the bed, near the dress.

I couldn't wait a moment longer. Engulfed by rage, I sprang forward and my clenching hands went through the girl's shoulders, passing through her body. I ended up on the other side of the bed close to the door. I burst through that door, intending to rush to my mother, but I suddenly stopped, realizing that I shove myself into the void again. Neither Mama nor her bedroom could be seen on the other side, only a deep, scary void. Stunned, I sprang back to my bedroom. The girl continued with the routine of matching cosmetics, jewels and shoes this time. Her face glowed with happiness, while admiring her new look in the mirror. At the same time, Mama's roars and lamentation filed the atmosphere.

Regrets and remorse, followed by horrific thoughts and fear of the unknown possessed me. "Oh, my Lord, why hadn't I helped my mother... why so much foolishness...? Where had my mind gone then?' Deep down, my soul knew that the only target I had had at that time had been the conquest of John's heart — my first hook on society's ascending ladder. 'John' — his svelte, tall and handsome body paraded in my mind. I sighed. "An evil encased in a diamond shell."

My mother's groans increased for a while, then slowly faded away together with my bedroom and the girl tiding her things. And the entire sad scene glimmered for a few more moments, letting another one vividly patronize the sight. This time, I found myself in-between John and 'I', the same high school girl, seen before. She even wore the same outfit: blue jeans and a blue Nike T- shirt. The three of us were in front of the school's washrooms.

"How come it took you so long to get here?" broke John's irritated voice.

"Arrogant idiot," I thought, searching his eyes, though very conscious that he could not hear or notice me.

"Shhhhh! People are swarming around, John," warned the girl, abashed.

"And what's that tatter on you?" John's eyes stared at the girl's T-shirt. "Where is the prom dress I bought you?" Disgusted, my eyes followed the girl's hands, trying to cress John's chest and calm him down. I thought: "How in the world had this scorpion been capable of bowing me like that? How could I been fooled by his ill-bred courtship? Had it been a self-imposed passivity in order to accomplish my goal — the main support for the jewels in my aspired crown, or a pure and simple naiveté, specific to that age? Was I a humble hazel hen or a sly fox?" My scrambled thoughts mingled with John's behavior and domineering words, as well as the girl's apologetic excuses.

I didn't know how long that particular scene was meant to be unveiled for me. What I knew was the fact that it filled me with rage, fear and remorse. I wanted out. No, I actually wanted to deepen more and more into it. I wanted to restart my life right from that point, from that stage. I wished to reverse the past, transforming it into a 'present' once more. Humanly speaking, there are no comparisons or descriptions to the remorse I experienced. I felt that particular moment being the cause of all bad things happened later in my life — the beginning of the gangrene that had ignited all evil occurrences in my life.

I waited with John in the hallway until 'I', the girl changed her clothing in the washroom. People moved up and down the hallway, but I eyed only John. I followed each of his arrogant eyes' movements, seeing him now, in my mind with other eyes. The girls in school were crazy after him and had the guts to show him that. He liked it and I knew it. I had known it all my life. He wore the look of someone expecting compliments.

"Alone?" whined a blonde girl, tossing her long bleached hair right under John's eyes.

His crafty smile replaced an answer.

"Alone?" scoffed another blonde.

"Alone?" mimicked a male student this time. It was Tom, the school's clown. John's look made Tom vanish like a hunted mouse. John was pacing nervously in front of the washrooms, looking as if he was calculating each of his moves. He eyed the group and with a matter-of-fact voice uttered:

"No… I'm not alone." After a brief pause, moving his piercing eyes from one student to another, he added: "As a matter of fact, the queen of this night is with me."

"Wow!" I sounded.

"Wow!" The group exclaimed, laughing derisively and departing.

I gasped. Emotions flooded throughout my body. I had never heard the words there in the front of the washroom's door at the time it actually happened. I remembered myself rushing behind the door, putting on the make-up and the eye-catching prom dress.

Even alone as John seemed to be, I noticed he was the center of attention. Visible waves of emotion rose as the washroom's door opened widely and 'I', the girl, entered the auditorium. I jumped near the girl, mimicking her graceful walk. The relived emotions electrified my entire body. They were the same ecstatic seat of passion I had then experienced as a graduating high-school girl. The girl stared ahead with pride. I did the same thing, copying each of her movements. She gazed at John. I gazed at him, too, but there was a difference in our look. She adored him with her eyes, though my looks showed him hate. The 'wows' around us brought even more people. Students from the hallways rushed inside, attracted by the occurrence. I realized only now that not all those 'wows' were genuine. Most of the comments were part of an embarrassed mockery. I had not noticed then how exaggeratedly elegant I had been for that prom night inside that modest high school. I had not noticed it then, but painfully got it now while listening to students' and teachers' remarks. I looked gorgeous — yes, very gorgeous. And John rose in rank, parading me around the school. Dragged by the envy, some students were mimicking my walk and even the way I talked and tilted my chin. Even teachers raised their eyebrows when I walked and talked.

"What a display of stupidity...arrogance...and ridiculousness!" I found myself yelling, "Stupid John! Oh, stupid... stupid, idiots... stupid life and stupid haughty world!" disgusted by the entire scene unveiling in front of me. "What a snooty...idiotic... pervert world!" I said to myself, staring at the entire crowd, though alone and unnoticed or sensed. I saw no place or reason for me to be there. I dared to spring out the doors, heading toward the parking lot. A strange feeling made me believe that I was fooled again by another 'already lived episode of my life'. My fear made me stop right in the hallway, while something inside me cautioned me that there is no 'outside' for me there. In my case 'outside' meant returning to the same eerie void.

I wanted to chaperone the two in John's car, but I couldn't. I was meant to witness everything from the outside — an 'outside' that wasn't in fact a road or a parking lot. It looked like a serene, summer evening on a county lane. I was outside. It seemed that I was actually floating into darkness, while the car was placed there in front of me, surrounded by that summery serenity. The girl exalted, rolling her arms around John's neck. I hated her for that — and I hated her a lot. John liked it, although his passion and 'chameleonic' nature stalled the animal in him. The girl played with the tip of his ear, flipping its bottom edge between her well-manicured fingers. From time to time, she moved her fingers down his neck. I needed to bite those fingers and be able to kick that foot off the gas pedal.

"Skunk...son a viper! Oh Lord...and how much I loved this evil... then!" I found myself saying, when I saw his face grinning. I hated him, and hated him even more that moment. I pitied myself, as I was wandering aimlessly among worlds and times, scared by an eminent end of my existence, while him being well off, living happily married and father of a small girl. This thought brought protest and rage inside my hunted soul. "I deserve to live, not him. He has to be here, wandering inside the worlds, not me. He has to be tormented with remorse, fear and uncertainty, not me. I am good. He's a crook... a con artist, smuggled mysteriously into the elite. Oh, God, what inequity... what a shame! He lives and I'm here in limbo… in this nowhere." I feel betrayed…betrayed by fate… betrayed by life… betrayed by You."

My hateful outbursts rose in me, blinding me to the point of not realizing when the revelation faded, leaving me in the void again. From there, I pleaded deliriously to have myself moved back to my 'real existence' as I called my real life. "Don't place me into bits and shreds of my pre-existed life," I begged, shivering. "I feel those shreds are the precursors of my real death," I thought with fear. "I'm exposed to what I've done and then killed… I'll be through with my existence. Dee-Anna dead… Dee-Anna Turner dead forever. Oh, God, don't let that happened! I'm still very… very young… and I have small kids that need a mother in their life." I felt so lonesome. I pleaded, made promises, cried, screamed, even threatened. I didn't know if I was lying down, sitting or standing. I only felt that exist — that's all. I didn't know even my real form, I only felt that I was in a form, but not how that thing looked like. I also felt that all my memories, including the childhood ones, were stuck in a box — relics squeezed into a tiny, rotten box.

Snapshot after snapshot appeared before my eyes, even forcing me to enter and conjoin them. Everything faded the same way it had appeared — swift and momentary; leaving me in fear, and ruled by remorse and uncertainty.

"If I could only get back my bedroom," I thought, I might be able to get my life back… but how do I get there? Oh, God, show me the way… put me there in my house, good Lord!"

And I was dropped back into my house, right into the bedroom, but not the one I wished for. I found myself in a bedroom in my parents' home instead. My bed, night table, mirror and closet — all mine, but not desire to see them in that moment. Hanging up the mirror there was the vulgar amulet that John had once offered me. "Ugh! It made me sick." I walked around the room examining my things — some long time forgotten. Suddenly, while turning around, my young figure came out of the blue. "My goodness! She… I mean 'I'… 'me'… what ever… wasn't there before. When did she sneak in?" I gazed at the ghostly white face of the girl. Gorgeous, slim, pale, weary and shocked — these is how I saw myself — the girl sitting on the edge of the bed, reading a letter. I was standing right beside her. I looked at the letter, and recognized it at once. It was John's marriage proposal. I hated the letter, and hated deeply each of its words. My frantic instinct was to grasp that letter from her and make it invisible as if it had never existed. I thought: "If I'd had someone destroying that destructive letter on time, I would never have ravished my own life. But fate… fate… fate… doomed chance. How clearly I see all now!"

As I anticipated, I couldn't reach the letter. My hands went through it, while the girl, unaware of my presence, continued reading it — dancing in front of the mirror this time. The more happiness she displayed, the more rage I felt. On the bed, I noticed another letter. I knew that, too, very well. It was another stupidity of mine. The girl read it lustily.

"It's approved," she shouted, bursting through the door. I burst with her, but instantly sprang back, realizing that I went into void again. I remained in the bedroom, standing near the door, baffled and disoriented. "Oh, God, when is these nonsense going to stop?" I dared. Still quarreling with the 'invisible', voices came from the other room, which physically did not exist.

"Approved what?" I heard Papa's grave voice thundering from there.

"My name… what else?" came up the girl's insolent voice. "I am not Ana any more… From now on I am Dee-Anna Kazlovsky… and…"

"Whaaaaaaat?" Papa roared.

"Whaaaaaaat?" jointed him Mama.

"And… more," added the girl, her voice mingled with Papa and Mama's yelling. "To be more exact… soon I'll be Dee-Anna O'Neil. I am going to marry John… with your or without your blessing." Her last words gushed out without even catching her breath.

A deep, deep silence followed and then a discharge of screeches, slams, moans and even threats filled the atmosphere. I visibly witnessed nothing of them, only heard them, recalling vividly the moment. My soul anguished. "I wish I would have never been born. My parents would have been better without me. They could have been lived for the rest of their life in Russia, respected and having noble jobs… not washing the floors in those American factories and banks. Why… why did I bring so much pain to their lives… why me… why me, Lord?" My lamenting thoughts mingled with Mama's voice:

"I wish you'd have never been born, my girl… we would have not suffered as much… oh, how you have changed! From such an angelic child into… into… into…"

"A bitch… the most notorious bitch," thundered Papa. "A slut," he added, trying to cover the girl's yelling and threatening. "Don't leave the room, slut," he yelled. "Stay here and listen to our grief… see how we put up with your coquettish manners… impudence… dirty flirt… and sick mind… you a Russian girl. Pew!"

I remembered the hate that had sprung from my heart then, seeing Papa spewing in my direction. My both parents have been born in a communist country, governed by a group of strong atheistic leaders, who imposed on Russians the atheistic education, while never being bothered if Russia's population learn a well-mannered comportment and correct vocabulary. That's why my parents didn't pay more attention to the language they used, and I copied them exactly.

"I hoped you both… be happy for my success, not roaring like caged lions," threw the girl with an insolent voice. I was sure neither of my parents heard her last remark. They both were shouting unintelligible words, their voices overlapping. Their delirious eyes and looks full of enmity came vividly to my mind, though I was unable to see them now. I felt like a snake thrown into boiling waters. I thought: "My reckless… lousy egotism! Lives destroyed… lives mutilated that are all I could harvest. Oh, God… have pity on me!"

The girl burst unexpectedly through the door. I started. She shut the door behind her. Papa followed immediately, striking the door with his foot. I started again. I experienced the same horrifying feelings as then, the same shaking legs and tossing heart.

"You will marry a 'good-for-nothing'… whose arrogance makes everybody kowtow around him," Papa yelled. "He'll put you on your knees soon… if he hasn't done that already, you idiot. Don't even think to bring that bastard… that scam… into my honorable Russian family. I don't want to meet him… I'll twist his damn neck… you hear me, girl?"

"I'll marry him… even if an army of opponents lines up in front of me… Nobody will stand against my will," dared the girl, moving like a ballerina right under Papa's nose. "Listen well, Papa… I want to become somebody in this damn world. Look at you! Both of you put out by all those ignorant bosses of yours." She raised her chin, slashing out at the air, while smiling like a fiend. I hated the girl. I hated my foolish guts, displayed like a clown. Mama's sobbing invaded the room, interrupting from time to time Papa's yelling and the girl's disdainful speech. There were moments when I did not know which voice to listen to first. They all combined, creating chaos in that tiny room. I moved near the corner of the room, turned my face against the wall and cried. It was hard to cry without shedding tears. In fact, my soul cried, my form was shivering uncontrollably. Sounds of lamentation, grief and threatening buzzed my ears for a while and then slowly faded along with the room, 'I' the girl, and Papa. Only my form remained, suspended into a 'dark nothingness', shaking with fear, sorrow and an incurable remorse. I felt thrown into more confusion than before. I didn't know which 'I' was represented, which 'I' or 'She' really existed. The married to Paul 'I', lying on the bed in our master bedroom, the dead 'I', lying down on the street's asphalt, near Oakland Plaza or the chased, baffled 'I', wandering among worlds and times. Nobody was there to help me, not even 'life' existed for me to live. I waited in vain, and I waited for a long time, trembling, crying and screaming, but still hoping.

CHAPTER 16

ACQUAINTED WITH THE ELITE'S TALL ORDER

"For now we see through a glass, darkly; but then face to face... But if any man be ignorant, let him be ignorant...

And now abideth faith, hope, charity, these three..."

(Recited by Mr. Tony Blair, England's Prime Minister, from I Corinthians 13: 12,13 and 14:38 in the Bible at the funeral of Diana, Princess of Wales, on Saturday, September 6th, 1997).

If I opened my eyes I saw, as if my eyelids were firmly closed, and if I unplugged my ears, I heard as if they were blocked. If I walked, I felt as if I never moved, like walking inside my mind, wandering around its snaky lobes. Each time a minuscule spot showed up, my entire self concentrated in capturing it, as the only sign of life. Every spot became a revelation of my life — my already 'used up' life. Witnessing my own life had been like enduring self-inflicted thorns all over my soul. The endurance brought about a weird patience, which existed vis-à-vis my incapacity of redressing my life's failures and damages — self- inflicted pain or agony inflicted in others.

Staring blindly into that undefined emptiness, I saw that the misty void before my eyes took shape. It was in extremely slowly motion. The only thing I could obscurely discern between some rotating, tiny particles were petals of flowers, or perhaps only an illusion of them. Everything appeared white at first — flat white. Then slowly, pale pink petals showed up, followed by red and yellow and then blue and dark blue. The leaves' different green shades showed up at last, followed by mauve and indigo flowers. With those last flowers the contour of beautiful vases appeared: some small and large, others extremely tall and thin. At first, I was under the impression that they were hanging in the air like stars in the sky, and that all contained gorgeous bouquets of fresh flowers. I gasped for air and then slowly exhaled a long, audible sigh. I recognized the flowers, and quickly glanced around, staring at the vases. I knew each of them well. The two foremost standing vases revealed contoured forms at last. Facing the church pulpit and beside the two standing vases, John and 'I', the bride, were standing in front of an old priest. I recognized in a moment that man who was hired by John to officiate at our marriage, exactly one day before our wedding day.

The priest couldn't refrain from staring at the bride's splendor and her husband-to-be, John's sylishness. His wife, too, was all smiles, so were my friends, Alice and Dana — both arrived from England especially for the event. "Wow... Sue is here... Sue... Sue... my sweet friend Sue!" My heart was jittering. "Oh... I haven't see you for ages! I haven't... see... you..." I repeated, staring at her gown — a long, splendid dress, which was another gallantry of John. That gown hadn't had the ability to capture my attention then, though I'd been too preoccupied with the completion of my ambitious dream. "I have never thought we had been looking so elegant," I thought, unexpectedly overwhelmed by the elegance of John and I, and our wedding party. They all radiated charm — beauty that emphasized even more a striking contrast between our splendor and the modesty of that priest and his church. At that time, during the ceremony, I'd seen everything unfolding perfectly, as planned. Witnessing from the outside world and at the same time re-evaluating everything, I raised in my soul's awareness, while still trying to fight stigma. My wedding day had been a crucial moment for me — very dramatic, in fact — with my pride trailing behind me. I could see that even better now, while standing alone at the back of the church, shaking in fear and also baffled by the scene of my own wedding. Everybody in that small audience was whispering and elbowing each other, while scrutinizing Mrs. O'Neil's, John's mother, and my parents' faces. Mrs' O'Neil was standing a good distance from Mama and Papa. I had never known that, either. It was only now I sadly discovered their glacial first encounter.

"Is this a funeral procession?" came out Tom's sarcastic, whispered comment, his look piercing Mrs. O'Neil's eyes. I, too, looked at her, though I've never had eyes for her. I caught her face and noticed that it was too long compared with her tiny, acid eyes, spooking everybody around with them, while hiding them under the brim of her immense mauve felt hat. She was dressed all in that specific 'queen's mourning' mauve, and was staring up at the decayed, wood-beamed ceiling of the old church, about twenty miles from Detroit.

"It may be a funeral for them... man!" nodded Ian, John's other best friend. "Look at them, they seem to be made out of wax, not flesh... and look at their eyes! Oh, my gosh... these boneheads! Cheer up... you dummm'b... you booby! It's you're child's wedding...come on!" My parents' faces looked as if participating to a funeral procession indeed. I didn't care much about Mrs. O'Neil's face and feelings. I looked at Mama; her pain punctured my soul. I knew I had washed away all the dreams linked to her daughter's marriage. Since I had been a small girl, I had always heard her mentioning the splendid dress she had wanted to wear at my wedding. I hadn't given her that chance. Seeing her now dressed in a simple, white silk blouse with a distinct Russian motif embroidered on its collar and also her long, elegant black skirt, my heart shrieked with deep remorse. I eyed once more that Russian motif. I knew why my mother had that blouse on. It was one of her unspoken messages to John and his beloved mother: she wanted to show them that he's marrying a Russian girl. Both mother and son had hated 'outsiders', people belonging to nations outside their own. I had always known that, although according to them, I had been an accident in their lives.

The priest was close to ending his reading. My eyes concentrated on the bride's face. I knew what was to follow, and I didn't want that to happen. In that moment, I wished to have a super power capable of erasing the moment right from its beginning. 'I', the bride, was shaking, while dressed in a long, lace gown, with long sleeves and deep, oval décolletage. The dress train looked too fancy and pearly in comparison with the church's filthy, rotten floor. My eyes were attracted by the brilliance of the pearls on the dress next to the floor's tanned dust. The veil covered half the face, professionally covered with fashionable make-up. The bride's lips trembled. I eyed her bouquet of flowers, not made of white anemones as I remembered asking John to provide, but of white lilies instead. My eyes moved rapidly from that bouquet to the veil, then to her face, arms and moved back to the bouquet again. The bride looked astonishing — thanks to the generous bank check of John's father, presented a few days before the wedding and before his departure to California. This check, including our honeymoon in Europe, paid all the wedding expenses. Well, she made her first paces into the elite's orders.

I moved, heading toward the other corner of the church, sitting on the last bench in the church, like a bird in a cage, waiting for its captor's next move. Perhaps, I was expected to wait calmly, while witnessing, absorbing, immersing and self-judging. I couldn't do that; I wasn't use to it. Every snapshot of my life frightened me, thinking about the reason of its unfolding and fearing upon its consequence. The fact that I was still capable of thinking, seeing, fearing, judging and grieving told me that I was still alive, though not sure in which world, form or time. Besides, I have never heard somebody experiencing something similar, such a bizarre tribulation. But was it really an experience or my own brain's travesty? My only wish and hope were to burst out the entire misery and confusion as fast as possible. Yet, there were times when witnessing some sequences of my previous life, I have somehow become a little calmer, melting myself into that scene and time. I saw everything happening to me as an accident — terrible, abashing accident. I thought: "… an accident is overcome with calm and dignity." I have forced myself to have that dignity a number of times during the ordeal, including during that wedding disclosure — a scene of delight versus anguish.

My thoughts were suddenly interrupted by the bride's "I do" words. I stared at Mama's face. She gasped. Papa, too, looked at her face. He nodded. Mama's lips trembled. Papa's huge hands patted Mama's shaking hands, resting on the back of the bench ahead.

"I do," said John, smiling down at the bride. I stared at Mrs. O'Neil's face. She smiled sarcastically, rolling her minuscule eyes towards the ceiling, while tapping with her knotty fingers on the edge of the empty bench in front of her, sucking her upper lip. Nobody comforted her. My friends as well as John's were all ears and eyes, examining the grimaces of my parents' faces, as well as Mrs. O'Neil's tapping fingers.

I've never been aware of what had happened behind my back during that wedding. My only goal had been my marriage. To my satisfaction, that had been done even better than I had figured and planned. Whispers, sentiments and tears — all kept outside my mind and heart.

From my spot, I could see the entire panorama, hearing each word and rustle. I even distinguished the irrepressible mouth's twitch of the priest's wife, perceived together with the death-defying cry of a fly, caught by a spider's web, up on the ceiling — above the bride and groom's heads. I gazed at the fly, examining the web for a short while, and then moved my eyes instantly, staring at the bride and groom again. Something inside urged me to make a correlation between those two events, which evolved parallel, though unaware of each other.

Examining attentively the small audience, I noticed that the only happy people there were the newlyweds and their young friends, as well as the priest and his wife. Although, the bride and her groom noticed their parents' morbid faces, they still radiated with happiness, showing smiling faces. With that wedding, the bride accomplished her first ascending dreams' flash, though the groom's ego, put down many times by my refusal of sleeping with him before the wedding, triumphed at last. In his turn, the priest had received a considerable amount of money from John, as a gift for his willingness to open the solitary church that particular Saturday autumn morning.

While still watching, it seemed to me that all the kaleidoscopic spattering colors of the outside view burst inside the church. I felt for a moment that all normal nature's and physics' laws were broken, letting the entire panorama with its perspective, sights and characters to mess disorderly around, while 'I', the spectator, obligated to make a sense of everything. I closed and then opened repeatedly my eyes — the same mess and confusion torturing without pity or hope. Snapshots of the of the 'inside view of the wedding officiating' mingled with snapshots of the 'rice-throwing moments' and 'photograph's and reception's occurrences', while 'I' the witness, forced to pick up something from all at once. I mysteriously sprang from the church's stairs where I got rice passing right through my body, to the park, where I was standing right in-between John and 'I', the bride. I was even present at the reception hall, sitting at the table with my parents and Mrs. O'Neil, witnessing the lack of conversation and their dishearten faces.

While sitting purposelessly beside them, my mind attempted to organize the snapshots in my mind, calling upon my recollections of that wedding's event. There were moments of calmness — gloomy tranquility. My incessant, hysterical struggle, fear and race transformed drop by drop into a placid awareness, followed by inexplicable rest and a dab of stoicism — but never a real serenity. My human nature, always struggling with the bizarre ordeal, professed an end to each action. According to that I, too, expected to be wriggled out my unexplained tribulation. Nothing happened as I wished. I hopelessly waited for an end whose beginning never showed up — and I felt responsible and accused. Fear of inevitable punishment engulfed me, but I saw no accuser. I pondered: "I'll go back to life… I'll live again. It must be a way out of here." The hardness of some moments of my life made my soul squall, capturing me in the moment. That wedding inflicted pain, incredible pain, also sorrow and remorse, but its revelation tricked me in some way. At first, I saw myself a victim, but the more it was unrolled, the better I realized that I was in fact the sole participant in my own destruction. My parents' sorrowful faces were still in my view, at the table inside that reception hall. A strange impulse urged me to kiss those faces, but I couldn't do it, of course. I yelled, pleading with the unknown: "Please, no more wedding sequences. I want to go back to my life… my life with Paul and my kids… the only life I called life. A life with touchable matter… with palpable faces and eyes… with flowers… with cars and stones… a life with real tears and laughter. Take this wedding away! Take it… take that mockery… take that farce away!" I spat, waving my arms as if wanting to pull apart an invisible movie screen displayed in front of my eyes. I felt like baby in his mother's womb — two worlds separated by a fleshy wall. I saw everything so real in front of my eyes — practically live disclosure

— though my own existence cut apart from that by a huge, invisible air bubble wall.

◀ ▶

My curiosity pushed me to nose into the newlywed's hotel room. I thought: "If I've been exposed to all these snapshots of my life… why not see this, too?" I wasn't present there though, but I knew what had happened — and I knew it intimately. It had been the only time when John had got rid of his vanity and arrogance, slaving at my feet, placing me where I'd always thought I belonged — at the top of the world. I felt like a queen with thousands of John(s) at my feet — I felt a prima donna. I had devoured the momentum, promising myself that from that moment on that it would be the only life chosen for me. I remembered crying in John's arms, not because of my happiness, but of my accomplished ambitions.

Mama, too, had cried that night, while in Papa's arms in their bed, and not because of her happiness, but because of my stubborn stupidity. They had never told me that. It was shown to me along with those mixed snapshots, while I was sitting at the table in the reception hall, alone and confused, gazing at my parents. Mrs. O'Neil didn't cry that night. I saw that, too, in the same unveiled snapshots. She didn't sleep either. I saw her being up for the entire night.

"How could this viper sleep?" I thought. "It's her only son's wedding night… she must be up making plans for this marriage." We looked at each other. I examined her disproportional face, and she stared through my face at the picture of her son, hanging on the wall in front of her bed. She grinned. I also grinned, thinking: "I can swear she had everything figured out by now." And I knew she had been well prepared for everything. A good example had been our honeymoon, which had been cut short. Mrs. O'Neil had called John home 'immediately for getting a prosperous position', while John had submissively complied.

It was almost 4:00 o'clock in the morning, and still dark outside. I could hear Mrs. O'Neil's old wall clock ticking, and also the rustle of her cellophane candy wrappers. Everything surrounding me seemed to be volatile. I could swear that if I had touched one of those things in that room, it would have slipped away like an eel.

Mrs. O'Neil was lamenting. I loved seeing her in that state. She seemed to be more human that way. I have never seen her like that — I've always seen her cold as ice, a viper ready to attack.

"Oh, John, why haven't you married the right way?" and with the same shrill voice, she added: "For crying out loud… I can't let my friends know about this scum… this 'nobody'. What a shame… what a shame! No… no! I won't let these 'packies' be introduced to my friends. She's beautiful, all right, but her situation counts… not her beauty."

"She's calling me a 'packie'… a 'packie! Hey… I'm a Russian, Russian… noble Russian…" I yelled, determined to approach, and confront her. I passed through her stooping body instead, both talking in the same time. She was blemishing my parents' roots, while I was cursing her venomous tongue and ignorance. My outrageous impulse and feelings blinded me, pushing me to the point of forgetting for a moment that we existed in two different parallel worlds, and could not touch, hear or sense each other.

Suddenly, my mind carried a wilder sound with it. "I'll burn this snake alive." I blasted my form through the candle's flame, hoping to ignite a fire. Certainly, it didn't happen as wished. The candle and its flame prevailed, undisturbed. As a matter of fact, everything looked unruffled, including Mrs. O'Neil. Outside there were sounds, including sparrows' chirps, mixed with pedestrians' footsteps, although I was sure it was not an 'outside' there.

One side of me was tempted to go outside, to search that 'outside', while the other warned me about the possibility of being thrown again into that 'emptiness', or worse — to march along with that mysterious, morbid crowd. So, I decided to wait in front of that viper, Mrs. O'Neil, although full of fury, outburst and fear. From my spot, in front of Mrs. O'Neil's bed, I could see her talking, planning, sighing and lamenting. At the same time, I witnessed snapshots of my life again — my life as a married woman. Intimate scenes of John and myself as well as scenes of quarrels and arguments with both John and his mother appeared in that tiny bedroom like huge air bubbles, engulfing the entire room and overlapping each other. I revolted: "How come I'm stuck with this viper here in her bedroom? I was with my parents before." Later, I found even more confusing the fact that Mrs. O'Neil appeared at the same time as those scenes. Her figure sitting up in her bed, while making plans, overlapped with other pictures of her. It looked like a retrospective album page, where the same person is portrayed in different positions and stages. Somehow, I felt stuck inside that woman's bedroom, and I was conscious of the fact that it was not up to me do decide when or if I should get out of there. I also had a feeling that there was a time set for witnessing those pre-lived life-moments. I thought for a second that I was actually visiting inside my mind, but immediately reconsidered my thought, realizing that people in those settings were normally and humanly breathing, walking, moving and acting. But one fact was certain — I was visiting my own life.

I was still in that bedroom, staring at Mrs. O'Neil's ugly face, when one of the disputes I'd had with John jumped into my mind.

"Is it because of all those stupid girls in your class, son?" I recalled Mrs. O'Neil's saying.

"Maybe, " her son replied smugly.

"What are they doing to you, Hon?" I remembered myself questioning him. I knew I had been beautiful, but full of jealousy in the same time. I'd been jealous, I had admitted that, but my jealousy had been ignited solely by John's actions. Even his protective mother had been concerned about her son's escapades — not for my sake, though. Her son's destiny had been well planned by that woman, and his crippled behavior, including our marriage, hadn't been part of her plans.

"John, you go back to school," I remembered Mrs. O'Neil ordering, and at the same time John jumping:

"W... h... at? Mom, what are you up against? Stop... for once all your tiring gimmicks!" He had spat, though curiosity had anchored him to the spot. Mrs. O'Neil had spread all smiles around, and I recalled the woman stretching her thin, long lips, while exposing her fleshly gums. Oh, how I had hated that venomous mouth — the sword that had pierced me for so long.

"Yes, son, you go back to school... you'll be a principal... yes, son, a principal. A few years... only a few years as a principal, son, and the superintendent position will be yours... and don't stare like an idiot, son. Be ready to go to school and Mother will take care of the rest. Shall we?" The remembrance of that scene pierced my heart again. I recalled the woman, grabbing her obedient son's arm and heading toward our living room, where 'I', the young, dumb wife had meticulously and aesthetically set the dinner table for all of us. I groaned — a cry of anguish, a cry of indescribable pain. I looked at the 'viper', sitting in her bed and something inside of me pushed to ask: "Are you aware of the pain you have caused me... or how many tears I have shed because of you? Who judges you? Why aren't you here... why am I here?" As I expected, there was no answer.

To my satisfaction, Mrs. O'Neil disappeared from my view together with her bedroom and everything around her.

"Where am I now?" I whispered, staring curiously around me. "Am not in that woman's bedroom... I know that... but what is this? Who are these?" I yelled hysterically, eyeing in horror at the people surrounding me. "Is this the same crowd... is this the same morbid crowd? Yep! I guess... I'm returned back into the same gruesome marching throng." I ran, galloping into a misty void. "No... no... nooo!" I screamed. "Take me to Mrs. O'Neil's room... take me back to her... I'd rather stay with that viper than being among these spooky lunatics".

In fact, my immediate problem was to find a way of making sense of the strange phenomena, presented to me in a new form each time. Although still screaming, deploring, pleading and panicking, it took me a while realizing that I was the entire time physically marching along with that endless, surreal crowd — never separated from it. Only my thoughts took live forms. They were displayed in front of my eyes as perfect live scenes, with I as an active participant. My mind was so-called 'physically' present in one place, making me participate normally to each unfolded scene, while my form or so-called body marched in confusion along with those stone-like figures. "Since when... this marching?" I wondered, forcing my mind to remember. "Yes... yes..." I murmured, "Things start to make sense. Thank God! Finally... a little light in this confusion! I have no doubt that my existence is divided in shreds — pieces of "I" wandering around worlds. Perhaps... one "I" is still lying down the bed in my house in Rochester Hills, with Paul and our kids panicking around. While... the other "I" is striding with this bizarre crowd right from the beginning of the ordeal. And only my mind is the spectator... witnessing the third "I" living my life as it had happened. A spectator wondering at a huge movie screen! Who knows? Maybe... I am not the only one seeing my life. Other beings are seeing my life unveiled, too." I tried to picture such audience. I whispered: "Judgement... I'm judged." Maybe... they are here with me... or they're somewhere else... witnessing from another world, forcing me to watch all these, so they can pour a verdict upon me. Oh God... oh God! Have mercy on me! I was silent for a moment, waiting. Then whispered again: "Is this death? Am I through with the real life? Are these unveiled scenes copies of what I lived before?" I looked around, staring at those people marching there with me. "Are these morbid faces seeing the copies of their lives, too?" Are witnessing your life, sir?" I said to a young man. "I'm re-living my life, dear, are re-seeing yours?" I elbowed a young blond, who looked to be my age. Nobody answered my questions. I thought: "Why this multiplication?" I stopped, letting some of those people moving ahead, while passing through my form. I pondered: "Why am I two entities? I'm groaning with these lunatics here, I'm panicking and crying while re-seeing simultaneously dear and heated faces from my previous life... and who knows what I'm doing in my bedroom in Rochester Hills." My entire life was spinning around me and I didn't know which part of it I must stop in order to enter into.

I closed my eyes and let my legs moving again along with the wired crowd. That gave me a little bit of relief. It worked for a while. I tried to gather together my thoughts. I loved myself, and I desperately wanted to exist as a sole entity, with its own personality, wishes, hope and ambitions. I urged myself to reflect calmly on each of those bizarre moments that have happened to me since the beginning of the frightening ordeal.

The previous scene came to my mind again. It was a normal thought this time, nothing materialized in front of my eyes at it had before. I thought of that cruel mother-in-law of mine. Her insidious ambitions had damaged my life irreparably. She had alienated John from me, taking advantage of the fact that I had been caught myself in maneuvering positions and connections, while never having time to detect her gimmicks.

Mrs.' O'Neil had kept her promises. In less then five years, her son had opened the doors of an important high school as its principal and a short time later as a superintendent at the same board of education. At first John had honestly protested his mother's maneuvers, mentioning some regulations. "Don't worry about them, son! Rules and regulations are for idiots." I recalled her replying. My opinion hadn't counted. "Don't wait for her approval, silly boy! She'll look after herself... and I'll take care of you, silly."

Mrs. O'Neil had relished the result of her performances. Both had enjoyed John's new job, but for me it had been the beginning of my marriage's disintegration. John's fulfillment had been a misfortune for me. At his request, a beautiful girl had been hired as his secretary, but she had left soon, because of her Christian principles — being loyal to her husband and faith. The recollection of that moment made me groan and then panic, although I was afraid it would be thrown right in my face. I had hurt that girl, I've always known that, and I had injured her reputation a lot. My jealousy had made me chase each of her steps. I had maneuvered my connections to throw her where I had been convinced she had belonged — "in the factory, on line, not in front of my husband's eyes". The second secretary had been hired by Mrs. O'Neil's connections. The young girl's devoted stay and attachment to her boss had damaged my fragile marriage. Recalling the moments made me instantly agonize with pain and savage remorse — remorse linked to my actions, linked to my stupidity. I howled, punching and kicking people around. I felt nothing, except my own pain, and I was convinced that they felt also nothing. I passed through them, while they waved through my form. They moved undisturbed, while my fists and legs boosted hysterically the air.

"Get me out... get me out! Why am I succumbing this way... why this slow way of dying?" My eyes stared at the impassible crowd and my arms waved around. "I hate everything... I hate my life... I hate all these cuckoos around me. They're not real... they're shadows... yes shadows. I'm alive... alive like never. I'm breathing, suffering, crying. Yes crying! Do you hear me? See... I'm crying, breathing... see?" I yelled, blowing air into my neighbor's ear. In my dementia, I didn't realize that the man walked uninterrupted ahead of me. Then I, too, continued walking and surrendering to the situation. I even had that sensation of walking, but had no idea of the kind of ground I was stepping on. I moved at the same pace as the crowd, but into another environment. People around me were gradually disappearing — dissolving into air, but I had the feeling that they still existed around me.

CHAPTER 17

THE BITTER FLAVOR OF HONEY

Unexpectedly, I found myself piercing slowly into a live scene again. Sounds, words and animation captured me once more. The same pain, remorse and confusion came tactically over me.

"During the day I seldom see you, because of your inability to cope with my 'moody face', and at night you are too tired to spend a few minutes with me, pretending to have an 'exhausting day'." It was my voice, and I recognized it in a moment. It was 'I', John's wife, talking. "You're accusing me of repeated nightmares, though you know well that I sleep as a baby, deep and quiet. I love you the same… it's you who have changed, John."

"You're annoying me, woman. I'm very young… and we're making a mistake marrying so young."

"It's too late now, hon."

"I want to live my life in full… you're in my way, lady." John said with a waspish look, as if ready to sting. Neither of them spoke for a moment. 'I', the wife, dragged her legs to the nearest chair. John showed no pity for her.

"I still love you, John." John looked indifferently in her direction.

I eyed my own crying face, while declaring love to John. But that did not own up the truth. I knew it. My red-hot love for John had faded, although I had continued playing an amorous wife and in the same time flirting with other men, Paul being one of them. John had been too busy with his own amorous life to be capable of noting my coquetries. On the other hand, Mrs. O'Neil had been suspicious, but had said nothing. My escapades fitted perfectly with her plans. She hadn't said a word to John, either... not for my sake, though, but for her son's love for me. Instead, she had used other tools of torture and had employed them fully. She had been a viper and I had transformed myself into a bird — a snake-hunting vulture, swooping in front of her with diplomacy.

"But John, what is annoying you? I am the same loving girl as you had married... but, still at the beginning of our marriage." I examined the crying face of 'I ', the wife, whining like a child. It was a striking difference in-between 'I', John's wife and 'I', the invisible one witnessing to the couple's quarrel. She was shaking, I was unusually calm, umpiring the game. I eyed the tears, rolling down her face, but their warm, salty taste invaded my soul. Both of us, 'I', the wife and 'I', the witness knew that those tears were purposely forced out — they had a job to accomplish. John, on the other hand, had been hypnotized by his own success and blinded by his mother's strings to notice the nature of my tears.

"Perhaps a child might be the answer in our plunging marriage, " John voiced. "It seems that you can't produce one."

"What are you going to do with a child, John?"

"Exactly what all the fathers do."

"There are two categories of fathers, the first formed by loving and caring fathers. To the other one belong fathers who procreate kids only. My guess is that you belong to the last one."

"How do you know?"

"I'm sorry to say it, John, but you're still suckling in your mother's arms... and that makes me sick. Admit, dear, that you're still a kid, and kids can't raise up kids." Silence. "And speaking about my potential of 'producing human beings', I would like you to know that in my both mother's and father's families, women had been capable of having more kids than they had ever been able to raise. Anyway... I'll see my doctor soon."

My eagerness of proving my legitimacy had induced me to consult my doctor the following day, submitting myself to a long process of visits to the specialists and medical tests. None of the doctors I'd seen during that lengthy investigation had found anything wrong with my reproductive organs. Exhausted by all those examinations, I had finally decided to leave my organs alone and concentrated, instead, on getting John in my bed. Soon, I had abandoned all my attempts, realizing that none of my tricks had worked.

The recount of the scene with John and 'I', the wife persisted before my eyes, and I was still part of it, in a sense. I examined both, as they were indifferently looking, one through the window and the other staring at the empty wall. The hot blood seething up and down their bodies added even more enchantment to their beautiful faces — gorgeous figures with evil hearts. John showed no sign of pity or kindness. He posted his tall body in front of the window, facing the garden, though I was perfectly aware of the fact that there was again no 'outside' in that setting. The glass reflected his body, appearing even taller than normal. Dressed in white silk pajamas, decorated with Japanese motif — a gift from his mother — he admired his own reflection in the glass window. I, too, admired that body from behind. He was tapping on the window's sash. He tried to show nobility, but couldn't fool me. There were many times when I had wrapped that back with my loving arms. I could hear his breathing — calm and in control. Suddenly, strange, new and grave emotions pinched what I felt to be my heart — human hate in crescendo, transformed into a kaleidoscope of colours: black hate, meaning no hope and red hate, threatening revenge. There was plenty of the last one there. I didn't know and have never known what had been in John's mind, while tapping on the window's sash, but I knew now what I had precisely designed in my mind, while crouched on the sofa in the other room. My plans of ascending and revenge were meticulously framed, blowing a categorical triumph.

While witnessing that exposé, a strong wish emerged from my own secretive ego. I wished to burst inside that living room and exchanged words with my own self — with 'I', the wife — hampering that exalted ego. I was left with John in the other room instead, although I knew that only my mind was active there. An unexpected emotion summoned all my courage and started to chat with John. I called his name, hoping for a miracle:

"John... John!" I shouted, but received no answer. "Let's make peace! Once we had been madly in love with each other... let's remember that time. We both cheated in our marriage, although I had been the smarter in covering it up. You might never know the truth — the naked truth." Silence, no voice, no sound heard, only my tossing heart made noise. John... John... you won. You're a winner, though I'm struggling here... up or down, who knows... with my own doom."

I expected no answer. John remained undisturbed, continuing to stare through the window, tapping the ledge.

Since the beginning of my ordeal, I have learned to adjust to some 'irrational' rules. At that point, I had no doubt that there was a parade of worlds around me — shining atmosphere bubbles, passing or bumping into each other. My bubble passed through and then melded with John's, though I knew it was just for a while. So, I talked — vibrant, fascinating words of sorrow and remorse. As before, my words came back to me unanswered and uncommented. I had no doubt that John had been a sinner, a cheater, and everybody had seen him as such. I had been the perfect sinner instead, making everybody around see me as a victim — an innocent lamb in the jaws of a handsome wolf. John had always had only one lover at a time. I had been involved with two or three at the same time: one for amorous escapades, another one a money provider and others to just flirt with — 'good connections' suppliers. I had been the one knowing all the tricks of the trade, and John's mother had known which side my bread had been buttered on.

My routine had helped me to wiggle out of the blame, invoking circumstances that had never happened. Many times I had been stuck in my own lies — dazzling lies, results of my own foul play. The revelations pertaining to my own life — naked as they were — unfolded in my mind and before my eyes, forcing me to the wall, experiencing a terrible terror of punishment and death. Frightened and damaged as I was while tossing in death's jaws, I still had the power to hope — humanly hope. A thought crossed my mind, trying perhaps to boost me up a little:

"Every cloud has a silver lining... every cloud has a silver lining... every cloud... every cloud..." but I immediately cracked up again, full of the same pain, horror, hopelessness and remorse. "See for yourself... see for yourself... see your actions... see your cunning acts... see the damage you have produced…" such words tortured constantly my mind. Discouragement took over. "I think this is it… this is it. Some of the people inside those airplanes that had collapsed World Trade Center twin towers, had predicted over their cell-phones what hell they had deepened into — some even discussing their own approaching end. It had been clear to everyone that they couldn't have stopped the advancement of their own fate. So, why was I expecting miracles out of my own hell? I'm going to die… succumb… perhaps be annihilated… history forever. Maybe my real body had been put in a grave long ago, already decaying now… and this is my soul… or maybe mind, wandering among worlds and times… while exposed to the presentation of my own pre-lived life… and longing for a peace and reconciliation that seemed nonexistent. I felt cold as ice and mimicked a sort of crying — tortuous crying without tangible tears. There were elusive tears that hurt more than the palpable ones. "Oh God, have mercy on my soul…I'm only a shadow… only a mist. I'm not a strong worrier who deserves your attention. Please, put a halt to all those unveilings of my failures and… those stupid stunts of mine!" I yelled of the top of my soul. "They kill me… they torture me… and in fact… who's perfect? Who can be perfect… who can be clean on the earth? I know I had done wrong, I have spoiled my life many… many times, but am I able to correct something now? You know better that I can't. God… God, why have you forgotten me? Answer me… answer me, I beg you to say a word to me! Stop throwing my rubbish in front of my eyes!" No answer. I pondered: "Maybe it's too late for me… maybe I am condemned already and left to wander with this bizarre crowd… this sacrificial flock wax-like figures."

The unbearable silence that followed was tormenting and in the same time confused me. It partially frightened and partially calmed me — the calm of death, modeled after that macabre crowd. I felt like someone stuck inside a huge glass balloon, placed on top of a high tower that is expected to collapse in seconds, while scratching desperately against the inside wall for a way out. I continued among those placid faces. "What world is this? Hey… sir, what's the meaning of this transit? Can you see me, sir? No? Yes? Here… here…" I waved my arms in front of that man. "I can see you, though… who are these… who are you, sir? Where is John… my husband… I mean my former husband? He was here before… oh, God! Oh God… what am I doing here?"

I rummaged through the foggy surrounding, progressing ahead through people's bodies. Nobody complained that I didn't stay in line or that I advanced irrationally. I was allowed to do what ever pleased me. The crowd's components continued undisturbed in their rhythmic stride, their eyes staring horrifyingly upward in the same direction. That guise around me glued a little determination to my wobbly feelings. "I'll stay here… I'll march with those waxy kooks… perhaps they know something. They know the end to it. There must be an end to it, anyway… everything has its own end. Maybe, I'll have my chance in a million to escape it if I stay with this crowd… and I'll go for it." I was too frightened and confused to care whether I had a good view over that cohort or not. I was only determined to keep walking along with them and wait for my chance.

As soon as I began bargaining with the situation, through my eyes, appeared my young figure again — John's wife — I assumed. I couldn't characterize exactly the aspect unfolded in my eyes. It confounded with the crowd. The scene appeared as if it came from somewhere up above, floating slowly above the crowd's heads, mingling with them, though making them melting gradually into it; taking me into it as well. That last integration helped me to understand a little why all those ghostly figures looked up in one direction. Figure after figure, vividly contoured in my sight, left the crowd in a dense mist.

'I ', John's wife, came first to my attention, followed by John and then by a large number of people swarming in and out of an impressive building. All those people normally and physically existed, but it seemed something artificial was there — a sort of a fabricated production. Everything looked exactly as I remembered it having been or happening once, including my figure, talking, walking, behaving lucidly and even breathing normally. And the surrounding was exactly as I recalled it, but I felt — perhaps for no reason — that everything I was witnessing was, in fact, a copy of the reality. While pushing myself to approach that last scene, something struck me even greater. I noticed that those appearances were vastly different, and they were indeed. Since I could not find a single contradiction, my mind struggled to point there a clue that conducted me to that last upshot. My inquiry accentuated the verdict of my common sense: an event happens only once, what comes after is a carbon copy, it doesn't matter how accurate its similitude is. Therefore, according to that last corollary, deduced from my own theorem, I acceded to the moment, hoping that it would be an unintended consequence and not a deliberate one. I was able to get those barred pictures out of my head — new phenomena for that moment. A feature, as all those new and bizarre characteristics experienced since the ordeal, which had made me ask over and over about their realm and verity.

John's svelte and elegant body glowed in the morning sun. Next to him, his mother's tall and bent-back body contoured also into the same ray. She was radiating happiness around, shrilling lustily. John was sad. 'I', the wife, also looked sad. I knew for a fact that we both had still loved each other; two unbridled stallions in the claws of many wicked people.

"Helen... Helen..." I yelled, discerning my friend's figure. Helen, a beautiful young black woman, had been my best friend for years, until her husband's jealous arms had pulled her away from me — a friend with a solid mind and heart. I saw her sitting on the bench, consoling me — John's wife — during that day, our divorce day. She naturally displayed passion in her consoling, patting my back at the same time and dragging Mrs. O'Neil's enthusiasm down. The scene made me suffer like part of the process again. During that time, with the irony ultimately defeated and Helen's wise persuasion, I had been able to jump unhurt over many stumps spread across my life's path after the divorce. Re-living them again, I felt a strange impulse to rush near both young women and embrace and kiss Helen. I could even smell her delicate perfume. My friend had been a lady in all descriptions — a sophisticated lady. I had learned a lot from her, and I have seen her as an embodied angel, descended especially for me.

Paul was also there, lurking around. At that time, I hadn't seen him and was not even sure if he had been present, but now I was able to distinguish him among the people walking around. He was standing up under an Italian archway, staring at the group, and from time to time frowning at John's brassy face. Paul looked extremely elegant and even more handsome than John. Meanwhile, one of my former bosses came there, too, and a few moments later his friend showed up — both my ex-wooers and both wealthy and influential. All four men were paraded in front of me like playing cards on a game table; a farcical interlude that I have never remembered taking place in reality. The four men were standing, one in the judge's room, another one under the arch and the last two, chatting coldly near a window in the hallway. Mysteriously, I was able to see all of them at the same time and even hear their discussions. Just when and where the unfolding scene happened, was not too clear to me. I remembered another setting around that day. What I recalled was the fact that the day had been an immediate success for me in terms of money. Mrs. O'Neil had been willingly determined to pay all parts satisfactorily in order to get her son free in her arms. She had lacked appreciation for love, tears and regrets — idiots' manifestations — as she had stated. In all fairness, I assumed she had been right. It had been applied to my case, also. When I had stopped feeling sorry for myself, acting instead as Mrs.O'Neil said, like a 'stoic fox', good things had inundated my life.

All those memories and recalled thoughts oppressed my soul. I groaned deeply, and I had a strange feeling that the entire waxy crowd was groaning with me. I closed my eyes, refusing to be part of that scene anymore or even reviewing the morbid figures. It was dark inside my mind and my soul. I reviewed in my mind what I had witnessed in the previous scene, revising my own deductions about it. I marched and thought, and it seemed that the morbid cohort did the same.

One of the most interesting things happening to me at that moment was the fact that none of the snapshots portraying my life as an apostate ex-wife were unveiled to me. Practically everything and everybody linked to that shilly-shally stage in my life has not rewound for me. Matters grew increasingly complicated for me when snapshot after snapshot bombarded my eyes and mind with pictures of my life linked to the time before my marriage with Paul.

CHAPTER 18

'I' THE INCRIMINATOR VERSUS 'I' THE PERFIDIOUS

As I was walking along with the crowd and desperately trying to escape those illusory thoughts — judgement versus life — another scene appeared out of the mist. As I said before, each of those scenes interpolated, squeezing themselves between other scenes, and the entire interpolation mingled along with the marching crowd. The new scene sucked me mentally into it, or I at least felt that way.

That scene revealed myself lying nude on my bed in the modest apartment that I had rented after my divorce. 'I', the divorcee, was thinking — bargaining with own fate, and I took the moment to my heart. I knew that night, I remembered it well as a beautiful, full of shining stars night. I refused to watch the moment again; it was too painful — a quill full of chagrin. Although I tried to sweep the unveiled setting away, rebel thoughts dominated, surfing among my overheated determination and ambitions.

I stared at my body relaxing insolently on the bed, and a flux of disgust pumped my soul. I felt anger mixed with disappointment.

"Bitch... bitch... scamp!" I spat, frowning with furry, while completely forgetting my status or the governing factors that had brought me into that roving state. I didn't know why I suddenly hated myself so much. One presumption — I assumed — was the fact that I had been the sole being sensing, noticing or talking with my own soul since that bizarre ordeal came upon me. Therefore, I had assiduously quarreled with my ego, detesting every element affiliated with my person. My fiery love for myself had been mysteriously transcended into a revolt and aversion against my own self.

"You brought me here… your damn lust dragged me here… your unbounded ambitions pushed me into this limbo. I'm rambling among these worlds because of your crazy appetite." A burst of immaterial tears and screams blew my words away with a thump, but that immediately echoed back. I jumped horrified: "Echo… echo… here?" I wondered, petrified.

"Oh Dee-Anna…Oh Dee-Anna…what have you done with your life?" I yelled. "You run…run and run after your glory…glory…glory…" the sounds of an echo burst the atmosphere. In panic, I eyed the faces of those people marching close by. Their bodies appeared to diminish in the beaming scene.

"Did you here this echo, ma'am?" I dared, shouting at a dim image of a woman behind me, but her impassible face made me believe that she was not seeing or hearing me. "Hey! Listen… listen to this echo… just listen… it's coming down! Seeeee? Seee?" I tried to stop the woman, holding her arm and forcing her to listen to the echo. It was like wanting to grab the hand of a person who walks in the same impenetrable fog. The woman surfed undisturbed through my form… her arm, too. It seemed that even her image was also a scrap of that mist. The crowd, too, paced smoothly forward into that haze, obviously untroubled by any sound. Though still part of the crowd, I moved with them, and it seemed that the unveiling retrospection of my life moved with all of us at the same time.

The beaming scene stood still there, portraying the same 'I' figure, lying on the same bed. My naked body looked like a piece of marvelous light-pink marble — the kind seen only in the masters' paintings. I kept staring at her, although I hurled toward her my damning words — words of hate and abhorrence. I didn't know why, but an impelling force tempted me to stare at her body.

"Gorgeous… gorgeous, indeed," I thought, looking at the body, legs and arms, and then at the hands of both of us — 'I', the naked body and 'I', the frightened witness, gazing at that nude. My hands — joined in prayer position and hers — relaxing under her head, while the fingers entwined the lace edges of the pillow. I frowned with repulsion. My heart cried and my legs trembled.

I needed not guess her thoughts. I knew every single one of them, and I remembered them well. The moment made me immediately realize that the unspeakable dourness of my plans at that time — although achieved as planned — had crucified me and also brought me to that actual state. Suddenly, the aversion against myself grew out of proportion.

The room was quiet. I heard only the blower of the air condition, while forcing its air throughout the ducts. The atmosphere was tense, upsetting. Two beings were there: 'I', the incriminator versus 'I', and the perfidious. A choking stir made me gasp for air. I knew what had happened with those meticulous plans. I had precisely accomplished them one by one during that time — exactly as I had planned them. I looked around in fear, trying to see if somebody else is witnessing with me the same scene. I even tried to distinguish some of the figures from the crowd, to see if they, too, looked at the intimate scenes of my life. I couldn't distinguish people around, though I was well aware of the fact that they were marching with me there. I've been among them for a long, long-time — unaccountable time.

After all, there was a new feeling tormenting me, coupled with the progression of all those intrinsic life-moments — a sense of contrition, irreparable guilt. My main feeling was to throw everything on others' shoulders. That was a burden too hefty for me to carry, incriminating also. After a stark silence, there came my heart's drubbing, giving me the feeling that its walls were about to burst apart. The horror within me was unimaginable — it frazzled my entire existence.

In my mind, I was convinced that tribulation was intentionally set. I was also aware of the fact that it had stolen a good amount of time out of my life, although I couldn't tell the difference between a real time and a fake imagination of time. Challenging my notions about the earthly time, I concluded that those unveiled life-sequences had taken forever. Each of their scenes had been playing a great number on me. I felt aging with each of those moments, even though they were fast-forwarded for me — the frightened bystander. After having my identity invaded and my soul thrashed along from one scenario of my bare life to another, I felt that my status had been gradually changed. One could have said that I was still a witness, but the last unveiled scenarios made me feel like another entity — another individual. I wasn't the same 'put-aside witness' as I had been during the entire, lengthy trial. Yet, my inner feeling made me believe I was an active participant to each scene, instead. I had neither physical pain nor other special feelings during that metamorphosis. The inquisitive conversion had purely and simply happened progressively, together with the change of each scenario.

Therefore, I became a character — a physical partaker, seeing the same sights, saying the same words and interrelated with the same people as I had been connected with once in my life. As strange as it sounded, that was a reality to which I had to adjust, albeit not perceiving much — a vexing present rooted in my own past. Consequently, that 'I', the witness of my own unveiled life-moments merged gradually into the 'I', the character, becoming one 'I', the ostracized pilgrim and actor, condemned to relive the same misery. My new state of existence brought more pain, panic, perplexity and torture. Before, I could at least keep my mouth shut, witnessing my own acts in life. Now, I had to endure the pain of saying and acting forcefully — as imposed, dramatizing the dialogue and performance that had once happened in my life. All these made me rebuff the idea of going any further. I deserted, opposing the changes. I stopped walking or moving in any form, fearing that it was another gimmick placed in front of me as a stump for more incriminatory plot — another accusatory proof. I said to myself:

"This smells like a closure… this is the last account of my life… the bottom line. My life must be over this way… the verdict pronounced. That's it… I'll soon be devoured by death… oh, God, have pity… have pity on my poor soul! At least… let Paul and my kids find out about my disappearance."

CHAPTER 19

ADVANCING TOWARDS THE JUDGEMENT

Crying, begging God for help and hoping for an immediate deliverance, I cowered like a dog under his master's stick. From time to time, I fearfully opened my eyes to find out if I still was part of the same setting or not. Yes, I was, and had no idea how long I spent there in that cowering position, bewailing my misery, disdained and timorous, begging my Creator for mercy.

Humming droned above my head, resounding all around me. I knew its origin. They were the same sounds of pain heard before, within that bizarre crowd. That told me that I was still there with those lunatic marchers, but I couldn't see them well. I must say that I was able to hear their pain more than see their stone-like faces and bodies. To me, they looked like shreds of creamy gauze weaving outside in a dense fog, and they all wove in the same direction — forward into 'nowhere'.

The entire scene became like an infinite stage — a boundless arena in which many changes took place. I had an even harder time telling the difference between the reality and the vividness of the appearing images. No matter where I moved, fear, uncertainty and desperation followed me. But none of these horrific feelings compared with the dismay endured while constrained into the next experience. Yet, buoyed by a strange hope, my soul seemed ready to accept whatever ordeal came next.

The haze became thinned — only on one side, though. I forced my eyes in that direction. Sun-like rays were penetrating throughout the haze, making the marchers look like shadows built of aluminum foil. The rays flooded the area. An alien, warm sensation engulfed me and the rays crawled all over my form.

"Life," I whispered. "Life… real life… life is coming back," I cheered up, yelling and crying. But my enthusiasm dropped when I noticed the slow pacing of a tall, glowing image emerging from those warm rays. The more she approached the better I could distinguish her face. It was the image of a blonde, young and gracious woman. My wide eyes put forth effort to capture her face. Unfortunately, the radiance of her face hampered me from distinguishing her exact features for some time, but then:

"Mel… Melie! Melanie… you here?" I screamed, full of surprise and conflicting horror. "Oh, no! No! Oh, please no… no… o!" I yelled, hiding my eyes in my palms. "Oh… o! Ah… h! No… o! Not this! God please… please! Don't! Dear Lord… don't show me this! Please, please! No… no! No… o! I don't want to recall this again!" I shouted, spreading my arms in the air and trying to shove the young woman's figure out of my sight.

The gracious blonde was staring calmly at me, although she was the last being on the earth I ever wanted to encounter. However, she stood there near an old oak tree, gazing at my dreaded figure. Her peaceful looking but reproachful eyes made my body shake unmanageably. I stammered, while trying to find words to address her, forcing my tearing eyes to catch the significance of that look — it was denunciation, no doubt about it.

"Please, forgive me Melie! Please, do not denounce me! Don't denounce me! Don't tell anyone! I be… bbb…beg…I beg you forgive me!"

I was petrified, yet watched her every move. Suddenly, I swooped into that void surrounding me. "No hope! No hope for me…no hope whatsoever. I'm lost… dead lost! Oh, Melie… please forgive me!" I burst into tears, but not palpable ones — they were my soul's misery. I felt my eyes burning aggressively. I rubbed them with my palms. I felt no tears, nor eyes.

"This candid face... is my accuser." I yelled, kneeling down into that nothingness, while scratching the void around me. My mouth was drooling, while imploring the 'unseen' around me for help. "Alas... alas... oh... alas! What have I done? What have I done? For crying out loud, what have I done?" My insides felt in fire. "I'm shattered. Oh, Melie... please forgive me... please... pleeese! You know I didn't do it... you know you did it. Please, don't blame me! Don't turn me over, please. I beg you... have pity on me, Melie! I didn't do it!" My eyes burned my tongue hurt and my mind turn insane. "My Lord... oh, my Lord... what have I done to this soul? Please, don't listen to this woman. I didn't do it... she did it. I have my right to defend myself... too... isn't it?"

My eyes darted, moving constantly from the woman's face to what I assumed being a sky. "Oh, God, please be good to me! Oh, dear Lord! Oh, my Lord... oh, my Lord! Please, don't condemn my soul! Let me live... let me live again! Let me be 'me' again, dear God! Don't drag me into that scene... don't let me face that woman! I can't ... I can't see her face again! Please, let me go back to my children, please! I have two children... you know! I want to go back to life!

Where is that crowd? Where are those weaving bodies? There were here a few moments ago. Oh, my... oh my! What's happening to me? Let me go back with those bodies. I want there! Where are you... people? Get me out of here! Let me go there, please... let me go the... re... e! Alas! Oh! Oh my... oh! Take me out of here... take me out of her sight."

Nothing moved — nothing changed.

Melanie continued to smile at me. That inflicted even more pain and panic in my already wracked soul. Tears, crystalline drops, came down her face. "How come she has tears and I don't?" I pondered, staring in horror at her glowing face. I sprang around, intending to rush away. Behind me, the same weaving crowd surfaced again — one by one. They were continuously marching undisturbed, but I could hardly distinguish their faces — shadows in a solid nebula. Again, I sensed them more than saw them. I tried to push some aside, but I passed through or was sucked into their bodies. In my agony to escape the scene, I didn't mind the way I moved backwards. I felt like a stone in a brook, washed by its water's waves. Panting and boohooing, I proceeded successfully, passing backward through a number of lines — interminable rows of morbid figures on foot.

"God, please, let me out! Let me... let... out... out... o... ut!" I screamed, hastening throughout the lines.

However, Melanie's figure followed me like a shadow, like the moon seen through the window of a speeding train. First, she was in front of my eyes, then on my right side, and finally ran all around me, surrounding me totally.

"Please, go away! Go away Meli... e! Go away! Don't follow me... you did it... you did it... you did it... you... you and only you! Paul had been mine before you met... get out my life, woman! We're happy and have kids together... stay where you are! That's enough... enough... enough! You're a deceit... all these waxy people marching along with me in this weird 'here' are gimmicks and... the entire occurrence is an illusion... an imposed chimera. You're dead Melie... dead... dead. I'm alive... and I'll be alive for a long time, Mel, living happily with Paul and my kids. You can't trick me into all this misery, girl. No! You can't... you can't... you can't, Melie!"

"Boohoo! Boohhhhooo!" My chest was shivering out of control, bursting forth into cries. There was silence — unendurable calm that put me out of countenance. Melanie was still there, crying — perfect streams, sliding down her glowing face. One of her hands was pressing against her chest, over her heart, and the other hand clenched a small plastic container with pills. I instantly recognized the pills. With repeated gestures, she rubbed the container against her neck, as if she wanted to say something to me. I knew the meaning of her indication, and instantly threw myself at her feet, begging for mercy.

"Meli... e! Melie... please! Melie... don't... don't," I cried, grabbing her legs with despair. I jumped back in a flash, realizing that I was practically sipped through her legs and body. "This woman can't even see me, how come I'm asking for her pity? She is not real... she is not real, for sure. You're tricking me, Melie. You're not for real. She's paying me back. She's the evil's tormenting instrument. You're the devil's tormenting tool, aren't you, Melie? You want to condemn me, hah? Nobody has ever condemned me, Melie. Nobody! Nobody has ever dared to incriminate me... and... nobody has ever proved me wrong. You killed yourself. I'm guiltless, Melie … and people see me as such. Paul, too. Hey, you people, " I turned around begging those weird faces to listen to my plea. "Look at that woman, lady! She did it… she killed herself. Yes, she did. Confess, Melie! Tell these people the truth. Confess your fault, Melie. Have the courage… and do it! You did it… not me! Sir… sir, please don't listen to her. Don't look at her! Can you hear me, sir? That woman tries to condemn me for her own fault. Please, don't listen to her! Please, people help me!" People's faces and eyes were orientated toward Melanie's face. "Go away, Melie! Don't lie to these people! Go away… you… shadow! You're another gimmick Melie. These lunatics are also shadows. Go away all of you! I've had enough of gimmicks in this falsehood. Oh, God take me away from these shadows!"

I managed to get up, changing my mind and refusing to bow in front of Melie's feet. "Well, you can stay there if you wish. I know you're not for real," I shouted, although not very convinced about my thought. Her figure and the entire setting were mostly seen on my right side, and I gazed at her with fear and uncertainty, moving ahead into that misty surrounding, traversing through people's bodies.

Melanie's tear-stained face remained put for a while. Then later, her glowing image diminished gradually. I managed to avoid seeing her face and those non-stop dripping tears for a while. I knew the gist of those tears. It was Paul and our fight over him that had brought both of us into this state.

CHAPTER 20

WHO WAS MELANIE DUPONT?

Melanie Dupont had been Paul's on-and-off girlfriend for a long time. She had not been seen as a beauty. She had a big nose and small eyes. But her elegance, candid nature and graceful body had made her a very attractive person — affectionate and dainty — and I had always known that Paul had made a connection between Melanie's and my resemblance. Her qualities and youthfulness had added even more hate to my soul. Consequently, I had done the impossible in order to intrude into that young woman's life. I needed Paul. He had to be mine. There hadn't ben room for the three of us. So, Melanie had to be out. Thus, I had used all tricks and bounds to accomplish that, and I'd done that, easily, even without Paul smelling a trace. I had never been able to find out whether Paul had indeed loved her, and that had really worried me, although my motto has always been 'what's mine is mine from start to bottom'. I have never accepted 'shreds', so I had started different strategies in managing the conquering fight. So, how I've won that fight?

    Paul and I had been lovers shortly before my divorce from John. In her innocence, Melanie had had no clue about our love affair. As I had understood later from Paul, she had been a virgin and I, an initiated mistress. Paul had loved Melanie's innocence, but could have not faced a day without me. I had known that very well, and I had never lost a chance of profiting from that. He had used all his potential in order to get me into his company, where he had held a notable position. From the day I had set foot in his company, I had made sure that I had been in his sight each moment. In my decision to get him as my husband, I had had been determined to do away with all his, insignificant or serious, amorous relations — Melanie being my foremost target. Therefore, I had ingeniously arranged my way near her, making sure I would impale the right nail in their 'at death's door' relationship. Everything had progressed as vigilantly planned, including the complicity of an escape goat.

Don, the chosen escape goat, had been one of my subordinates, famous as an unbeatable womanizer.

"Don, I want you to meet a girl… she's something, you know," I had intentionally accosted the young man.

"Wow… who's that?" he had agreeably jumped, volunteering immediately to walk me to my car. "Who's that, Dee?"

"Well… a good friend of mine," I'd replied, spying on his face.

"How is she… I mean, is she pretty… tall, short… blonde… what?"

"Well… she's not Sophia Loren, but I'm sure… you'll like her. Anyway… do you want to meet her, or not?" I'd forced a bit my intention.

"Whoaaaa! Wait a minute! But is she single?" He'd rushed, noticing my precipitation. "Yes… yes… yes! Of course, I want to meet her, but I'd like to find out more about her." Don had explained, flummoxed in the same time by my spontaneous camaraderie.

"Well! She's a virgin dumped by her boyfriend… perhaps ready to weep for him in the arms of a new boyfriend," I'd clarified, smiling malleably.

"Is that right?"

"Anyway, Don, I don't have much time now, but call me tomorrow… no, no. Wait! Not tomorrow! Friday after 2:00 is better, and I'll let you know more."

The next moment after our discussion, I found myself in my car rushing toward the Wal-Mart parking lot, close to the main entrance, waiting for Melanie. Through my connections, I had found that she had worked there as a floor manager.

"Melie… Meli… e!" I'd shouted, seeing the girl, quickly walking toward her Honda.

"Hey, Dee… you here?" The girl's happily surprised face had pleased me. She had rushed immediately toward my car.

"Yea… I came to buy something, but… I didn't know they close at 9:00. Anyway, it's O.K now. I'll come tomorrow. So how have you been, Melie?"

"Fine… fine" she had answered melancholically, obviously uncomfortable with my question.

"How are the wedding preparations carrying on?" I'd insisted, determined to get the news that initially brought me there. There had been only a week since I had forced myself into her life through a so-called 'accidental meeting'. During our conversation I had subtly tried to pump her for all the details linked to her and Paul's relation. Thus, fearing an eventual wedding I had pushed my actions a little.

"Well… there is no wedding coming soon…or maybe never…" Melanie's sad face had encouraged me to attack even farther.

"What… what?" I'd said, pretending to be inquisitive, although my heart was trilling. It had been the exact, wanted answer.

"Yes! I don't think we'll be marrying… at least not soon." She'd evaded her full of tears eyes.

"Hey… don't say that!" I'd feigned. "What's going on here, Melie? Why this delay? How come…whose fault is it?"

"Definitely, not mine," had come Melie's firm answer. "I think our relationship is almost dead. I guess Paul is seeing somebody else. There is a long time since we haven't gone out for a date or so…"

"Is that so…?"

"Well… He calls from time to time, but… a social call… you know? It's no more than that. It seems that he doesn't have… eyes… or heart for me anymore."

Her last words had mingled with her sobbing. A wave of happiness had swept my heart, but I showed her a grievous grimace. My first endeavor had been accomplished. "She must be out, I should definitively prevail upon his heart for ever," I'd thought, full of satisfaction and visualizing the final victory, wile staring at her tearing eyes.

"Oh! I'm sorry to hear that. You'll be fine, Melie! Don't worry! Don't cry! I know the feeling. I'd just divorced my husband… and I've been crazy about him. You know… first love, etc."

Melanie had smiled compassionately. I had smirked back.

"Beeeep... beep... beep!" Somebody had tooted his car's horn.

"Oh, my goodness! For crying out loud... chill down, man! Have some patience! Will you?" I'd shouted, showing a face to the unquiet driver. "I'm afraid I have to move," I'd said to Melanie, "but wait a minute, Mel give me your phone number. I have some thing in mind... it might work for you," I'd added, beaming while pretending to grab a paper and write her phone number down — a number that I'd known it well, but not wanting to boost her suspicion. "I'll call you tonight," I'd shouted, slowly moving my car out the parking lot.

I had rushed toward home and the first thing in my mind had been to call Melanie again. The plan for that day hadn't been completed.

"Melie?" I'd voiced. "While driving home I thought... maybe you and I might meet together. How about going out for dinner? I know a cozy restaurant where we can dine even on some tropical delights ... would you be interested, huh?"

She had instantaneously agreed, and I had immediately set the place and hour to pick her up, and then I had called Don the same day, telling him the news.

At the restaurant we both had praised and blamed Paul, as the only common element of our discussion. We had chatted for a while, then suddenly Don had showed up:

"Don... Don... Don!" I'd hissed, noticing his silhouette walking near the restaurant's window. He had also pretended to just see us, and played his role perfectly.

"Hey... you little one, it's a long time since I haven't seen you," he'd lied, staring insistently at Melanie. "How have you been?"

"Fine... fine, thank you! Oh, I'd like you to meet Melanie, she is one of my best friends," I'd also lied, catching Melanie's embarrassment in the same time.

"Nice to meet you, Melanie," had bowed politely Don.

"Nice to meet you, too," had come out Melie's meek voice.

"Are you with someone, Don," I'd pretended not knowing.

"No... I am single. In fact I'm single every day," he'd philosophized, smiling cunningly.

"What do you mean?" I'd intentionally questioned him.

"I meant, I'm not seeing anyone now… unfortunately, I'm a 'solo' bird, Dee. No girls, no dates… ha, ha, ha," he'd chuckled, casting a glance at Melanie.

"I can't believe… you running out of dates, huh!" I'd laughed too, glancing also at Melanie. She'd smiled politely, not knowing what was indeed going on there. "Then sit down here with us, Don… we are 'solo birds', too… Ha, ha, ha, ha!" There had been a burst of laughter among us.

"Certainly! But… I pay! O.K.?" He'd said.

"Fine!"

Melanie had looked at me. She had been evidently very embarrassed — her face red like a lobster.

"It's O.K., Melie!" I'd tried to calm her down, but she'd continued to move in her chair.

"Oh, it's O.K… really!" Had supported me Don, also concerned about Melanie's flashing face.

After a little while, pretending an urgent phone call, I had rushed out to the other room, leaving Melanie and Don alone most of the time.

Melanie's happiness had impressively grown day by day, and I had not lost a chance to observe the progress of her rendezvous with Don. Their love had budded. In less than two months, Melanie, who had been close to losing her rented apartment, had rented Don's second bachelor-apartment. As for my part, encouraged by swayed passion and romantic conventions, I had driven Paul to seeing me more often. This, I had used the best of mine to seduce him even more — It had worked. Melanie and Paul had stopped seeing, and even calling, each other. Melanie being Don's last obsession and vice-versa. Don had followed her like a shadow; an unexpected attention that had made Melanie fall rapidly in love with him, and things had worked perfectly for me until she had called me with her latest news. I have never forgotten that day, although I've always wished to eradicate it out my mind and consciousness forever.

My phone had been ringing for a quite a while. My plans that night had been to go out with Paul. A group of most influential people in our town had arranged to meet together. Paul had been one of them, and I hadn't had any intention to lose the chance of being known by the elite. So, I had let the phone ring. It had stopped for a while, and then it had rung again.

"Hello!" I'd said morosely.

"I'm pregnant," Melanie's soft voice desperately told me the staggering news.

"You're what?" I'd shouted over the phone. "Idiot…miserable Casanova," I'd thought, remembering how many times I had reminded Don about her virginity. Her pregnancy hadn't been in my plans. "Oh, Melie… that's not good at all. But calm down, Mel. Don't cry like that! Do you hear me… Mel… Melie… Melie? Hello! Hello! Hello!" The phone had died. I had dialed her number. "Melie, please don't panic! There is a solution for everything… wait! Stop crying, girl! I'll come there to see you. I'll come right the way…O.K… O.K… I understand… fine… fine… I won't. Fine, we'll discuss that also… I'll see you, bye!"

She had called me back, but I hadn't been able to understand a word, her sobbing mixed with yelling had made her words impossible to hear.

"What did you say, Melie? No… not the same address. Repeat please, you not living at the same address anymore? No? Yes? Is that right? Well… give me the right address then!" Pause. "How come you have the same phone number then? A… a… a, you kept it." Pause again. "Good, say it again… say the street number again. Good! Good… aha! I'll be there soon… and be a good girl! Bye! Bye… I will… bye!" I had hung up the phone and pondered. "What an sucker… what a sucker… I told him many times to be careful with this virgin. Oh, he wrecked everything, deepening me in more trouble. I'll pay you back, Don!"

Instantly, tens of tormenting thoughts had stormed my brain. One side of my mind claiming liberation of those thoughts and events, while the other side deepening me more into it, giving me no way out. "That's the last thing in my mind," my soul had echoed. "Oh, boy… why this pregnancy now? Wait a minute! In fact that's not my problem… she messed with him, not I. It's her problem. No! It's my problem, too. Well… I'll deal with it," I had said, and a chain of names, places and possibilities had paraded in my mind. "I'll find a way out of this, I know enough people… I won't worry. Oh, silly… silly girl! Welcome to the womanhood, Melie!"

I'd got lost for a short while, but when I had finally found Melanie's building, I'd rushed upstairs to her modest apartment. A well-maintained, large park with many old, impressive trees had surrounded her building.

The park had looked more like a forest than a city park. An oak tree with strangely shaped branches had exquisitely attracted my attention. I had looked at it with curiosity, while searching for the main entrance, and I'd then gone up. I rushed upstairs, afraid of not being late for that night gathering. Melanie had discretely opened her apartment's door for me.

"Hi Melie," I'd greeted, staring at her face. "You promised me to be good, what's this face, huh? You think…"

I hadn't been able to finish my words. Melanie had burst into more tears, mixing words with her sobbing. I hadn't understood a word.

"Oh, come on, Melie… it's not the end of the world," I'd uttered, taking my pullover off and intending to sit comfortably on the edge of her bed. "Women get pregnant every day and night… and what?"

Melanie had locked the door and made herself also comfortable on the bed, beside me. I'd wrapped my arm around her waist saying:

"How did you end up sleeping with him?" I'd started, patting her back this time. Melanie had stared at me as if seeing me for the first time, and fetching a deep sigh she'd replied:

"He was very tenacious, bombarding me with gifts and favors I couldn't resist. You know, I'm not doing well with money… and everything he did for me, I considered being a miracle in my life." Her lips had been trembling, her eyes shining.

"Hmmm!" I'd sounded.

"Well… his nonstop insistences bossed me around… and I ended up in his bed," she'd said with one breath.

"Oh, silly girl… silly, silly girl," I'd said, eyeing her shaking body. "How many times did you sleep with him?"

"?!"

"You don't know?"

"No. When I've moved in his second apartment, it has been the first time… then it has followed. I don't recall exactly how many times we have slept… perhaps many."

"Oh, you silly goose, he took advantage of your dumb innocence… as most men do." My last words had mingled with Melanie's burst of tears.

"Shhhhh! Melie… Melie, calm down. Please, calm down… it's all right. It's all right. It's not the first time you'll get pregnant."

"Yea… but, I'd be married then," the girl had yelled, hiding her face in her palms.

"Perhaps," I'd replied bluntly.

"He has abandoned me, Dee," she'd yelled again, as if seeing him in front of her eyes.

"No! I don't think so," I'd rushed to say

"Oh, yea… oh yea! I've seen her… I've seen both of them," Melanie had hysterically shouted, braking in tears again.

"Seen… who?"

"The new woman in his life… who else?" She'd gesticulated with her arms in the air.

I'd said nothing. The room had been quiet for a while, only Melanie's sobbing and grouching had been heard. Both of us were tense, upset. Then, throughout her sighs, I had heard: "I want desperately to have a child, but not in these circumstances." She had cried again, whimpering in her palms.

"Then get rid of it," I'd thrown. "What's such a big deal?"

"I can't," she'd replied, staring with curiosity at my placid face. I'd got the look.

"Why?" I'd questioned her with the same voice.

"I can't… I absolutely can't. I'm against abortion… I don't want to kill'm."

"Why?"

"I think it's a sin…" she had barely sounded as if being ashamed of what she had said.

"Yeah, but… circumstances like this are…"

"Please, Dee… I won't do it, believe me… no matter what." I hadn't intended giving in.

"Fine! Then?" I'd asked.

"Then what?" Melanie asked.

"If Don would decide not to come back to you… what in the world are you going to do with this child? This is not an answer, Mel… please, take my advice and do something till is time left. When is the last time you had your period?"

"I guess two month ago… or less."

"You're sure?" She had nodded. I'd etched a smile, encouraging her. She had pouted her lips, ready again to burst with tears. We had kept silence for a while, then suddenly asked:

"Did you tell Don?"

"No." She's answered curtly. Her eyes had been saturated with tears.

"No?" I had shrieked in disbelief.

Suddenly a sinister thought had crossed my mind: "This might be Paul's child, and this perfidious woman is hiding it from me." I shook with fear, as if wanting to get rid of a chimera off my mind, and abruptly asked:

"Have you only slept with Don, or with other men, too?"

Her looked had denounced a hurting soul. I had regretted my impelling force of placing my question, but hadn't apologized. I had been petrified at the thought of that child being Paul's, but I'd masked my fear. She'd smiled candidly saying:

"No, only with Don, Dee."

"Then tell'm." I'd said, with my heart free of suspicion.

"No… I'm not ready yet," she'd replied, looking me in the eyes.

"Do you want me to tell him? I can do it. He's my subordinate. Do you know it?"

"Yes. I know, but I prefer to be the one telling him this."

"O.K. as you wish… but, I can do it."

"No, thank you."

Thinking that my suggestions might be alien to her standards, I had refrained from going on with my 'what's best to do' advises. Her tear-stained face had still alleged her innocence. "Above all," I had said to myself, "she should take care of her pregnancy, not me." I'd turned toward her saying:

"I'll do something about this although, I prefer not to, Mel. I have an excellent idea, but give me a little time," I had said, getting up from the bed, ready to leave. "I need to go, Mel… I'm seeing some friends tonight. Wow! It's already late."

"What… whhhhat idea," she'd jumped, getting up also, while trying to get all from me. Her flowing tears mixed with her candid smile had animated her face. Out of the blue, a strange thought had lightened my mind: "Pills… pills," the voice had cried out.

"Pills," I had repeated louder, smiling at Melanie.

"What?"

"I said pills, they might help you out… it's not that late," I had made it plain.

My answer had anchored her to the spot. Her eyes full of tears had been questioning me. It had been obviously that I had aroused her suspicion. I had felt loosing good ground.

"Mel… it's O.K.! Believe me… it's O.K.! It is at very beginning of your pregnancy… pills or shots might help a great deal now. Think about that… pills might get your period flowing normally again. Don't you want that? I know you do. Now, I really have to go, Mel," I'd said, opening the door and getting out. I had turned my head and whispered, avoiding that way to be heard by Melie's neighbors.

"Oh, my goodness… how should I fix this impasse?" I'd questioned myself. "Well… tomorrow is another day… I'll think about something, but most important is not to let Paul find out."

Paul hadn't found out about Melanie's pregnancy from me, but from her. Hopeless and desperate as she had been, Melanie had called Paul, trying to get an advice from him.

"You did what?" I'd yelled into the phone's receiver when hearing her news — my blood boiling, my heart throbbing. "Gosh, Mel… why did you do that? What did you involved Paul into this? I can't help you now."

"What do you mean… why I involved him? He's my friend… he's still my friend, Dee." That had been the last thing I had wanted to hear. "He's mine, girl… he's mine and he is going to be mine forever," I'd said to myself, but continued to speak nicely to her, playing trifler in that matter, while moving the discussion deviously towards my contrivance.

"Yes… I know that, Mel… but… but you're not together anymore." In my furious attack I'd stuttered, and felt everything around me spinning. My thoughts had been ambushing my mind: "Gosh… they're together again after such an effort I made to keep them apart. I'm losing ground here," I'd thought, panicking, but still having enough vigor to question her more. "How can Paul help you with your pregnancy? Do you think is fair to let him take care of a situation that had been created by another man?"

"Well… I still see Paul as being my friend…"

"That's why you slept with his good friend? They're friends… you know that, Melie?"

"Not really… Don never told me that, " the girl had whispered.

"Well… I'm telling you now. They are longtime friends. I see them every day chatting in the corridors. Don didn't tell you, but perhaps he told Paul about your intimacy. Who knows?"

"Did he tell you?"

"Who?"

"Don."

"No, he didn't, but Paul seemed to know something, Melie." I'd lied.

"How do you know… did he say something?"

"Not specifically," I'd lied again, "but I sensed something."

"Really?"

"Really."

"Well… maybe I did the wrong thing by calling him, but I needed him with me in my pain, Dee." Her last words had made me ruffle her, but managed to control my temper, asking her calmly instead:

"To solve what, Mel?"

"Maybe nothing… but…"

"Don't you think you put yourself down by informing him of you sleeping with a man before getting married? He knows you as a girl with high moral standards."

"In fact, why you're making such a big fuss about this? Why are you so concerned about my secret being carried on to Paul? I can't understand it, Dee."

"Oh, my goodness! Don't misunderstand me, Mel, really. What I'm trying to say… is… that you're not being diplomatic. That's all! Don't involve the whole community in this problem. It's not wise, Melie. What I'm suggesting… and believe me, I'm being very honest with you… keep Paul out of this and concentrate instead on involving Don in it. Get him back into your arms, too."

"But, Dee… I want…"

"I know what you want to say, Melie, but just listen to me! You're not diplomatic, Mel… not at all. As I said before, keep Paul out of this and you'll see…"

"But, you don't understand… just let me… Dee, please let me… just one second…"

Actually, I had had no intention to let her continue. Nothing had interested me more than Paul not being involved, and I'd struggled hard to brainwash Melanie using that thought. Consequently, I'd interrupted her immediately, actually talking at the same time for a short while.

"O… o… o, no, Mel… I understand you perfectly. I understand you much better than you think. You don't understand me, " I'd snapped. "You don't see my support in this… perhaps never noticing my crying heart for you, Mel."

"Thank you," had murmured Melanie.

"Really, Mel… I get nothing for this, I only want to help you," I'd lied. "I like you, Mel, and I like you very much. I see you differently than any other girl, you're so sweet and gentle… I don't want you to ruin your life."

My own falsehood had been buzzing like a bazooka in my mind. For a moment the entire situation had seemed like a blind alley, particularly with Melanie's puerile bravura.

"Mel, the bottom line is… my help is sufficient to you. A situation like yours needs to be kept mostly as a sacred secret… and a secret is a secret. So keep it as such, Mel. Don't invite everybody into your life. Stop seeing Paul… stop seeing Don, if you wish, and concentrate instead on your problem only… and when you're free of this pregnancy, then sees whomever you want. There are plenty of other fish in the sea." Her taciturn mood had made me worry a little. "Melie do you understand what I'm saying?"

"Hmmm!"

"Now as I promised you, soon I'll bring those pills to you… please, Mel… make no mistake… this a very serious matter. We both can be in a very, very big trouble if you whisper a word. Understand?"

"I'm not so sure if I want this, Dee… is it…"

"Hold on, Mel… You just told me yesterday that you want the pills as soon as possible. Now you're changing your mind?"

"Do you already have them?"

"Almost," I'd lied.

"Then… O.K.! Bring them to me! I'll see after… I might…"

"Melie, you're acts are so unforeseeable. Do you want to try them or not?"

"O.K...O.K., bring them to me."

"Sure?"

"Sure!" Melanie had said, a little bit vexed by my persistence.

"Now be a good girl and say nothing to anyone. Be sure I am with you and I won't let you down, and remember... I'm doing this toward helping you. Bye now, Mel... see you soon!"

"O.K.! Bye! See you soon!"

"Hmmm!" I'd sounded, hanging up the phone. Help you... help! Hmmm! 'No one can sincerely help another without helping himself' — that known line had fitted perfectly with my controlling factor over Melanie's decision.

The will behind that, the determination to get Paul urgently as my husband and Melanie away from his side had made me sleep less and plot a lot. I'd visualized my life as being a chessboard and me the winning king. I'd played with the adversaries in front of that chessboard, spying like a tactful spider for the prey's next movements — although my final move had dazzled even myself.

"Whew!" I'd taken a deep breath. "I'm good... I'll succeed! Everything works together for the sake of my worthy goal." I'd laughed — hysterical laughter, full of contentment. Visualizing Melanie being pushed aside, my mind had gone farther, seeing myself climbing upward — with Paul being the ladder. "Melanie out... well, at least, I naturally displayed a passion in helping this girl with her accidental pregnancy. She should be appreciative... she should recognize my act of kindness."

Sitting on my sofa, I had let my thoughts flatter my soul and my eyes stare at Paul's face in the picture on the table. There had been a misery combined with mystery in my actions. Alongside the mystery and my maneuvers there had been a good side of mine, inherited from my mother — a docile soul. However, even this had been used to attain my goals. Melanie — I'd rushed to help her, impressed by her anguish, brought upon herself by her silly conduct, and also by her inability to solve it honorably. I would have not done it if she hadn't been in the way of my winning Paul's heart and name.

Paul's professionalism, sobriety and semblance had made him gain reputation and implicit good position and higher rank in society, and his dashing feat had perfectly coupled my burning desire. Consequently, I'd decided not to let any chance slip away. Melanie's pregnancy had come as a stump in my way. Therefore, I'd taken action. First, I'd called Paul.

Paul and I had been facing each other, both standing up in my office. It had been a foggy winter day. Our moods had matched the weather.

"Dee, please, don't hurt this girl," begged Paul, searching my eyes... "What does he mean?" I'd thought. "I hope that girl didn't tell him about the pills." I'd stared at his face. "I still have some kind of feelings for her," he'd added, his eyes pleading for my consideration.

"See, Paul... this part really frightens me," I'd shouted, snatching my arm out of his hand. "You still love her and define it as 'still feelings for her'.

"Don't be foolish, you know better that I love you... that I'm madly in love with you... that I can't live without you... and..."

"And that's why you're marring her soon, hah?" I stopped him.

"What?" Paul's wide eyes scared me.

"Well?"

"Who told you that?" Paul had jumped.

"Who told me that? Well, Melanie did... recently. Melanie, your fiancée... remember her?" My sarcasm hadn't moved him a bit. He'd calmly asked instead:

"Is that right?" He'd looked different with those bulge eyes and puzzled face. "Melanie, huh? How recently was that?"

"Not even a week ago, dear." He'd evidently disliked my gibe, though I had read it in his eyes.

"Not even a week ago... hmmm!" he'd repeated, thinking.

"Can you be more specific and... tell me the date?" Paul had insisted.

"What's that exactness, man?"

"I'm trying to figure out when, for crying out loud, have I possible set a 'soon date' for a marriage I haven't been sure of," he'd replied, looking me in the eyes. I had felt somehow an accomplice to that plot — my blood throbbing inside my cheeks and ears. Paul had scrutinized my face. I had smiled annoyed.

"But you'll get married, Paul... what else should I say? Besides, I don't think that girl would lie about such serious matter. Don't you agree?"

"Are you crazy? I haven't seen the girl for ages. You told me that she's seeing Don. Am I right?" I'd nodded. You're not seeing each other… you're the only one I date."

"Well…"

"She's impregnated by that guy, isn't she?"

"Yes… I guess," I'd replied.

"So… what do I have to do with this? It's over, Dee… over for ever."

"Really?"

I'd received no answer. His lack of words concerning the subject had inflected my determination of taking action — attacking, no matter the risk. Therefore, with the help of one of the caretakers from my previous job, I had contacted a middleman who had provided me with some ecstasy pills — well hidden in an envelope. I had kept them in a safe place for a few days until my next plan had been accomplished. Taking advantage of Paul's caring nature, I had faked being sick all those days. He had visited me every day, worrying about my health.

"I think I need a short vacation, Paul," I'd said one day. "I haven't been away for ages. I need my time out this stress."

"Well… take a few days off if this well put you on again," Paul had suggested.

"Yea… but you see I hate going alone anywhere. Since my divorce, I've never been out the town alone."

"I can't come with you, Dee, if that's you imply. See… I really can't."

"But Paul… I… can…"

"No, Dee. No! I can't! Believe me… I can't. Where do you want to go?"

"First, I didn't say I'll precisely go. Well… I don't know, Paul, perhaps Bahamas, or no… let see Las Vegas. Yeah! Yeah… Las Vegas. I really want to see the place. I've never been there. Please, Paul let's go there. If you don't come… I'll never go. I won't take any day off and for sure I'll get sicker and sicker. Look at my arms… look at my neck! See? Seeee how red they are?" Paul had examined them dumbly. "See? What does it tell you?

That… I'm very sick. Believe me, Paul, I'm very seriously ill and need to go out somewhere." Paul had said nothing. In fact, he hadn't been able. My intentionally, noisily yapping had had that purpose. So, what do you say?"

"O.K! But…"

"O.K. I'll by the tickets," I'd rushed to say.

"Ooooo… not that fast! I need to talk with my superior first."

"Do you want me to talk to him?" I'd dared. "He… likes me," I'd burst with laughter, which had also contaminated Paul. We both had laughed for a while.

"Yea… he likes you a little bit too much, I guess!" He'd replied, refraining to laugh. "No, please, Dee, leave it up to me!"

The following day we had had the tickets and the next Sunday, I had been on the airplane, with my head on Paul's shoulder, travelling to Las Vegas. Therefore, Paul had ended up accompanying me, and not only that, but he had paid for everything, including for a luxurious hotel right in the heart of Las Vegas. Two days prior our departure, while faking a visit to the pharmacy, I had sneaked inside Melanie's apartment and handed her a small medicine bottle full of ecstasy pills, together with instructions.

In Las Vegas, after two days and two nights of craziness, Paul had rushed with me to the nearest 'walk-in-chapel' where we got married 'á la minute'.

All my drafts and dreams had snapped one after the other, each of them conceived as planned. That had given me the courage to press for more luck. Consequently, I had called some of my acquaintances back in Detroit, including Don, bringing them the 'good news'. As I had always known, Don, hadn't been the type of person who would keep a secret for himself. Thus, I had intentionally told Don about our marriage, so he must convey it farther to Melie. She had indeed heard the news as expected, but not right away as I'd thought; one day before our triumphal return from Las Vegas. As I had found out from Don, Melanie had been more puzzled than upset when heard the news. Don had been saying that she'd kept saying: "I can't see the liaison… I really can't. I never assumed to see them together." I had played my role perfectly; she had never suspected a thing.

After my return, I had tried not seeing Melanie immediately. I had needed a little more time to work on my impressive, mawkish speech in order to make her believe my reason for marrying Paul. The speech had been all kept in my mind, including chilly examples and tearful 'granting pardon'.

More than three weeks had passed. Then, when I had considered myself prepared enough to face the girl, I had called her, having in mind the exact time and place where to meet her and make the news known. I had received no answer. The next day I had called her again, no answer that time either. I had persisted with that phone call a number of times, but not even her answering machine had been on. I had decided to wait two more weeks, though still calling from time to time, each time my concern increasing. "Is she secluding herself in some way," I had wondered. Seeing that I had been down on my luck and in the same time concerned about her pregnancy, I had decided to meet that challenge directly. I'd driven straight to her building, determined to wait hidden in my car, twiddling my thumbs until she would come home. Soon I had realized that I had been in fact facing a blind alley with my silly investigation. The entire situation had seemed to be under fire, though I had had a feeling of being responsible for what had been happening to Melanie. I had also felt under my own steam to solve everything wisely and with calm.

Deciding not to wait any longer, I had driven toward Wal-Mart and waited for her there. Something inside my soul — premonition perhaps — told me that I'd been about to get the shock of my life.

I hadn't had any shock though; I had waited there for a while — bored and tired — then decided to enter the store and talk with one of her colleagues.

"I'm sorry, Melanie didn't show up for a number of days already," had come her colleague's replay, staring at my wide eyes. "I heard she's sick and my boss said… that… she's…"

I couldn't hear her last words. "Gosh… something is going wrong," I had thought, rushing toward the exit. I had driven like a maniac back to her apartment. While in front of the door, I had mutilated the dumb doorbell, pressing and squeezing it all around. I had even called her name aloud many times, never minding manners. I had pressed my ear against the door, but I had heard no sound, only a tormenting silence. Even her little budgie had been silent, though he had always made a lot a noise when someone had been at the door. I'd called the bird's name: "Coco! Coco! Coco!" Silence.

On my way back home, frightened thoughts rolled up in my mind, imagining all the evil in the world. I hadn't eaten and avoided Paul's company. The same tormenting question tossed me over and over: "Should I tell Paul?" "No" my common senses dictated all the time. In spite of that command, I'd dared approaching him:

"Hon, have you seen Melanie recently?" I'd said, though trying not to weak up his vigilance.

"Melanie? Me? Dee... what's this now, Hon? Don't you remember? It's over... it had been over for a long time."

"O.K... O.K... just asked!" I'd nervously reply, avoiding looking at him. "It's nothing in particular... believe me. I've been to Wal-Mart a few times and she hasn't been there. Usually, she is there most of the time," I'd added in order to wipe out any bit of suspicion. In the same time, I'd rushed down in the basement, pretending to take our laundry down.

That night I had slept only two hours, and even they had been interrupted by frightening nightmares. After I had sat up in bed a number of times, I had finally given up sleeping, letting my mind go free with terrified thoughts and fixing solutions.

"What did that girl do with those pills? I told her zillion times how to use them. I don't think she's that ignorant, not knowing how to swallow a pill. Maybe she took them all intentionally. She took them on purpose... she killed herself. I hope it's not because of me marrying Paul. Oh, boy! How come I have such suspicion? She loved Don... not Paul. Paul is all mine. Yeah... but how about if they had secretly met ... and... who knows? Maybe the child was indeed Paul's. No! It can't be! She was madly in love with that coward... not with Paul. Yea, but Paul had been her first date. No! The man you sleep with the first time counts and fall in love, not with 'a date'. No, it wasn't Paul for sure. It was that sucker. Oh, Lord... oh, Lord! What a mess!" I tossed in the bed like an earthworm on the heated seashore. "How about if this is an accident... maybe she's in the hospital, very ill from those pills. I'll call all the hospitals in town tomorrow."

I'd got up and put my housecoat on my shoulders, and left the bedroom. "How about if she she's sick in who knows what house... and needs help? Well… in fact… this is her problem, not mine. She must deal with it. But… she's dying. Well… if she dies… she dies, and so what? She was in my way, anyway." I had tiptoed back in the bedroom and gently removed my pillow and lain flat on my sofa in our living room, avoiding exposing Paul to my anxiety. I had waited there with my eyes shut tight for a trace of rest. "She's for sure in trouble… and… I, too, might get in trouble because of her stupidity. But, I, in fact… intended to harm her, didn't I? So, why am I so frightened? Why am I tying myself in knots worrying about her? Her trouble is her trouble. I'm happily married with the man I wished… and that's all I want for the moment. That girl may go to hell if this she wishes. She has been in my way enough… and also idiot enough to believe that playboy who impregnated her first night she slept with him. Well… what should I expect? She's stupid… doesn't know enough to come in out of the rain… and no wonder she's pregnant.

I'd entered the kitchen and poured a glass of milk from the fridge, then tiptoed back to the sofa. Again, thoughts after thoughts had been buzzing in my mind. "Well… I've got this girl the red carpet treatment. I hope she'll appreciate it one day." I leant against the pillow. "But… how about if she misunderstood the use of those pills. Who cares? But, I might be in trouble. Huff! That's the last thing I needed. Hmmm! I'll tell Paul tomorrow. Oh, no… for crying out loud, I won't do it. Gosh! What a foolish idea!" I had jumped out the bed, pacing the room that time. "I'll better talk with Don about this… but, I'll not say a word about those pills…of course. But Paul might see us whispering. O.K! Let's see! Tomorrow morning I'll sneak near Don's desk, telling him I need to see him urgently. From my gravity of my voice and language of my eyes he'll understand the urgency. Well, he's an excellent improviser; he'll come up with a perfect excuse. This way I'll keep Paul out of the problem and I'll get what I want from that sucker."

The night had been compromised anyway. Thus, I had renounced the few minutes left for sleep. Then, I had dragged myself to the kitchen again and prepared an extremely quiet breakfast for two, making Paul perfectly unaware of my sleepless night. I hadn't mentioned anything to Paul — neither at home nor in the car. We had exchanged banalities; Paul had been too sleepy to entertain a discussion and I had been too frightened by Melanie's lack of vital signs to intend going through any other conversation.

At the office, I'd had a tough time tempering my anxiety attack. My only wish in that moment had been to seeing and talking with Don.

"Have you seen Don?" I'd dared asking one of my subalterns.

"No, ma'am. I haven't," the young man had answered back.

"Oh, my gosh... why is he so late?" I'd asked myself, staring at my watch.

"Have you seen Don?" I'd questioned a girl whose eyes had always spying on Don.

"Not this morning, Mrs. Turner," she'd replied.

"Hmmm!" I'd sounded. "Don... Don... where are you? I need you... and I need you now," I'd murmured entering my office, after I eyed for a while his empty desk.

Don had come very late that morning. I had been tormenting in my desk while waiting for him, and the whole incertitude had been playing me up. Although, I had pretended to work, busy with piles of papers, in reality I had only worried like crazy, my eyes watching the corridor where I had expected Don to walk in.

Suddenly, my office door had sprung opened. I'd jumped up the chair. Don had stormed inside, his lips trembling.

"Dee... Dee... Melanie's dead," he'd shouted, covering the mouth with his palms, tempering this way his burst of emotions. "Melanie is dead," he whispered, coming close to my desk.

"What?" I had yelled, rushing energetically to shut the door behind Don. In my despair, I had grabbed his arm, pulling him close to my chair, while staring duped at his morbid face. "Calm down a little... will you?" "Oh Dee! Oh... Dee... what a shock... what a misfortune. Oh, poor girl! I can't believe she's dead... oh... oh!"

I was stunned. My mind had dictated me to talk, but my lips hadn't move.

"Melie... dead... oh, my goodness! That's impossible! How that happened? When?"

"Drugs... she overdosed herself with drugs." His face turned red, with the veins around the neck visibly quivering.

"Drugs?" I'd shouted, exhibiting intentionally a petrified face.

"Drugs… Melie? No! It should be a big mistake here. Melanie is not the 'booze and drugs' type. Are you sure, Don… drugs?"

"I swear, Dee… that's exactly what they said," Don had explained, puffing.

"They?"

"Yeah… the police… the officers, well whatever…" He had bubbled.

"The police?" I'd blathered.

"Yes, Dee… the police… the investigators," Don had replied. He'd stopped for a moment, trying to read my emotion-stained face.

"Investigators… investigators…?" I'd repeated. "Don what's going on here? Why the investigators?" My heart had been on the edge of bursting out my chest. "Investigators… investigation? Oh, no! They might interrogate me next," a sick echo tormenting my mind.

"Dee, are you all right?" I had heard Don asking. "You're white like that wall."

"Never mind me! Oh, poor girl… Oh Melie! What have you done? What have you done with your life? Oh… such a candid soul. Don, are sure she's dead?"

"Come on, Dee… I just came from the police station. Why do you think I'm late this morning?"

"Well… I hoped it was a confusion of names or some thing like that. When did it happen?" My mind had already started to calculate the time I had given her the pills with the time returning from Las Vegas.

"I don't know when it exactly happened… they didn't tell me, but there must be quiet a time, I guess. They investigated a good number of people she knew… perhaps they'll ask Paul about her, too, maybe you… who knows?"

"Paul?" I'd jumped. "Me… for what? No! They won't"

"Why not?"

"Why Paul, Don?"

"Why me, Dee?" It had revolted Don. "Paul had been her boyfriend, too… hadn't him?"

"Unfortunately!" My word had slipped uncontrollably out my mouth, unmasking for a moment my discontent — maybe jealousy. Don had caught that.

"What did the police say?" I had changed the subject.

"They said that she abused drugs and that she…"

"What kind?" I'd interrupted him.

"Ecstasy… I guess, and she…" Don had said. "Ecstasy… ecstasy… ecs… ta…" The echo had screamed in my ears.

"Ecstasy?" I'd bubbled, eyeing Don. I had felt the room spinning around me. I'd managed to drag myself near my chair, not realizing when I had dropped my body in it. "Ecstasy… ecstasy…" I had kept gibbering. "I killed her… I killed the girl," I'd repeated to myself, panicking and staring desultorily. "I killed her… she trusted me, and I stabbed her in the back… I killed her…"

Don had been rummaging through my desk drawer, perhaps looking for something, his face full of fear.

"Dee, I think you need some water… where's that dumb mug?"

"Oh, Don… never mind… sit down there! I'm O.K. now. Ecstasy, you're saying, huh? Hm!"

"Yes! Ecstasy… they found a bottle with some left over pills… and asked me about her lifestyle. They even mentioned about her epilepsy that she…"

"Epilepsy?" I'd shouted terrified. "Epilepsy… since when? Oh, Don… she was…"

"Yeah, she was epileptic… and some kind of heart malformation… or something similar… I don't know, Dee… all that medical terms and…"

"Heart malformation? Wow! I never knew she was epileptic. Did you know?" Don had nodded.

"Yes, I knew. The last time we've been together… you know what… she was so excited… and bang! An epilepsy attack." He had stopped, staring at my widened eyes. "That was the last time I saw her. Honestly, Dee, I am scared of those sorts of things. I recognize… I'm an ignorant in the field. But that's me…"

"Oh, poor Mel!"

"I know… I know, but…" Don had shown signs of compassion. "I know she suffered a lot… and perhaps cried her heart out to you, but I can't put her down. I have always respected her. She seemed to be different than any girl I have ever met, but her illness and all staff scared me. I really don't know how to handle such situation and…"

"Stop excuse yourself now… it's your problem… really, Don. Well it's too late anyway. Let's see how we might help her…"

"Help her?" Don had jumped as if burned. "Dee… the girl is dead… dead. We can't help her now… God have pity on her soul!"

"I know … she's dead, but we were her best friends… remember? Friends in moments like these are needed. Besides we…"

The door had largely opened. Paul had majestically entered the office. "Ahhhha! You're chirruping, hah?" He'd kidded. I'd said nothing, so did Don. "Hey… what's this mystery? You guys have secrets? May I intrude?"

Silence again. Paul had bewildered, staring at our faces, pulling a chair and making himself comfortable.

"Melanie… dear… she's dead," I'd braved.

"Whhhhat?" He'd wheezed, eyeing both of us; his look reading our distressed faces. "Are you serious… who… who told you that?"

"Don," I'd rushed to answer, pointing with my eyes in Don's direction.

"Who told you that, man?" Paul had asked Don.

"The police," Had replied Don, his face read and eyes bulging.

"The poooolice?" Paul had queried, frowning at Don. "How come?"

"Yea… the police. The interrogated me this morning… I spent three or four hours there."

"Interrogated for what… man?"

"Her death… I guess," Don's nervous voice had obviously raised Paul's suspicion.

"Don, can you be a little more clear? You guys are keeping something from me, can you…"

"Drugs, dear… drugs," I had interrupted Paul, trying to ease Don's bewilderment. "Yes, she was found dead… overdosed by ecstasy. At least that's what the police told Don."

"Ecstasy? Come on guys… what's that ecstasy?" Don and I had stared dumbly at each other, then at Paul. "I don't think… you guys intend going through with this ridiculous idea."

"Well… Paul, is hard to believe, isn't it?" I'd dared. "I think those officers don't have any reason to lie, huh?"

"Wow! Melanie… dead… drugs… wow!" Paul had shook his head. "I can't believe this. Sorry, but I pure and simple can't swallow it. What kind… anyway?"

"Ecstasy," we both Don and I had jumped to answer. "We just told you before, " I'd added.

"Ecstasy… ecstasy… yeah, yeah! Ecstasy for what?"

"Come on, Paul, all people in this town know about ecstasy… all the country… and even the world, and you don't know?" Don had said, staring Paul's puzzled face. "It boosts you up… what else? Hey, don't look at me like that. I never use this stuff. I know I'm a bad boy, but not that bad."

Paul's face had been pale and worried. I hadn't liked that look.

"Wow… Melie dead… I can't believe. Poor Mel!" Paul's words had cut my heart. Some kind of jealousy had surfaced again. Thanks God! She's out of scene," I'd thought, but said instead:

"Oh, poor girl… I suffer so much. Who could believe such a candid face vanishing by abusing drugs? Did you sense something strange in her behaviour, hon, when you were together?" I'd asked Paul, smiling agitated, though a little chaffed.

"Melieeee? No, never," he'd replied.

"Don said that he knew she was epileptic," I'd continued. "Did you know it?"

"Yes," had calmly answered Paul.

"And you never told me this… hon," I'd reproached. "Tell you what?" Paul had suddenly asked.

"That she's an epileptic."

"Why was it so important for you to know?" His irritated tone of voice had chafed me.

"Yep!" I'd popped. Paul had known well what that popping sound meant.

"Hon… forgive me, but there are some…"

"Never mind, Paul. I'm not upset. Let's move on with our discussion," I'd said, ignoring Paul's pleading look and Don's uncomfortable mood. "As I told Don before you came in, the three of us should do something for this girl. What do you say?"

"Hmmm!" had sounded Paul, his eyes questioning Don.

"No... Dee, please! No! Keep me out of this," had broken in Don. "I don't need those officers messing with my life again. Keep me out of this business... will you?"

Paul had been unusually calm, staring placidly at Don and I quarrelling. Then, he looked at me as if waiting for an answer.

"A wreath... a card perhaps?" I'd suggested Paul, never-minding Don's bubbling sounds.

"No! Dee... really my answer is 'no'," Don had interceded again. "She's dead... God bless her soul. She won't know if we give her flowers or cards, but the police might nose around us. Do you guys need such trouble?"

"Don you're annoying me. In fact, what are you afraid of?" Paul had jumped this time.

"Nothing... nothing! I swear to God... nothing," he'd bubbled, staring at Paul's and my puzzled faces. "Perhaps those guys at the police station... scared me... Anyway, you guys don't know how thorough those officers are with stuff like that."

"Maybe Don's right, Hon... we should stay out of things like this and..."

"Besides," interrupted Don, "maybe she's buried already... who knows? She was..."

"By the way, when did she die?" had asked Paul. "Do you, guys know?"

"I don't know, perhaps not recently..." had replied Don. My mind had immediately started to calculate the time I had given her the pills with the time I had heard about her death. "Perhaps three weeks," I'd pondered.

"Two, three weeks," I'd heard Don saying.

Suddenly, all my thoughts had pointed towards my precipitation of the scary reality — "I killed her," had been my predominant tormenting thought. "I killed her," I'd kept repeating, thinking also that I could have nowhere that reality been more frighten. The 'I killed her' verdict had been built on my own inner tension, born from the struggle of the truth and false thoughts — guilty or not guilty sentence. "Guilty", one side of mine had thundered. "You knew well that ecstasy and pregnancy don't match. So you gave it to her anyway... killer!"

"Not guilty!", the other side of mine had fought back. "No… is not pregnancy that killed her. Epilepsy killed her. How in the world was I to know she was epileptic? She's a killer, not I."

Don's constant excuses and Paul's 'hms' and 'wow' had hushed up my thoughts. I'd stared for a short while at both of them and then, calmly said:

"You guys… you know she was pregnant, huh?" The two men had gazed at each other. "Pregnant?" They both had uttered in the same time. I'd caught their look, and I hadn't minded Don's, but Paul's had raised my jealousy. He had known very well that Melanie had been pregnant. She had told him, and we had discussed about that sometimes. "Why is he faking?" I had pondered.

"Yes, pregnant," I'd calmly replied. "Now… it depends who the father was," I'd added, staring at Paul.

"Not me for sure, Hon," blurted Paul.

"Come on, Dee, don't look at me like that. I haven't slept with her for ages. No! It's not I, for sure. Did she tell you who the guy was?"

"No," I'd lied, piercing Paul with my eyes.

"Well… then…" Don had sounded, but nobody had paid any attention to him.

Paul had been plunged into his thoughts, and that had been troubling me a lot.

"Guys, if you don't mind… I would like to finish some work," I'd lied again.

Both men had gone out. I had heard them whispering in the hallway for a while.

"Wow!" I'd sighed, while alone in my office. "That's something! What a shook for them!" I had said while meticulously organizing a pile of papers on my desk; the hands working without my brain's command. "Well… Mel is out our life. There hadn't been room for three of us anyway". Then paused. "Now, I have to be calm and in control of this situation. I have to handle it wisely," I'd advised myself, already lining up an invisible chain of plans linked to my next move.

"My gosh!" I'd startled. "The officers… I forgot about them. If that silly girl left something there… they're sniffing me out for sure." I'd stopped piling for a while, thinking. "Oh, my… what am I going to do? I can't go to her apartment. That's for sure! Perhaps there's nothing there anymore… maybe it's rented already. What can I do? They might have my fingerprints on something. Let see! I gave her the bottle well wrapped, didn't I? I remembered carefully throwing the wrapping away. I never touched the bottled. She did. But… wait a minute! Did I get rid of the paper? Yes… No. No! my goodness… it's still in my car. I'll get there right now and destroy it. Gosh! I should do it now. If they investigated Don, perhaps the next person is me. No! I won't do it right now. I'll do it at lunch. I'll pretend to eat out somewhere… I'll avoid suspicious looks that way." I had moved back in my chair, continuing with my plans. "Let's not panic! Panic raises suspicions. One step at the time," I said, eyeing Melanie's smiling face, portrayed in the picture that Don had left for me on my desk.

"You foolish girl, you spoiled everything," I had talked with her silent face. I wonder how come your big nose couldn't smell danger there?" Her piercing eyes had been staring at me from that crumpled photograph.

CHAPTER 21

BUOYED BY FALSE HOPE

Day after day had passed. My mind had bathed thoughts of tormenting fear and plans of escaping 'pure as a lamb' from the incriminating situation.

My body had showed up to the office, and back home in Paul's arms, but not my mind and heart. Melanie had persisted to be the hub of my attention, and she would have perhaps been Paul's too, if not for my perspicacity of washing his brain of all the memories linked to her. Probably, the closest anyone had ever been to Melanie's sudden desperation and also disappearance had been I — the jealous and ambitious friend.

Nevertheless, my plans had budded, flourishing under my strict control and watch. There had been no doubt about that, and I had never left a trace with my actions. Naturally, with the help of the unvigilant and inexperienced investigators, I had been able to blind all conclusive facts. I had let Melanie's case end as an undesirable accident, though my hand had been all over it. Yet, for me, it had been interesting to speculate those officers' weakness. In all fairness, I had been wishing — and to some extend assuming — that my involvement in her death had been minimal. There had been people — Paul one of them — questioning if it had been indeed Melanie's decision to kill herself. "Why not?" I'd combatted him. "Maybe she thought that epilepsy and pregnancy don't match… and perhaps decided to end her misery that way. Don told me that he couldn't get intimate with her because of her epilepsy attacks. Who knows? Maybe she had it, and saw this as an impediment to have a normal life… marriage and kids… intimate relations with a man. Nobody knows what was in her mind in that desperate moments?" I had forced my thought into Paul's mind. It had worked.

My interest in denigrating Melanie had grown more — much more — coming to the point where I, myself had believed my own lies. Ironically, the indicators of the naked truth had narrowed — Melanie's reputation had been disparaged — very denigrated, I must admit — while my name praised. Even Paul had been impressed with my dedication put into that occurrence. Her act had been finally seen as a deliberate action not as an accidental one.

Basically, she had ended up dead. In my few moments of sincerity, I had recognized that deep down I had wished in my soul for her death to happen. My deceitful struggle to take Melanie's side had brought up Paul's even much stronger love for me and Don's fearful obedience. Don had been under suspicion for a long time and he had needed Paul's and my reputation to clear his name up.

Time had passed and Melanie slowly had vanished out my mind and plans. Paul had had promises to be transferred to an even higher position and I had worked things around so I, too, moved with him. I had felt us spin upward toward that elite platform and had no words to describe my well being. I had been more beautiful than ever — gorgeous in all descriptions — intelligent, successful, praised and courted by the most influential men. I was in heaven, picking the most gorgeous fruits and manna. We had changed two houses until we had established ourselves into an impressive mansion that I had decorated with the most expensive furniture and things. Michael and Daniel, our kids had come into our lives at the perfectly programmed time. We had represented the perfect American family — handsome, prosperous and noble. Suspicion and gossips had poured towards us, but I had walked over all hostile necks, triumphing at the end.

One day, entering incognito into Paul's office, I had found him staring through the window. I had stood up at the door, facing his back. He had had no intention to turn, continuing instead to look through the window.

"When I first met Melanie," he had started, "I thought I had seen the most gentle, innocent being of this world... and all her acts and thoughts proved her that way. What happened to her... then?"

"Oh, Hon, don't chuck that old crap around. People change. Besides, I thought we had closed that case forever... we still have so many things to achieve in our lives. Daniel is sick," I had abruptly changed the subject, trying to remind Paul that way that he belonged to me, to my family. "His babysitter took him home." Paul had looked indifferent. That had irritated me. "Paul... Daniel is sick."

"I heard you," Paul had finally said. "I know you'll take good care of him. I spoke with his teacher... it seems to be only a flu. This time of year..."

"O.K. Paul! If you're not interested in Daniel's illness and ... want to talk about Melanie instead, then let's talk! I know that hurts you... but she had been a loser all her life. She couldn't finish any class she had started... she couldn't keep any boy friend she had ever had... she..." Paul hadn't spoken a word. He had continued staring through the window. I had taken advantage of his placidity and continued: "Yes, people do change. My mother had always upheld that, saying that I had become an American coquette out of an innocent Russian girl." Although I had waited for his reply, Paul had said nothing. He had continued looking undisturbed through the window. "Well... Melanie had been an innocent, pure soul... all right, at her birth perhaps and later in her youths, but her doomed acts count now..."

Silence. I had waited a few seconds, then continued: "Maybe she had been hiding a darker side. A side you had never known... maybe she had suffered a paranoia besides her epilepsy, maybe..." Paul had suddenly turned around. His piercing look had invited me to shut up, but I hadn't. "Well... I know... it's not easy, but, Paul you must be realistic. She had lived with a man like Don... you know...while still unmarried. This is not innocence, is it? Then, she had been messing around with punks, perhaps shooting ecstasy with them. This is not innocence, either. Sleeping with a man before marriage... means concubinage. Concubines carry many nicknames, too. Drug addicts also are badly called. Yes, Melanie had been an innocent baby when born, but later... dear... Anyway there is some good time since she had died, let her rest in peace. Will you?"

I had left his office triumphant as always, satisfied once more that 'that woman' had been out my life forever.

CHAPTER 22

THE TWO 'I'S CONVERGE

While still moving along with that weird crowd, roaming inside the nihility I realized that the part with Melanie' story was purposely lengthily and deliberately replayed. Each aspect of that part was accurately exposed as had happened in reality. I knew for sure that 'Who' ever uncovered all these strange depictions in my eyes, mind, or what ever part of my body, disclosed right there into that 'nowhere', did that expressly for me and for me only. The more I was advancing, the better I understood that the crowd witnessed nothing of what I witnessed. I looked attentively once more at the people roaming beside me. I tried to get an answer while reading their mimics of their faces.

"No… no… I am sure they know nothing about Paul, Melanie or even Don. No they don't," I said gazing at their faces. "Who knows? Maybe they are witnessing their own life… their last judgement." I thought. "Did you see Paul?" I asked the young woman pacing beside me. "He's my husband," I continued, ignoring the fact that she paid no attention to me. "I have two children with him… both boys… I am looking for them… I can't find them… they are not here in this eerie place. By the way, where are we… what is this place called, do you know? What's the meaning of this place… where are we heading… I see no horizon line? I had no answer. I stared at her face over and over, hoping for an answer. "No… she doesn't see me. Perhaps she is witnessing her own life… maybe this is the rule over here. I am witnessing my own life, too."

Still gazing at those strange faces, I suddenly relived once more one of the unforgettable scenes that had happened during my marriage to Paul. He was staring through the window. To my horror, I found myself repeating absolutely the same dialogue and mimicking the same gesture, only my thoughts were different now than the ones I had had at that moment when the scene had really happened. I became an actress playing a character's role. Two people in the same body: one, a still-jealous wife, competing for the first place in life, and the other one, the wife, dominated by fear and humiliation, while wandering around strange worlds. The scene started to unfold the same like a movie. Paul came first in my sight. My first impulse was to yell at him, warning him about my 'peculiar transmutation', but I couldn't. I was forced instead to carry out the same play. I wanted to embrace his back, crying out to him about my strange wandering into another world, but I couldn't. I felt like I was in an immense, transparent womb, yelling and scratching to get out. I wanted to scream, shouting: "Paul get me out of this misery… take me home to our kids." I couldn't do that either. Something or somebody pushed me to repeat those words that once I had said, and I restated: "This is not innocence, is it? Then, she had been messing around with punks, perhaps shooting with them ecstasy. This is not innocence, either. Sleeping with a man before marriage… means concubinage. Concubines carry many of those nicknames, too. Drug addicts also are badly called. Yes, Melanie had been an innocent baby when born, but later… dear…"

That Paul, who was portrayed there for me, looked stunned. 'I' the wife shook her head and went out his office triumphantly. I followed her, but to my shocking surprise, Melanie was waiting for me outside in the hallway, right in front of the door of Paul's office. I was horrified. The building, its offices, including Paul's and everything around suddenly vanished, swallowed by a mysterious striking light. Melanie was in center of that light. It didn't take me much to realize that, I was in fact still part of the same bizarre crowd, and that Melanie had perhaps never left the scene. "Melanie Dupont! This woman still here… torturing me?" I challenged. "Was she waiting for my reappearance? Why? What does she want from me? What do you want from me, Melie?" Silence. I only heard the crowd's humming sounds. "Are you here to take me with you? Why?" I eyed, panicking at the crowd. I was convinced like never that that sightless audience — lurking court — has been always there during my tribulation, trailing my culpability. They paced placidly ahead. "They care less about me," I bubbled. They seemed to look at Melanie instead. I wasn't sure. I stared at the young woman, pacing close to me. Do you look at that woman, ma'am?" I dared, looking the young woman in her face. No answer heard. "Do you see her?" Silence. I turned around, grabbing an old woman by her arm. "Why are you staring at that woman? Are you indeed staring at her, ma'am?" She didn't say a word. One side of me tried to convince me that the woman was staring at Melanie, while the other side convinced me that they all looked, in fact, ahead through Melanie's body.

I had no options. I was forced to endure there, but I kept my dignity, refusing to beg Melanie for forgiveness and not speaking out, though my eyes continued watching her moves. She was levitating above the same floating bits of dust. Her entire body intensified its glowing until it came to the point of blinding me. I felt its warm touch. I yelled, trying to back down. I even tried hiding, though moving backward against the lines formed by that crowd. Their bodies interpenetrated, passing ahead one by one through my body. Melanie, too, passed through their bodies, following me with each of my moves. Seeing her passing through those human lines, I had the same sensation as seeing the moon passing through the clouds.

"Melie... stop... please, Mel, don't follow me! Leave me alone, Melie... noooo! Stop! No! Noooo! Ah! Ah! Somebody get me out of here! Melie, please leave me alone... please, please!" Her body almost pierced me, her face close to mine. "Go away, Melie... let me go! Let me go... you ghost!" Her nose touched my nose and felt her gasp — a warm, musty breath. "Melie... no, please no! Nooooo! Get away from me! Ahhhhhhhhhhhh!" I howled hysterically, grasping and elbowing around people, trying to escape Melanie and the crowd.

"Glug! Glug! Glug!" A sinister sound was chafing my ears. I raised my arms trying to cover my ears. I could move only one arm, the other one I felt being kept still. "Ah!" I screamed. Far away, coming from a long distance some stifling voices came to my ears. Then: "Glug... glug...

glug", followed by soft ringing sounds and "Snip... snip... snip!" cutting sounds. I tried to turn around, but my body felt heavy, like tones of dust. I tried again — the same feelings. Melanie's face almost fused with mine. I wanted to scream, but couldn't do that either. I was unable to breathe. I coughed instead, and felt better. Melanie's face and wide opened eyes scared me. I felt a few rows of those strange bodies passing through me, but Melanie stayed almost stuck on my body. Again, that musty breath warmed my face. Horrified by the moment, and thinking that she was almost entering my body, I screamed as loud as my lungs permitted: "Melie... please don't steal my body... please... please... go... go away! Go! Don't steal my body! It's mine... go away!"

"Hon... Honey, dear, please wake up! Dee! Dee! Wake up, Dee!" A familiar voice irked my ears. I forced my eyes to see clearly.

"Mrs. Turner... Mrs. Turner... Dee! Wake up! Wake up... can you hear me?" A strange voice, this time, thundered in my ear. I felt that the voice's sounds invading each cell of my brain. I still felt Melanie's face covering my face. Her nose touched mine, and then something like a metal was penetrating my ear. I had no pain. I tried to move away, but I felt a hand holding me down. I screamed again, thinking that it was Melanie's hand, trying to push and enter my chest.

"Open your eyes!" the same strong voice ordered. "Mrs. Turner, open your eyes!" I tried to open my eyes, and succeeded a bit. Slowly, Melanie's lit up face faded, taking more fleshly appearance now.

"Shhhh!" A voice whispered in the background. Thank Heavens... she's moving now. Let her wake up by herself. Don't force her!"

"Babooom! Babooom!" My heart was pumping into my ears. I tried again to open my eyes, though the entire time since that inexplicable ordeal has come upon me I have been sure that my eyes were wide opened — seeing everything around me. Things around me started to take shape, helping me to make sense of the surrounding. The crowd vanished away completely, taking with it its bizarre look. Melanie's face also vanished.

"Mrs. Turner, can you hear me?" came the same strong voice, pitching my ears. "Well... her blood pressure is stable now," he also said, softer now.

"Ahhhhhh!" I squealed and instantly came nose to nose with Paul. "Paul," I whispered, kissing his lips. "It's you, not Melie?" My question puzzled everybody around me, including Paul who immediately moved away from my bed, whispering with a man dressed all in white. "Oh… Dr. Sorensen! Why Dr. Sorensen here? Where am I?" I panicked. "Gosh… hospital bed? Why in the hospital?"

I looked at Dr. Sorensen for a while and then asked trembling:

"Doc, am I alive or dead?" He stared puzzled at me, so did Paul and the young nurse beside him. The man came closer, bending over my bed. I felt his breath. It was the same musty breath, felt before. Paul, too, rushed to lean over my bed. He took my hand in his. I felt my hand extremely heavy. The other hand was hooked to a medical device. The doctor whispered something in Paul's ear. Paul immediately moved aside, letting the doctor taking over his spot.

"Dee," Dr. Sorensen started, "you are very alive. You had a serious seizure, and we don't know its cause". Paul and the young nurse nodded both in the same time. I stared at the three.

"Why? Since when?" I puzzled.

"We don't know yet," whispered Paul, trying to get close to me, "but I found you this morning unconscious, when I came in your room. What did you take last night?" He rushed to ask.

"Nothing. I always take Excedrin for my migraines, but I didn't take any last night."

"Are you sure?" asked the doctor.

"Very sure.". The three gazed at each other. I didn't like their look. "I remember, wanting to take something, but I had nothing in the house." I stopped, and then added: "No, Doc, I am positive, I took absolutely nothing. I'm even recalling, eating a tuna sandwich and an apple. That's it." I paused again and after a short breath, continued: "We all ate tuna sandwiches… and even apples." Paul nodded.

The three people looked perplexed. I said nothing further. I just stared at them, as they were whispering. I felt like acting that way, I was preserving my dignity. Suddenly, I begged Paul:

"Take me home!" People around me looked even more bewildered. Paul snatched a glance at Dr. Sorensen, the nurse, too. Dr. Sorensen shook his head.

"Why not," I dared with a very frail voice, understanding immediately his 'no' answer.

"Well… the cat-scan shows nothing wrong, but after such a serious seizure, Dee… I don't want to take chances. I'd like to investigate it more." The doctor said.

"Serious seizure," I repeated, wondering.

"An unusual migraine type seizure… I should say," clarified Dr. Sorensen, smiling.

"Why?" I questioned him.

"We don't know yet, but a few more days of tests would clear up this mystery." He smiled again — a benevolent smile anyway.

"But I want to go home, Doc… I need my kids with me, please Doc, let me go home." And immediately turned to Paul, begging: "Please, Hon, bring the kids here… I missed them badly during my entire tribulation." All of them with me in the room gawked stupidly, evidently not knowing what to believe about my words.

"What tribulation, dear?" dared Paul.

"Nothing," I answered, understanding the idiotic situation I put myself into. "Please, Doc, let me go home to my kids," I insisted. Dr. Sorensen looked down. Finally, my stubborn insistence won. I was let home, but not that afternoon, the following morning with my promise that I'd return to the hospital for each prescribed medical test. Right after my revival, I was hardly able to talk, feeling my lips heavy as lead. Later on, everything went normally, amazing everybody around. Doctors and nurses went in and out of my room, and finally Paul left to bring my kids in. The nurses urged me to sleep, but I was afraid to do so, dreading a new coma-type state.

The scene seeing my kids, Daniel and Michael, was hard to describe. I felt like I was holding them for the first time in my arms, exactly the same feeling as when they had been born. Daniel ran, hugging me. I kissed his cheeks with passion and then asked:

"How is your flu?"

"Flu?" He baffled, staring at Paul. "I didn't have a flu, Mom." I immediately knew I goofed again. Paul's suspicious look made me feel forlorn.

After spending a few more minutes with them — hugging and kissing and kissing and hugging them — Paul took them home, promising me that he'd get back to me as fast as possible, and he did. While in my room, he tried his hardest to convince me to stay a few more days in the hospital.

"I'll bring the kids every day to you," he promised.

"Come on, Paul, is nothing wrong with me. I want to go home."

"How do you know?" He asked moving like a rustle all around my bed, tidying things up.

"Sit down, Paul, you're annoying me!" He immediately sat down, obeying like a grade-school student who seeks his teacher's favor. "I want you to pay careful attention to what I am going to tell you. I am not sick, and know that perfectly well. Don't smirk Paul! I am not crazy. Believe it or not, this ordeal was meant to happen to me."

"Ordeal?" I stared into his eyes, not knowing what to believe. He couldn't speak a word, and I didn't give him time to clear up his perplexity. I immediately came up with the whole story.

"Hon, please believe me. I wanted to wait until we get home, but I can't hold it any longer. I must share everything with somebody... and who is closer to me than you? I'm glad we are here by ourselves, so we can talk." Paul moved in his chair. "I want to warn you, dear, that what you are about to hear might scare you." Again, I didn't give him time to react. I continued uninterrupted: "Hon... now, just hear this! I think I was a guest in my own mind... and..."

"Please, Hon, stay here a little longer," interrupted Paul, shifting in his chair. His lack of understanding me made me furious.

"Hon... Hon... I... am... not... sick. Look into my eyes. I am perfectly normal. What was happening to me while — as you said — being in a coma is frightening. I need to get it out, Paul. Please, Hon, help me... listen to me! You're my husband - for crying out loud - bear with me. You are my husband for better and for worse... show it now. Even if I am sick, as you think, let me get every thing out, so as to find a cure. Oh, Paul, how little I know you."

"Hon... some things you're saying don't make sense. You said something strange in front of the doctor and that nurse, later to Daniel and... all this weird stuff to me now. Maybe, you took some tough medication, which you don't remember now and... Bang! All this cuckoo stuff." My tears stopped Paul's burst of explanation. "Hon, please, stay a little longer in this hospital. Let the doctors find out more about this strange seizure. I love you and I don't want something wrong to happen to you. You and our kids are the center of my life. My life doesn't have any meaning without either one of you. Didn't you learn this already, my Love? Please, let the doctors check seriously into this."

"Paul, I am not crazy and I am not sick! Don't stare and don't smirk like that!" I cried. "I am perfectly normal... normal than ever. As I said before, what happened to me is strange. Believe me, I understand you. If I were in your shoes, I might react the same way as you are reacting right now." We were both silent for a short while. I cried softly. He caressed and then kissed my hand.

"Paul, I killed Melanie," I suddenly whispered, staring at the door in the same time.

"You did what?" Paul chaffed, visibly vexed. "Boy, Dee... you're very sick. How do they call that illness that makes people incriminate themselves for something they assume..."

"Paul... Paul... Paul stop! Shut up and listen! I killed Melanie. I gave her that ecstasy... look here... with these hands." Paul grinned. He was evidently unable to believe me. I continued anyway. "I knew she was pregnant. I went to her house, trying to comfort her, lying to you and saying that I had to go to the pharmacy. Later, with the help of a middleman I procured the pills from a bad guy." Paul started to pay more attention. He looked down and asked:

"Are you serious? Please, Dee... don't push it!"

"Yes, Paul, I am very serious in everything I am saying. I can give you tons of details, so you can put them head to head and see if they match... or if I am imagining this or telling the truth." I looked at his puzzled face, adding: "Oh gosh, I must have done a good job trying to convince you at that time of my innocence in her death. That's why it's so hard for me to convince you now of the reverse. Can you believe me Paul? Can you, Hon?"

"I don't know, Dee, I really don't. I am still afraid you're making this all up because of that seizure you had. I am sorry, but I can't see you messing with those punks to get whatever... and... kill... Come on, Dee! You are going too far with these things. It's dangerous, also. You'd better wait a few days, take the medication Dr. Sorensen prescribed and then see if you have the same visions."

"Oh, Paul... oh, Paul! You have no idea how much pain you're inflicting in my heart. Man, believe me, I killed that girl."

"O.K... fine! You killed Melanie, but how in the world you killed her with some pills, which I am not even sure if they were indeed ecstasy or whatever?"

"Do you have another definition for my act? I knew she was pregnant... I told the middleman about it... and he warned me there is a possibility of death. I answered him that I didn't care... and I didn't really care. On the contrary, one side of me wished that to happen. And when it did happen, I thrilled, having little or no remorse at all." Paul listened quietly, his face red and eyes wide. "I saw Melie there," I continued. Paul burst suddenly with laughter. His burst made me furious. "Paul, I saw Melanie there. I don't care if you believe me or not. She was there... she was there. I saw her there with my own eyes."

"O.K., Hon, I must go home now. Get well and we'll continue this at home," he said rising from his chair, ready to leave.

"Sit down, Paul, I need you to stay a little longer with me. Sit down, please!"

He looked miserable. The first part of my effort to alienate his misery failed. On the other hand, to estimate my own risk, I needed to clarify Paul's position first. The bad thing about it was the fact that I didn't have much time to plan ahead, as I had always done. I continued to tell Paul about my bizarre encounter, vividly detailing each of my footsteps during the ordeal. To my surprise, the more I explained, the more I realized that Paul's mind wasn't there. His look seemed to display sorrow for my 'new illness' than sympathy for my misfortune of being thrown into a bizarre word. He even became blasé at one point, albeit feeling foolish. He stopped me a number of times, staring surreptitiously at the door.

"Shhh!" He warned. "Don't let everyone hear this craziness." I bridled with indignation at his peculiar reaction and lack of consideration.

"Did you see my mother there?" He suddenly interrupted me. I didn't know how to interpret his question — sarcasm or little bit of credence.

"Are you serious? " I asked suspiciously, eyeing his smiling face.

"Yes... very serious," he answered, smiling again, evidently trying to get my confidence.

"No, Paul... I saw none of our loved ones, only strange figures... and none of them seemed to notice me there. They looked normal... bones... flesh, eyes, legs... normal human beings as seen every where around us, here on this earth... but..."

"Gosh, Hon! I can't believe you're saying this stuff..." Paul laughed.

"Paul... Paul... Listen to me!" My burst of enthusiasm made me spring up from my bed. Paul gently pushed me down.

"Hon, don't get up... you need rest."

"But Paul... I'm so moved... so frighten in the same time. Hon, believe me, I've seen everything perfectly like I'm seen things around right now. As I'm seeing you right now. And believe me, I saw you there..."

"Me? What... where?" He laughed again.

"Yes, Paul, I saw you there a little younger, though. I saw John and spent time with that viper, Mrs. O'Neil in her bedroom.'

"What?" Shouted Paul, sketching a cunning smile.

"Hon, believe me, please! I relived my life exactly as I had lived years and years before." Paul looked giddy. Obviously, he didn't know what to believe. "I even saw myself as little girl, leaving Russia with my parents." The same enthusiasm made my get up again, and Paul pushed me down a second time. "You have no idea, Hon, how much, we, human beings wish to live. We love our lives... but unfortunately, we take it as a deserved privilege. The only thing I did the entire ordeal was struggling to get back to this life. Life... life... life with you and our kids! That's all I wanted there."

Paul burst with laughter. I felt offended and cried. He regretted and came closer and kissed my hand.

"Hon, I'm sorry, but it's so strange to hear all these things coming from you. You never talked about this stuff... you're always the optimist, full of life...full of energy. And now you're talking of walking into 'the valley of death'? You like partying and going out dressed like a queen. Please forgive me! Please don't cry! This episode in your life will pass away... I'm sure... and I'll get my queen back. The queen as I always have known you." He continued kissing my hand.

"I saw my dead body, Paul... there... somewhere on the asphalt. I know you can't believe me, but I saw my body there. I swear... it's true."

"I believe you, Hon… but I'm trying to help you lose sight a little of these queer things now… Your brain plays you up, dear. Understand that!"

"Paul, you don't understand… you don't understand it at all. I've been caught up in another world… another life. Believe me Paul, different from what we know as being life. Accept this, Hon, for crying out loud. You have no idea how hard it is for me to confess all this to you… especially when you know me as a person different than this one talking to you now. I feel humiliated in front of you. I am a very proud person. You know that."

"Yeah… but…"

"Hon, I have been out of this world… yours… mine, I should say swapped or something like that to places that I have never heard of them. Paul, when you and the kids were wandering around my helpless body… I was at the same time wandering around strange characters and events, trying desperately… as you're trying now… to make sense of everything surrounding me. Hon, I've even encountered war… yes… war. Don't stare like that!"

"War? What war?"

"I don't know, Hon, but it was something I never heard of… weapons… like I've never imagined existing."

"Boy, Hon… you should really reconsider your decision of coming home so soon, you better…"

The nurses coming in and out the room interrupted our talk. In fact, I was sure Paul was happy for that interruption. After a few minutes of trivial chatting, Paul left. I abided the situation, though very discouraged. "Paul, my best friend and lover, whom I have always trusted the most, not capable of believing me?" I needed him to believe me. It was imperative for me to have a human being feeling with me. I was even tempted at some moment to share everything with the nurse. "Perhaps Dr. Sorensen, will listen," I thought, but immediately reconsidered my impulse, fearing for the consequences. I didn't want to end up being treated as a psycho.

I didn't sleep that night. I was afraid that sleeping might deepen me into a coma or worst. As I found out later, Paul couldn't sleep either, having the same fear. The next day he seemed deep in thoughts. I, too, was silent. He told me that he let the kids go to school and rushed to the hospital to take me home.

CHAPTER 23

AT HOME WITH A BORN-AGAIN WIFE

Going back home was vibrant, fascinating and I couldn't wait to get away from all those hospital forms. After I heard doctors' and nurses' advice, we both dashed to our car and headed straight home.

In our car we kept quiet most of the time. Something seemed like it was not the same in our life. There was a kind of annoying disconcertedness among us. Paul seemed to be a changed man. Something disquieted him. I looked at him a few times, but he wasn't bothered by me gesture in any way. My impression, though, was that he preferred me not to talk. Thus, I savored each little detail — pleasant or less pleasant — from the view out the car's window. I felt like I was born again into the same life. I missed that life so much. "Life… life… real life," I thought.

"It's so good to be back home," I broke the silence.

"We're not home yet, Hon," Paul remarked.

"I meant back to life, Paul."

"By the way, Hon," he suddenly began, "I don't want you to mention any of that stuff you told me last night… especially to the kids… you know that it's…" I felt his words slapping my face. "So… that's why he's so quiet," I thought. "Gosh! He… my husband. Hmmm! I can't trust him… he doesn't believe me. He 's ashamed of me… he my husband… he, my body… he…"

"Hon, did you hear me?" He interrupted my thoughts.

"Yes, Paul... I... heard you. I won't say a thing to the kids, if this is what you wish. I'll tell Helen 'this'... she's my best friend. I tell her my most sacred secrets of my life. This girl... deserted by others because of her skin's color has been a priceless jewel for me. Yes, she is my best friend... and she'll believe me. Somebody should listen to me... and I know she will."

"Honey... don't do this to me. I'm your buddy... and best friend. You are married to me, remember?"

"Well... judging by your lack of understanding me... I am entitled to doubt that, huh? 'For better and for worse'... remember that line?"

"Dee... I love you... and you know that. I love you like a fool... I can't imagine life without you... and I love our kids, too. I know Helen is your friend... and I appreciate her very much...you know that, too. She is a distinct and trustworthy person, but you share your life... and your body with me, dear. She might be your friend for a while and ... who knows... tomorrow she'll be gone. I am your buddy for life. Speaking of my lack of understanding you... or 'this kind of out of this world stuff' I would like you to know one thing. People do not easily accept such things. We are accustomed to our 'touch matter' life, what comes beyond this is cast off, catalogued as fantasy... as craziness." I said nothing. I continued staring through the car window, disappointed and puzzled. "Believe me, Dee, it's hard for me to accept the fact that my beautiful, intelligent and stylish wife is going to turn into an obsessed 'life beyond' seeker." Although, my soul rebelled hearing his words, my mouth was incapable of making a sound. Paul continued: "We belong to a high society now, Hon... we have worked hard for these years. Do you want everything to collapse like sandcastles?"

"Life itself collapses like sandcastles for each being... one day," I grumbled. "I've been 'there'... I've tested it. My life collapsed in a twinkling of an eye. I assume the lives of those bizarre marchers had collapsed the same... though they, too, had probably belonged to a high society once... here on this dumb world." My words mingled with my tears.

Ohhhh, Hon... I didn't mean to upset you... or dispute your encounter. I only have a request... make it a plea: Do not tell people about this strange experience. I'm not prepared for stuff like that. I am also not prepared to have my wife… my family on everybody's lips. Imagine a person like Mrs. Little trashing your name because of 'this stuff'. Her envy and enmity can drag us down. I don't want to be down again, dear. Ooooo, wait a minute! Even Mrs. O'Neil, your former mother-in-law might catch the flying word. Oh, Hon, I can't even dare to think what might happen to us… in case she runs off with something like this." I didn't reply, though I madly wished. I continued instead to look aimlessly through the window. "Besides," He continued, "that stuff… with Melanie… I still have doubts about it. There might be people harassing you with unnecessary inquiries. Do you want that?" I didn't answer. "Imagine our family being stigmatized for something which it might be only a figment… only the side-effect of a chemical imbalance… in your body…a…"

"Oh shut up, Paul… your ignorance makes me sick… 'chemical imbalance', hmmm!"

"But, dear… I can't…"

"Oh, shut up, Paul! I've always thought I have been the most ambitious person from the world, but you are the worst… you and your dreadful high society."

"Look who is talking! Who first wove under my nose the smell of the elite… me… or you? I belong to it… I like being one of them… and I fight to stay with them on the same podium… and I'll force you with me, no matter what. Please, keep this bizarre stuff as a sacred secret, pertaining only to you and maybe me, too."

"God have mercy on me!" I muttered, and then with a louder voice I said: "Paul, I killed Melanie. It is not my imaginative… sick mind. It's a fact, a painful fact. I killed her, and I had been perfectly aware of what I had been doing. I had wanted her out my life… actually, out of your life, dear, and I succeeded. What can I do to make you believe me? Do you want me to go with you, tracking all my moves… people I'd contacted and so forth? Do you want me to disclose to you the source of those pills? Would you believe me then?"

"Well… God knows! You might say the truth, but I don't want to hear it… and I don't want to believe it. I refuse to be convinced… and I also refuse to be indoctrinated with that 'the other lives' stuff. Really, Dee, I don't! I still belong to this planet… I know the laws and rules of this life and that's all I want to hear and recognize." He looked at me, smiling. I didn't like his cunning look.

"Well, Paul…"

"Wait," he interrupted me, "again, please, try to wipe out of your mind that thing with Melanie. Consider it over. The police had their final verdict. Leave it like that… will you?"

"So, you have a little bit of doubt, huh?"

"Perhaps," he said, throwing at me the same cunning look.

We kept quiet for another while, and I promised nothing to him. We were close to home, anyway.

For the rest of that day, the weeks and months that followed, I enjoyed the love of my kids, and Paul's special — make it unusual — attention. Sleepless nights went on, one after the other, marking my face with their hardness. Although not interested in partying and showing off, as I had been before, I still participated in the special events, dragged on by Paul's ambitions. He realized that I'd changed. I, too, realized it, but could not help it. I felt a marked person. Every day and night bits of that experience bombarded my mind. At night I was afraid of not experiencing them for real, and during the day not discussing them with anyone. All the time the same question persisted: "Why me?"

I saw Helen a few times, and each time I was extremely close to divulging my secret. I couldn't do it, and I didn't know why. She saw me changed, and she expressed her concern, but each time I came up with a new excuse. My kids made remarks about my unusual behavior, also, but they, too, were forced to swallow all kind of excuses.

CHAPTER 24

OPEN LETTER TO THE READER

Every day that passed, it became a burden hard to endure, and I complained of pain all over my body. "Anxiety," Dr. Sorensen explained. "Overstressed," was a specialist's opinion. I was the only one who knew the truth. I needed to unburden my mind and heart, I needed to shift this torment to a listener, and I couldn't find one. So, during one of those sleepless nights, not capable of bearing my struggle alone, I decided to choose you — yes, you, my dear reader.

You might be the only one to believe me without stigmatizing my name. I don't care if you spread the word. On the contrary, I really want you to share my experience with others. Who knows? Maybe there are people who believe that one day they, too, will have a rendezvous with their own life's deeds, and be judged by their course of actions.

My last words to you? None other than these: "Vanity of vanities, saith the Preacher, vanity of vanities; all is vanity." (Ecclesiastes ch.1: 2)

CHAPTER 25

EPILOGUE

I, Paul, Dee-Anna's broken-hearted husband became her first reader — not by choice, but by chance. After her burial, I found her diary in a shoebox, well hidden among other shoeboxes. I read it. While devouring each of her words my mind was imaging her standing, behind me while sweetly whispering them in my ears.

I lost her — my best friend. A boy who threw randomly stones from a bridge crossing Hwy. 94 killed Dee-Anna Turner. Our Mercedes was found a few hours later, smashed against a bridge abutment. She was still conscious when transported to the hospital and whispered to the paramedic's ear a message for me: "Believe… believe… believe!"

The requiescat in pace at her tombstone recalls "Perhaps a witness to her last judgement". In front of her plaque — a huge bouquet of anemone flowers that she had always loved.

THE END

MISSION STATEMENT

Bookstores are filled with books dealing with afterlife experiences, and the majority are best sellers, but unfortunately they all seem to belong to the New Age section. Death and eternity, two fearful yet ancient subjects, make headlines today through books, movies, magazine articles, TV shows, and the like. The sad part is that the authors of these forms of expression take bits and pieces from the Bible and transform them into new-age propaganda, impressing with it waves of people who are ignorant of the Word of God and— true to new-age philosophy — advocating that everyone goes to Heaven, because there is no Hell.

The purpose of this novel is to send a message to my readers and say that although Dee-Anna, the novel's main character, did not undergo actual hell, there is in fact a real hell. Many people are sadly heading toward it and all the money in the world will not buy anyone a pass through to Heaven. I wish many hearts to be touched through Dee-Anna' story, but most importantly, the hearts of those who are taken in by the appearance of their life thus ignoring their perishing soul. I want to warn this category of people that crossing over to the other realm does not mean happiness for everyone — regardless of the deeds committed during their earthly life. The views of those who advocate that everybody joyfully interacts together on the other side are not realistic. Dee-Anna's story proves that terror and loneliness await there for those mocking God's laws under the effigy of a "good" Christian.

Through my market research, I have found that Dee-Anna's experience is unique in nature, yet it thankfully does not fit the ordinary pattern followed by authors who write on subjects pertaining to out-of-body experiences and life after death. My novel is more profound and it is exactly as a result of this that it garners readers' interest.

My primary audience is one formed by readers young and old who take the relationship between life and death very seriously, readers who moreover long to learn from such experiences and by no means discount them as science-fiction adventures.

CPSIA information can be obtained
at www.ICGtesting.com
Printed in the USA
BVHW071550200922
647490BV00002B/246